LIAN HEARN

SIBLING ASSASSINS

fi

For H

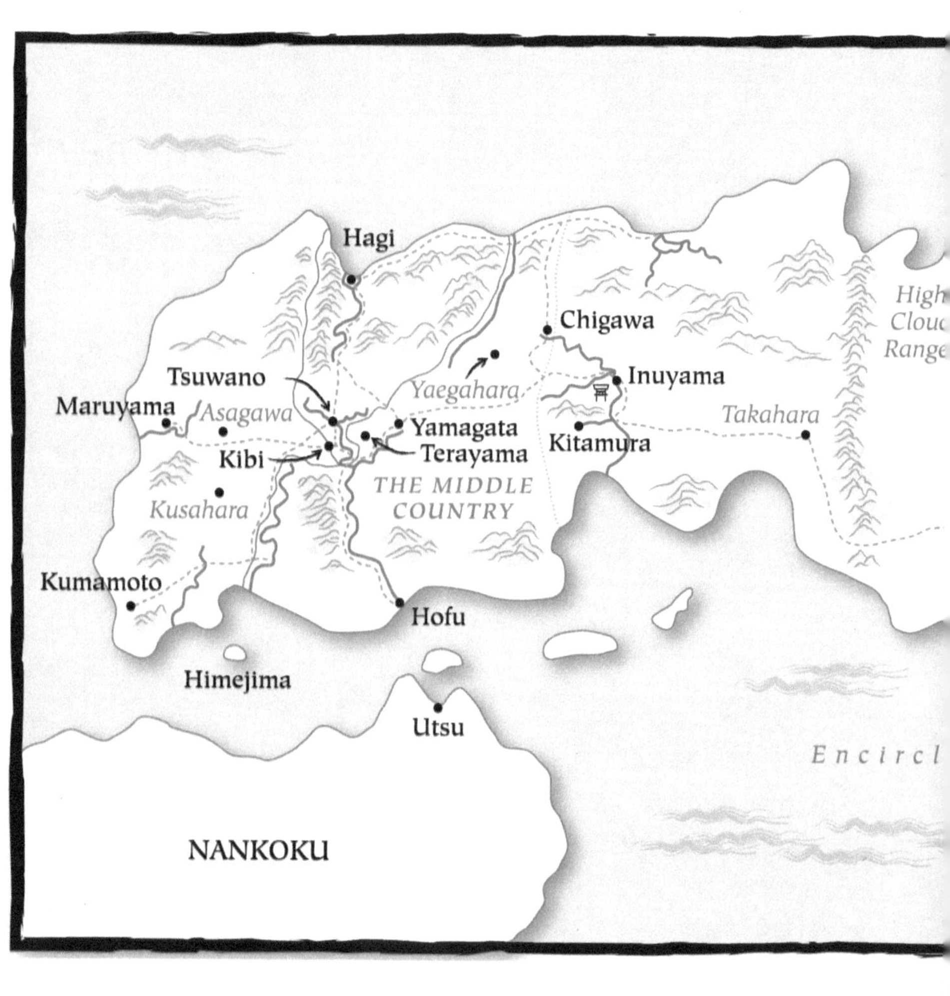

Hagi
Chigawa
High
Cloud
Range
Tsuwano
Inuyama
Maruyama
Asagawa
Yaegahara
Takahara
Kibi
Yamagata
Terayama
Kitamura
Kusahara
THE MIDDLE
COUNTRY
Kumamoto
Hofu
Himejima
Utsu
Encircl
NANKOKU

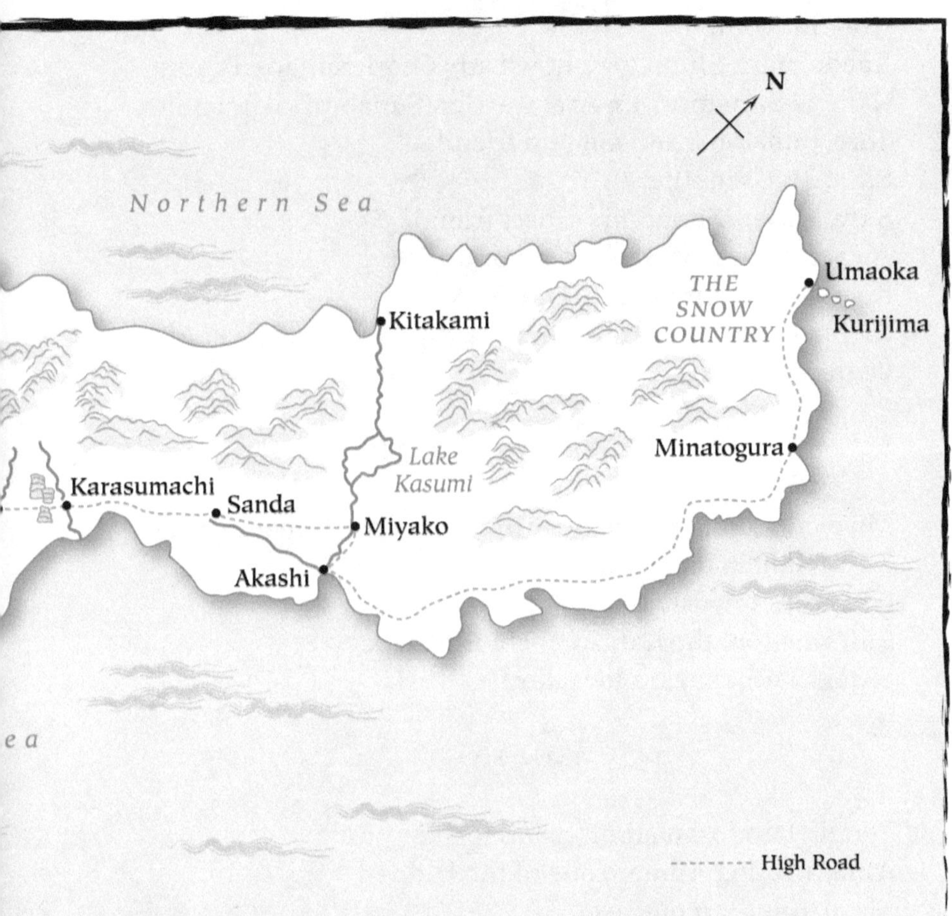

N
Northern Sea
THE SNOW COUNTRY
Umaoka
Kurijima
Kitakami
Minatogura
Lake Kasumi
Karasumachi
Sanda
Miyako
Akashi
e a
High Road

PEOPLE IN THE BOOK

IN MIYAKO

Arai Sunaomi
Kaede, born Shirakawa, now Lady Otori, Sunaomi's aunt
Kaneda Sunamori, an Arai warrior, Sunaomi's companion
Taro, Sunaomi's servant and friend
Saya, Taro's mother
Saga Masao, Sunaomi's oldest friend
A vagrant boy, Masao's companion
Kiyoko, Sunaomi's Muto cousin
Kichizo, her younger brother
Utahime, a ghost

ON THE ROAD

Miyoshi Kahei, commander in chief of the Imperial army
Kinu, Kahei's daughter
Genjiro, a townsman
Shinzaemon, the Karasumachi innkeeper
Sasaki Tsunenaga, a local lord

IN HOFU

Terada Fumio, an admiral and former pirate
Ame, a young woman, one of the Hidden
Maru Toma, an outcast
Renzo, an interpreter
Don Carlo, a foreign priest
Don João, a foreign soldier
Dr Ishida, husband to Sunaomi's grandmother, Shizuka
The Abbot at Daifukuji
Shomei, a monk and teacher

Hachizaemon, a merchant taylor
Mizuta Yasunobu, the Utsu lord
A Sillan groom
Lady Nin, the Sillan ambassador

FROM THE TRIBE

Muto Yoshio, now head of the Tribe
Mai
Nori, a servant

IN MARUYAMA

Shigeko, Kaede's daughter, Sunaomi's cousin
Sugita Hiroshi, her husband
Naida Sadaaki, a retainer
Miki, Shigeko's sister
Haruka, a maid

IN YAMAGATA

Lady Miyoshi, Kinu's mother
Katsunori
Kintomo, sons of Miyoshi Kahei

HORSES

Kiki, Sunaomi's ivory-coloured horse
Baku, Kaneda's roan
Hitare, a dark bay

DOGS

Chin, a gift from the Sillan ambassador to Kaede
Shishi, the Abbot's dog

虎穴に入らずんば虎子を得ず

Koketsu ni irazunba koji-o ezu.

If you do not enter the tiger's cave,
you will not catch its cub.

'I have a gift for you,' Sunaomi said, holding out the basket. It was carefully woven from bamboo and lined with red silk. It quivered slightly from the movements of the creature within. 'It was brought to Maruyama by envoys from Silla and entrusted to me by your daughter, Lady Shigeko. I've carried it for nearly two months on the road.'

He felt an unexpected pang of regret. Without realising it he had become attached to the animal and a bond had formed between them. He frowned to hide his feelings and looked around the reception room. He and his aunt, Lady Kaede, were alone, apart from the maids, who hovered almost out of sight, and the guards, ever present beyond the doors. It was a fine day in the fourth month, the air fresh, the breeze from the east. Bush warblers called from the gardens that surrounded the palace.

Kaede opened the lid and exclaimed in surprise. Her face, usually so stern and grave, softened. The lion dog jumped out, and she restrained it gently. 'We had one like this in Hagi, when the children were young. He was called Shin. I don't know what happened to him—lost, I suppose, along with so much else.' She was silent for a moment and then said with forced cheerfulness. 'Does this one have a name?'

'I've been calling her Chin, but you can name her what you like. The Sillans sent many other gifts which I dispatched by sea, but this one I wanted to deliver in person.'

The dog put her ears forward when Sunaomi spoke her name. They were black like her mane and her plumed tail. The rest of her fur was merging shades of fawn and white. Her eyes were dark brown and at night they shone with a reddish glow. She was about ten months old. She allowed Kaede to pet her but her gaze did not leave Sunaomi.

'The Sillans value them very highly,' Sunaomi said. 'They are temple dogs, bred to keep the monks company and guard them while they pray. They are small but fierce, they don't eat much and they hunt rats and mice like cats.'

'I'm afraid she will be bored living here with me in the palace,' Kaede said, signalling to one of the maids to take the dog away. 'I'll make sure one person looks after her but I am too busy to occupy myself with a puppy. I will send a message of thanks to the Sillans. Did they give any indication of what they want from us?'

'Their envoys have gone on to Hofu and hope to be summoned by you to the capital. I believe they would like the Red Seal ships to be reinstated and to trade on a regular basis.' He could hear the dog whining, the sound gradually fading away.

Kaede said thoughtfully, 'We already trade with the foreigners but they become ever bolder and more demanding. And the people of Miyako have become addicted to the luxuries they supply: furs, glass vessels, all kinds of cloth, and of course firearms. Perhaps some competition from the Sillans will be good for everyone.'

Sunaomi bowed his head. His aunt was the most powerful person in the Eight Islands, ruling in the name of the Empress and the retired Emperor, maintaining peace for the past seven years, keeping the powerful warlords in check, negotiating with foreigners not only from Silla and Shin, but also from the Southern Isles and beyond: the half-mythical countries, possessors of great ships and dangerous weapons, that lay far to the west.

He was as close to her as anyone, after her daughters, and believed she was fond of him, but he had been away for a year in Maruyama and now he found her cool and remote. He did not want to displease or disappoint her.

Kaede must have sensed his feelings for she smiled more warmly and reached out to take his hand.

'I am so pleased to see you, really. I've missed you. How long have you been back in the capital?'

'Two days,' he replied.

'You did not come straight to me? I should scold you for that! But where are you staying?'

'At the scribe's house. It's a little neglected but it is convenient. You remember the Arai warrior, Kaneda Sunamori, who has been with me for years? He's arranging repairs. There's a woman who can keep house and cook for us. She and her son, Taro, have been living there ever since Master Minoru's death. Taro became a sort of servant to me and accompanied me to Maruyama.'

'You are nearly a man now,' his aunt said. 'You must make your own decisions. I will ensure the house is made over to you.'

He smiled and bowed his head again.

'We must start thinking about your coming-of-age celebration, now you are in your seventeenth year. We will have a splendid ceremony. It's a miracle that you are alive after all the dangers you have passed through ... but let's not dwell on the past. We must plan for your future. Your teachers speak highly of your ability and talents. You are old enough to marry. I must give some thought on how best to employ you and who will be your bride.'

She still held his hand and now pressed it more firmly. 'You are going to serve me, aren't you, Sunaomi?'

'I will vow it now and at the ceremony,' he replied. 'I have only one request to make of you: that Masao may attend.'

Masao, Saga Hideki's grandson, had been his closest friend ever since they had met as fellow orphans at Terayama. They had grown up together in this palace, had studied and trained side by side.

'Of course,' Kaede agreed immediately but a slight shadow crossed her face. After a moment she said, 'You have not seen him yet?'

'No. Is something wrong?'

'There have been some difficulties with Masao. I'm afraid you will find him changed. He's made some undesirable connections. To tell you the truth, I am thinking about sending him away.'

'In exile?' Sunaomi said, alarmed.

'Not as harsh or extreme as that. Maybe back to Terayama where Makoto and Genba can control him and where he will be away from the remnants of the Saga clan who want to reinstate him as Hideki's heir and their lord.' She had been gazing into the distance, but now looked directly at Sunaomi again. 'He is the only survivor of Lord Hideki's family, you know. All the others were either killed in the fighting or committed suicide afterwards.'

'On your orders,' Sunaomi said.

'Not exactly. They were offered the choice to submit to me but they declined and accepted the consequences. Masao was spared, mainly because of your friendship and all you had been through together. In the year you've been apart he has become troublesome. Let's hope you can rescue him.'

'I will do my best,' Sunaomi promised, certain the old friendship would be renewed and they would become as close as ever.

'To change the subject to something more pleasant, what news do you bring of my daughters, and the grandchildren?'

'They are all well,' he replied, smiling at the many happy memories of the past year spent with Shigeko, Hiroshi and their two daughters, four and two years old. 'The little girls are delightful. Their father already has them riding ponies. They called the older one Naomi.'

'So the Maruyama descent is secured, though I should not tempt fate by saying so.'

'You must have known Lady Naomi?'

'All too briefly,' Kaede replied. 'I was only a girl and she died so soon after our meeting. One day I'll tell you the whole story.' For a moment she seemed lost in the past, her face sorrowful.

Sunaomi said, 'Lady Shigeko seems to have fully recovered

from the birth of the second child, runs the affairs of the domain and finds time to breed and train the Maruyama horses. She gave me one, a real beauty, ivory coloured with a black mane and tail and black points. She has written herself. I have letters from both her and Miki.'

He took the bamboo tubes that contained the scrolls from inside his robe.

'I'll read them later,' Kaede said, placing them on the floor beside her. 'How does my younger daughter seem?'

'Miki? She seems well.'

A silence followed.

'You know it was my husband's wish that you and Miki should marry when you came of age?' Kaede said finally.

Sunaomi had been aware of it but he had tried to put the idea out of his mind. His cousin was five years older than he was and they were close friends. She had never spoken of the subject. But she was still unmarried.

'Maybe it is something we should consider,' Kaede said when he made no reply. 'Although Lord Miyoshi Kahei has hinted that his daughter Kinu would be a good match for you. Do you have any preference?'

'I feel I am still too young,' Sunaomi said. 'There are many matters in my life that need sorting out.' He did not intend to tell his aunt the true reason. It was a secret he had never shared with anyone and never would. It was, naturally, flattering that the most powerful families in the realm were considering him as a bridegroom, he who eight years ago had been an orphan, destined to see out his days in a remote temple, never to ride a horse or hold a sword, certainly never to marry. Yet he would have to find a way of refusing them. He could not become the husband of either Miki or Kinu.

'The most pressing matter, I assume,' Kaede said, 'is the Arai inheritance. Have you come to a decision on that?'

'I visited Kumamoto on my way back here. My grandmother is there with my brother.'

'Yes, Shizuka writes to me from time to time with news of his development. You know you are both as dear as sons to me.'

'Then she will have told you that Chikara is very popular with the people of Kumamoto. They say he is the image of our grandfather, Daiichi. He loves hunting and martial arts and he is not averse to the day-to-day affairs of the domain, despite still being so young. He prefers to live in the provinces whereas I like being in the capital where I can pursue my studies.'

'You must not renounce your heritage lightly,' his aunt said. 'You are the Arai lord and I would prefer that you remain so. But if you and Miki were to marry you would become my son. We must think of the future of the realm and in whose hands I can safely leave it, for I will not live forever.'

'Don't speak of such things,' he said, aware of the cords of her will closing around him like a net. He was bound to obey her—she was his aunt as well as his ruler—yet it was impossible for him to marry Miki.

'Let's leave tomorrow's wind to blow tomorrow,' Kaede said. 'First, we must arrange your coming-of-age ceremony. Lord Miyoshi is expected any day. He will officiate and you will swear allegiance to both him and to the Empress for whom I will stand in stead. You may seek out Masao and decide if you want him to attend. But impress on him I am doing him a considerable favour.'

Sunaomi bowed to the ground. He could not imagine any reason he would not want to invite Masao.

There was a sudden pattering of paws followed by running footsteps. Chin sprang into the room. As Sunaomi sat up she leaped onto his lap and tried to lick his face.

Kaede laughed as a flustered maid crept forward on her knees, apologising.

'You had better take the dog with you,' his aunt said. 'It's obvious you have become her master. I will appoint you official guardian of Chin, the dog from Silla, and allow you an appropriate stipend.'

'There is no need to pay me for what my heart desires,' he replied. 'I only hope the envoys will not be insulted.'

'You are my nephew, Sunaomi, and maybe my future son. They cannot take offence. I will write to them, thank them profusely for their gift, and tell them I am open to discussions on the subject of the Red Seal ships. That should deal with any hurt feelings.'

At the palace gate Taro was waiting with the horse, Kiki. He grinned and took the dog, scratching her behind the ears. She moved her plumed tail in response. After Sunaomi she liked Taro best, for he sought out meat for her, game birds or ox flesh. She ate fish and rice if nothing else was available but meat was her favourite.

'It seems she is to be mine, after all,' Sunaomi said, mounting the horse.

'I'm not really surprised,' Taro replied. He had grown into a strong, sturdy young man, self-confident and bold. He had been raised in the city and knew all its back alleys and drinking places. They had met as young boys when Sunaomi had been a fugitive orphan, and Taro had never treated him any differently since. Next to him Sunaomi knew he himself looked slight and unworldly. It was an appearance he cultivated to some extent, preferring to keep his true nature hidden.

'Only you would have a matching dog and horse,' Taro said mockingly, as he handed Chin up to Sunaomi. She balanced like a cat. She liked being high up.

'Will you see if you can find Masao?' Sunaomi asked. 'He may be at the old Saga place. Otherwise you'll have to track him down in the city.'

Taro nodded. 'Shall I bring him back to the house?'

'If he'll come,' Sunaomi said. He knew Masao was inclined to stand on his dignity, very conscious of rank and status. 'If not, I'll go to him. Just get him to tell you where and when.'

Taro bobbed his head and walked swiftly away through the crowds.

Petals from cherry blossoms covered the ground and fell

like unmelting snow on the horse's dark mane. Sunaomi rode with a loose rein, relaxed yet alert to everything around him. He followed the main avenue as far as the river, where he crossed the narrow wooden bridge. Water birds lined the shore, herons, cormorants, ducks and geese, while terns, gulls and swallows wheeled overhead. The air was full of insects, making the dog twitch and sneeze.

On the far side he rode into a maze of back streets and lanes, some so narrow they barely allowed room for a horse. As they drew closer to the old house Sunaomi recognised people in the street, the weavers taking a break from their looms, the rice-wine brewer at his door, the bath-house owner. They all called out greetings to him.

At the gate of the old house he tucked Chin under his arm and dismounted. He set the dog down and led Kiki past the shrine, through the neglected garden to the small horse yard, where Kaneda Sunamori was fixing up new ropes and tidying up. The yard was already supplied with dry grass and water buckets.

Kaneda was a man of about thirty-five years, unusually tall, rather old-fashioned in speech and dress. Kiki whickered to him and Chin ran up, her tail wagging.

'You were allowed to keep the dog?' he said. 'I hope that will not cause any trouble.'

'My aunt insisted,' Sunaomi replied. 'I am grateful to her.'

'I trust Lady Otori is well?'

'I think so.' Sunaomi realised concern for his aunt had been lurking just below conscious thought. 'The affairs of state must be a heavy burden.'

Kaneda nodded, seemed about to speak but then thought better of it. Sunaomi made a note in his head of both his concern and the warrior's reaction. Later he would discuss the matter further but for now he wanted to be alone. He said, 'I'll be in the old house for a while. See I am undisturbed.'

'What about something to eat? It's nearly midday.'

'Thank you, I don't need anything.'

Kaneda looked him up and down. 'There's no need to starve yourself,' he said disapprovingly.

Sunaomi raised his eyebrows.

'Forgive me, lord, but you have become very thin!'

'I am no longer a child for you to fuss over,' Sunaomi exclaimed.

'It's hard for me to break the habit,' Kaneda admitted, a little shamefaced.

'Within a few days, as soon as Lord Miyoshi returns, I will have my coming-of-age ceremony. So you must get used to the fact that I am a man now.' Not wanting to hurt the warrior's feelings he added, 'You have taken care of me for years and I am very grateful.'

'It takes more than a ceremony to become a man,' Kaneda grumbled. 'You have to act like one.'

Sunaomi let this remark pass without comment. 'Masao may come,' he said, 'but don't let anyone else in.'

'Masao?' Kaneda questioned.

'Yes. Is there anything wrong in that?'

'We'll find out,' Kaneda said, turning to unsaddle the horse.

Sunaomi walked away, Chin at his heels.

Taro's mother had opened all the doors and shutters and swept up most of the dust, mice droppings, feathers and dead leaves that had accumulated in the rooms and on the verandah. There was no vestige of the man who had died here, executed by the women of the Tribe. Sunaomi's skin shivered as he stepped past the place where Hisao had sat and called for the wine that had poisoned him. The dog's ears flattened against her head and she whimpered, reluctant to follow. Sunaomi went back and picked her up. Her chest was vibrating as she growled silently.

He paused at the room where he had had lessons with Hiroshi. It seemed like a lifetime ago, seven years in fact, nearly half his life. Now Hiroshi was in distant Maruyama, married to Lady Shigeko, father of her children.

The scrolls and texts had all been taken away. Only a low wooden desk remained. Taro's mother had tidied up and dusted and had placed a vase with a spray of blossom near the doorway. Its smell transported him instantly back and he stood for a moment, recalling in his bones the child he had been.

He went on to the end room, half under a spell. He had slept here the previous night, alongside the old lacquered box which still stood on the floor seven years on. It had once been a tea room and had a tiny crawl door in one corner. Sunaomi put the dog down and opened the door so she could come and go as she pleased. After a few moments sniffing around she went to the patch of sunlight, lay down and fell instantly asleep.

Sunaomi had placed a small carving of a bear on the lid of the box as if to set a guard. Now he picked it up and ran his fingers over the silver collar that encircled its neck. Hisao had made it long ago in Terayama and had destroyed it. Kaneda had recovered the two pieces and repaired them. It was always warm, as though the creature within were hibernating. Sunaomi had once woken it and knew he could do so again.

For seven years he had avoided any contact with sorcery, magic or *that other world*. Alongside Masao, he had received the education of a young warrior, the art of sword and bow, the strategy and tactics of war, classics of history and poetry. But now, back in the old house where so much sorcery had taken place, he felt a thin insistent craving, like a needle in his flesh.

The box had been filled with dolls, effigies of the dead whose spirits had been captured. Sunaomi had seen the dolls crumble to dust and since then the box had remained empty, until last night.

He placed his sword on the floor and sat cross-legged. He thought about the doll that lay within, her slender limbs, her wistful face, her silken black hair.

Spring filled him with desire, a longing to seek out the hidden, the forbidden, the unknown. He was trembling.

'Utahime,' he whispered. 'I have time now. No one will come.

Did you wait for me?'

But even as he reached out to lift the lid of the chest he heard the creak of the garden gate and a shrill whinny from Kiki.

Taro's voice called, 'Lord Masao is here!' He treated Masao with far more deference and respect than he ever showed to Sunaomi.

Chin awoke from her sleep with a deep bark that sounded as if it came from a bigger, fiercer dog. She was snarling as Masao came through the crawl door. She ran forward and nipped him.

'Get away from me, you rat,' Masao said, fending her off. 'I leave my sword outside and come in on my knees, unarmed, and this is how I am greeted.'

'You surprised her,' Sunaomi said, restraining Chin as she continued to growl and show her teeth. 'She will soon learn you are not her enemy, or mine.'

'I don't care for these little lap dogs,' Masao said.

'She is more than just a little lap dog; she's a temple dog from Silla, a gift for Lady Kaede. She became attached to me on the journey so I am going to take care of her.'

'Everyone and everything becomes attached to Lord Sunaomi,' Masao said.

Sunaomi was not sure how to take this remark. In the past he and Masao had been lovers in the way of young boys becoming men, exploring each other's bodies and their own emotions, strengthening their friendship into an unbreakable bond. A strong attraction still pulsed between them, yet he sensed some new bitterness in Masao's words.

'You are more beautiful than ever,' Masao said, gazing at him frankly. 'I suppose I should tell you how much I've missed you.'

'I have missed you too,' Sunaomi replied, still puzzled by the hidden resentment. He returned Masao's penetrating gaze. His friend had grown and broadened out. Two years older than Sunaomi, he was already a man. He wore his hair in an unusual style, shaved in the front and long and untied at the back. His clothes were flamboyant, a red robe with a golden sash.

He remembered his aunt's words. *There have been some difficulties with Masao. I'm afraid you will find him changed.*

And Masao had changed. At first his features had been animated as though it really was a pleasure to meet again, but now in repose his expression was sullen and brooding. His fingers moved restlessly, touching his own skin, his clothes, the floor.

'Is something wrong?' Sunaomi said tentatively after a few moments of silence.

'No. This is always a bad season. It is so many years since my parents and my sister died you would expect me to have forgotten them, but as soon as the cherry blossoms appear my grief is reignited. Every year without them seems harder.'

'I understand.' For Sunaomi the bad season was towards the end of the year, the eleventh month when he had been told of his parents' forced suicide. He had come to dread the change in colour of the trees and the beginning of the frost.

'You still have your aunt and cousins, your brother, your grandmother. And as I said, everyone loves you.'

'I lost my youngest brother,' Sunaomi said quietly, remembering the child he had hardly known, Hiromasa, whom his mother had taken with her into death rather than leave him. And then he remembered his other cousins, whom he tried not to think about, the siblings, Kiyoko and Kichizo, who certainly did not love him at all. He had not seen them for years and he had never told Masao about them.

'I did not know that,' Masao said. 'Well, I have no one—only you. I need to know that you still love me.'

'Of course I do,' Sunaomi said.

'You will never turn against me? You will never betray me?'

'We swore that we would be friends and comrades forever, that even death would not separate us.'

Masao smiled a little. 'What boys we were!'

There was a moment when the pull of desire seemed so strong that neither would resist it. Sunaomi felt his pulse quicken. Yet Masao made no move towards him, and he found he did not dare either.

'What did your aunt say about me?' Masao asked.

'Only that I might find you changed.'

'Changed! That's one word for it.'

'How would you describe yourself, then?'

'I made an important discovery: life is no more than a dream. Let yourself go wild and you find out who you really are.'

Sunaomi frowned. 'I don't understand what you mean.'

'Come out with me tonight and my friends and I will enlighten you,' Masao replied.

'These friends, who are they? Who do you spend your time with now?' Sunaomi tried to make the question sound innocent but Masao guessed his hidden motivation immediately.

'So, Lady Kaede doesn't approve of my companions? It's true they are a rough crowd but they amuse me and we enjoy ourselves together. We like everything new and foreign. Come with me and I'll show you what fun we have.'

'Another time. I am still a little fatigued after the journey.'

'*I am still a little fatigued,*' Masao repeated mockingly. 'I am never *fatigued*. I hardly sleep, it's a complete waste of time.'

'Stay and eat with us. Taro and his mother would be delighted.' Masao made him feel uncomfortable but at the same time Sunaomi did not want him to leave. He wanted to save him from something though he did not know what it was.

'I have to go.' Masao stood, making Chin, whom Sunaomi was still holding, growl. Masao looked at her with dislike, and then shook his head as though scoffing at both the dog and her owner.

They walked through the house and out onto the verandah where Masao retrieved the sword he had left outside. It was somewhat longer than usual, sheathed in a red scabbard. As he slipped it into his sash Masao said, 'My sister, whom we called Utahime, was in her seventeenth year, the same age you are now. She was born in the late spring. Maybe on this very day. I have outlived her now by two years. I was her younger brother but now I am older than she will ever be.'

There was a moment when they might have spoken of Uta-hime. Sunaomi longed to open his heart to his friend but they were interrupted by Kaneda coming through the garden.

Kaneda raised his eyebrows at the sword and Masao's attire, but his voice was scrupulously polite. 'The housekeeper wants to know if Lord Masao will join us for the evening meal.'

'Another time, perhaps,' Masao said, barely acknowledging the warrior's presence. 'My companions are waiting for me.'

Sunaomi sensed he was losing him and said quickly, 'I haven't told you about my coming-of-age ceremony. It will be held as soon as Lord Kahei returns. I hope you will attend.'

'For your sake, I will,' Masao replied, 'even though I find such things unbearable.'

He turned and walked swiftly away with no other words of farewell.

Kaneda maintained a steady silence.

'What?' Sunaomi demanded, putting Chin on the ground. She immediately let out a flurry of barking and ran towards where Masao had disappeared.

'Did I say anything?' Kaneda asked.

'Your thoughts are shouting at me!'

'And what are they shouting, tell me, if you are clever enough to discern them?'

'I think you are longing to disclose who Masao's companions are.'

'Street gangs of ruffians, masterless warriors, a few courtiers, servants, some young boys—a real mix. They brawl, cause trouble, set fire to things.'

'Why?' Sunaomi asked. 'Do they have grievances? Are they the victims of some injustice?'

Kaneda gave a short laugh. 'They imagine they are: the colossal injustice of being ruled by women. They tell themselves they disapprove of her policies—trade with foreigners, protection of sects, growth of the city guard, strict laws about forestry and agriculture, her attempts to punish corruption—but the root of it all is that your aunt is not a man. As a result they profess to hate women. They have an ugly side. It is not just youthful excess and high spirits. They actively seek out women to punish them. And they believe it is a man's right to kill.'

When Sunaomi made no reply, Kaneda went on. 'It might have been wiser not to mention your ceremony. You should not associate too closely with Masao.'

'He's my oldest friend,' Sunaomi said. 'I can't break my ties with him. I will never abandon him.'

'It's my duty to warn you. Don't let him pull you into his world. You risk losing everything.'

'You are exaggerating, as usual,' Sunaomi said, regarding the warrior with affection tinged with exasperation.

Kaneda bowed his head. 'I will inform Saya that Lord Masao is not eating with us.' He walked away, his back stiff.

Sunaomi called to Chin and bent down to stroke her. 'Now he thinks I have rebuked him,' he said to the dog. 'He will be silent and offended all evening.' He crouched for a few moments to compose his thoughts, letting the sounds of the spring evening wash over him. People were so quick to take offence. They raised themselves up as rigid as oak trees and then were amazed and outraged when storms ripped through their branches. They should learn to bend like willows, flow like water. A calm mind, a peaceful life of learning and contemplation. That was his goal in returning to the city.

Chin was attacking his feet in play with half-growling noises, nothing like the fierce snarls she had made at Masao.

He heard Masao's mocking voice. *Let yourself go wild.*

CHAPTER THREE

Night had fallen when Sunaomi returned to the old house. He had told Kaneda to remain in the newer building where Saya and Taro lived, saying he wanted to be alone.

'I'll keep guard near the horse yard,' the warrior announced.

'There's no need,' Sunaomi said. 'There are no dangers; no one threatens me in the heart of Miyako.'

'There are always bad people in any city, robbers, horse thieves. Taro can replace me in a few hours.'

'I'd be glad to,' Taro said eagerly. 'Come and wake me.'

Kaneda had taken Taro under his wing and taught him all the same warrior skills as Sunaomi. Taro loved them and excelled at them. They were both so enthusiastic about exercising these skills Sunaomi had to agree.

'Keep Chin with you,' Kaneda added. 'If she barks I'll be there in an instant.'

The dog followed Sunaomi to the former tea room. Saya had been in to light the lamps and their glow made the room look inviting and intimate. When he sat down Chin curled up in a fold of his robe and fell asleep. Carefully he undid the sash and slipped his arms out of the sleeves, leaving the robe on the floor and the dog undisturbed. The night air was cool on his skin. For a few moments he sat, trying to slow his breathing and his pounding heart.

The bear still remained on the lid of the box. He picked it up, placed it on the floor, lifted the lid of the chest and took out the doll.

He had carved it himself, given it locks of his own black hair, dressed it in clothes made from ancient fabric. And when he had been in Kumamoto, city of blacksmiths and metal workers, he had had made an exquisite nail of silver which he carried in a silk pouch on a red cord around his neck.

The doll's white face had a remote, wistful look and the reddened lips an expression of repose.

In the distance an owl hooted and cats were yowling in the street. The creatures of the night were awake. His whole body was alert. He had never felt more alive.

Holding the doll in one hand he slid the nail from the pouch. For a moment he hesitated.

'I don't want to hurt you,' he murmured. His fingers trembled. The lamp light glistened on the nail and the doll; the shadows deepened on the wall. He held the doll up and with his right hand drove the nail into its chest.

He heard distant music, a flute. He sat without moving as it grew louder. Someone was approaching, along the ghost paths of the nighttime city. The dog whimpered in a dream and her legs twitched.

A shadow on the wall grew and took shape until it was no longer a shadow.

She moved towards him, smelling of incense and earth, the flute at her lips.

'Utahime,' he whispered.

'Sunaomi,' she said, in the grave voice he had treasured for over seven years.

He carefully put the doll to one side, his eyes never leaving her face. She had not changed; she was still the girl on the edge of womanhood he had met in *that other world*. She wore the same white silk robe, the bloodstains fresh on it, and the red still flowed from her throat. Yet he was not afraid of her. He loved her for what she had suffered, for what was done to her. No one understood or even knew her but him, and no one understood him but her. She knew his grief and shared it.

She halted a little way from him, tucking the flute into her sash. 'I've been waiting for you.'

'Has it seemed a long time? I'm sorry, I had to grow up. But not a day has passed that I have not thought of you.'

'It has not seemed long. Where I am there is no time. It is no time since you came to the temple, no time since we last parted on the battlefield.'

'Where have you been? Where are you now?'

She shook her head slightly as though it was too hard to explain.

'Now I am here,' she said, coming closer and taking his hand.

Her touch was both icy cold and arousing. She did not feel insubstantial as he had imagined a ghost would but she did not feel human either.

'You know I love you, Sunaomi. I loved you when I first saw you, for your innocent courage. It was that love that tied me to this world. After my desire for revenge was slaked I could have moved on. But a thread bound us together and so I waited for you. Now you have brought me to life and for that I love you even more intensely. Let me hold you. Let me give myself to you.'

She was both terrifying and irresistible. He was on fire with longing and her body was as cold as snow. In her he found relief from loneliness, yearning and grief.

Afterwards he must have slept for a little. When he woke she was holding him close, touching her cold lips to his neck. 'Do you love me, Sunaomi?' she whispered.

'Yes,' he replied. 'Yes, I do.'

'We are the same age now,' she said. 'But you will grow older and leave me behind one day.'

'Never,' he promised. 'We will stay here together forever!'

'No, I cannot stay where people might see me. If any one comes to know about me, they will prevent you from being with me. I trust you. I have given myself to you. You may use the doll to summon me when you are alone. Now, take out the nail and let me go. Don't be afraid, I will wait for you.'

He hesitated. 'Doesn't it hurt?'

'Only a little. Nothing like the pain of dying the first time.' She smiled at him and for a moment seemed like any human girl.

He wanted to lie with her again, to be with her eternally, but even as he reached out to take her in his arms, Chin began to growl. Till then it had been completely quiet outside but Sunaomi heard a sudden disturbance, a few streets away, a cry as if for help, running footsteps.

'Someone is coming,' Utahime said. 'Let me go now.'

Sunaomi drew the nail from the doll and the ghost girl faded back into the shadows. The lamps spluttered and one went out. He felt around him in the dark and touched the silky fur of the dog. She was sitting up and growling deep in her throat. He wrapped the doll swiftly in the silken cloth, slipped the nail into the pouch and put them both inside the box, replacing the bear on the lid. Then he sat without moving, listening. Silence had returned, yet after a short time he suspected there was someone outside.

Holding Chin firmly so she would not bark he crept to the small door. On the verandah he could see it was growing lighter, the sky paling in the east. One bird started a tentative song. It was nearly dawn.

Years ago Sunaomi had spent a summer in a Tribe village where he had been subjected to weeks of rigorous training alongside his cousins. He had none of their innate skills but he had learned how to discern them. Now he was convinced someone was using invisibility not a pace from him.

His first swift thought, that they had come to kill him, was followed immediately by the realisation that if they had intended it he would already be dead. Chin struggled, trying to yelp. He held her muzzle closed.

'Kasho!' It was his old name, whispered by a voice he recognised at once. 'Let me inside. I need your help.'

It was his cousin, Kiyoko.

He had not seen her for years. They had once been almost friends; they had not parted on friendly terms but there were still bonds between them, thicker and deeper even than blood.

She was the last person he wanted to talk to now but if she was asking for help he had to respond.

'Go inside,' he said, 'through the crawl door.' He felt the air move as she went past him. He followed her in, and pulled the door across.

When he put Chin down she began barking shrilly, circling a spot in the middle of the room, her mane standing up on her neck.

'Make it stop,' Kiyoko said as she let her form come into view. Chin flew at her, growling fiercely. As Sunaomi grabbed the dog he heard footsteps and then Taro's voice.

'Is everything all right?'

Sunaomi said, 'A rat ran across the floor. Where's Kaneda?'

'Still sleeping, I think.'

'Whatever you do, don't wake him.' Sunaomi slid the door open and pushed Chin out. 'Take the dog and give her something to eat. Keep her with you for a while.'

Taro walked away and Sunaomi turned his attention to Kiyoko, moving the remaining lamp closer so he could see her more clearly. She stared back at him defiantly. She wore what looked like men's clothes, a jacket over leggings, but the leggings were torn at the waist and the jacket stained with dark splashes. Her hair had been tied back like a man's but had partly escaped its cord and fell wild around her shoulders.

'It's been a long time,' Sunaomi said.

'You can forget the formalities, cousin,' she said, raking her fingers through her hair and retying the cord. 'Get me some water. I'm covered in blood.'

'Are you hurt?'

'No, it's not mine.'

'Whose? Have you killed someone?'

'No. But someone may have died. Don't let anyone see you.'

Once her mother, his other aunt, by marriage, had said to him, *She is your senior. You obey her.* As if still following that order he walked through the house to the stone basin by the gate where he filled a bowl with water. Saya had left cloths to dry on the stones and he took those back with him too.

Kiyoko took one without a word of thanks, dipped it in the water and washed her hands and face. She slid a short sword from her waist and carefully wiped the blade. Then she slipped off her jacket and began rubbing at the stains. She wore nothing underneath; she had the muscles of a man. She was quite unselfconscious; they had seen each other naked often enough as children.

'What happened?' Sunaomi asked.

'I got caught by one of those street bands.'

'I don't understand. How did they see you?' She had all the skills he lacked: invisibility, the second self.

'I don't know. There was a young boy among them who was able to perceive me. He must be from the Tribe but I'd never seen him before. I don't know who he was.'

'Is he the one who died?'

'No, he's still alive. The dead man was a nobleman judging by his clothes and his hair. Really, I'm not clear what happened. They were going to rape me. One of them was holding me down. The others were arguing over who would go first. Then someone was crying out and someone else was shouting ... I ran while I had the chance.'

She looked up at Sunaomi. 'One of them was your friend, Masao.'

Sunaomi found it hard to breathe. 'Not the one who died?'

'No, but he deserved to. And if I ever see him again I'll kill him.'

'Why did you come here?' he said. He had so many questions and her story made little sense to him.

'It all happened just around the corner. The guards turned up and I had to get off the street.'

'But how did you know I was here? I've only been in the city for three days. Have you been following me?'

'No!' she said immediately.

'You promised once always to tell me the truth,' he reminded her.

'So I did, but I don't think I'm obliged to keep my promises since you broke all yours when you ran away.'

'I was a child,' Sunaomi said. 'I was abducted. Your family had no right to demand my life.'

'Well, that's how it is in the Tribe,' she said, smiling for the first time. When he shook his head she went on, 'There are compensations.'

Sunaomi was silent. To some extent he understood: the thrill of belonging, the dark skills that no one else possessed, the permission to kill in so many different ways ...

'The truth is, Jun was keeping an eye on you while you were in the capital, and when you went to Maruyama Kichizo took over.'

'Your brother followed me to Maruyama?'

'I can't believe you never noticed him,' Kiyoko said, a note of pride in her voice. 'It shows you how skilled he is. He is everything you are not.'

It was not only her contempt that chilled Sunaomi to the core. He could see her face now the light had strengthened. She was studying him in a way that made him feel deeply uncomfortable.

'Kasho,' she began.

'No one calls me that anymore,' he interrupted. 'For years I have been called Sunaomi.'

'All right, I'll call you Sunaomi. It suits you. You are so beautiful—more than ever. My mother used to say it was the Shirakawa curse and was the ruin of that family.'

He remembered Kiyoko's mother, Tomiko, as jealous and spiteful, terrifying to a child. 'Where is your mother?'

'She is dead,' Kiyoko said. 'That's why I am in the capital. I buried her a week ago.'

'I'm sorry,' Sunaomi said. 'Did she die suddenly?' A memory came back to him of Tomiko clasping a tree-trunk column in a shrine, telling him to pray for a swift death.

'No, it took months. She suffered a great deal. She was ill for a long time and could not eat or drink. It was agony for her and unbearable to watch. She wanted to see my brother one last time, but he was so far away in the west and you took so long on your journey she died before he got here. When she finally went it was a release for me, as if a lid had been lifted off a box I'd been trapped in. My limbs knew freedom for the first time. I could say what I wanted without being judged. Even the air I breathed came rushing unrestricted into my chest.' She stopped abruptly as if she had said too much. 'I don't want to talk about it. She's gone now. What I was going to say before your beauty distracted me was, something smells strange. What have you been up to?'

'What do you mean?'

'Have you had a girl in here? I suppose I shouldn't be surprised. You are old enough now, after all. Where is she?' Kiyoko sniffed the air. 'Definitely a girl, a lover, but with incense and earth mixed in.'

'It's not what you think,' he said abruptly. 'There's no one here.'

Kiyoko smiled. 'I think I'm a bit jealous.'

'Don't be ridiculous.' To change the subject he asked, 'Which way did you come in?'

'Over the side gate. I'll leave the same way. You should keep it guarded, by the way. Anyone could get in like I did.'

'There are guards on the other gate, between this house and the next, where the horses are kept. They are the most likely target for thieves.'

'Oh yes, your man's roan and the new one from Maruyama, ivory with black mane and tail. You call him Kiki.'

'Is there anything you don't know about me?' Sunaomi asked.

'Probably not,' Kiyoko said. 'You are wrong when you say the horses are the most likely target. You aren't aware that there are many who want to see you dead? Remnants of the Saga clan,

Otori who cannot forgive the Arai, noblemen who resent your aunt and your closeness to her, not to mention the Tribe.'

'You could have killed me but you didn't,' Sunaomi said.

'I have a different plan.' Kiyoko laid her hand on his arm and said in a mock angry voice, as if she were his older sister, scolding him. 'Everyone knows who you are. You are always so flamboyant. You make no effort to disguise yourself.'

'Why should I?' he replied. 'I am proud of who I am. And I have no fear of death.'

'You need someone to look after you,' Kiyoko said. She turned her head. He could hear nothing but she whispered, 'Someone's coming. Don't say anything about me. I'll be in touch soon.' Soundlessly she slipped away.

CHAPTER FOUR

Kaneda was approaching with a heavy, urgent tread. Chin's claws pattered on the boards as she bounded after him. Sunaomi closed the crawl door, and went swiftly to the main entrance of the house. Chin greeted him ecstatically as if they had been separated for weeks.

'Your aunt has summoned you to the palace,' Kaneda said.

'What's happened?'

'There was a street fight. A young man was killed. Masao was recognised by the city guard but he fled. The dead boy was from the Kono family, nobility, related to the Emperor.'

'What was a young nobleman doing out on the streets at that time?'

'As I told you, Masao attracts many young men from all walks of life.'

'I will go as soon as I have changed my clothes,' Sunaomi said. 'You can prepare the horses. And ask Saya to come to me.'

Saya helped him dress carefully in wide formal trousers of a colour between mauve and purple and a dark broad-shouldered jacket marked with the bear-paw crest of the Arai. Both garments were of high-quality silk. Kiyoko had been right when she had accused him of being flamboyant. He loved the finery that he had had to give up when he became an orphan, and when it was restored to him along with his rank, he resolved never to forgo it again.

Saya combed out his hair and tied it back, murmuring, 'So thick and silky, like a girl's.'

Sunaomi picked out one of his favourite fragrances, placed his sword in his sash and wore the carved bear on a red silk cord around his neck.

'Where is Taro?' he asked.

'In the late master's study, going through the books that I moved there. Since you taught him to read he cannot get enough of them.'

Sunaomi was about to say he could stay there but Kiyoko's words came back to him. Maybe he should be accompanied by more than one bodyguard as he rode through the city.

'Tell him we're ready to leave,' he said.

Guards were everywhere. Kaneda had mentioned that their increased presence and powers were among the complaints made against Kaede, but Sunaomi had not realised quite how numerous they were. Many were from the Otori armies and had served Miyoshi Kahei. They wore their hair in a distinctive style, cropped short, and their jackets bore the heron crest of the Otori.

Otherwise there were few people on the streets and no sign of Kiyoko. He imagined her disappearing unseen into the maze of the city. No doubt she would appear again when he was least expecting it.

Despite being woken so early his aunt was as composed and as carefully dressed as ever. She wore the layered robes of a court lady in spring shades of pink and green and over her head, as always, a shawl. Sunaomi looked with admiration on her fine features and slender wrists and could not help recalling Kiyoko's words: *the Shirakawa curse*. People said the only woman who had surpassed the young Lady Kaede in beauty was her sister Hana, his mother. Hana was dead and Kaede scarred. Maybe they had been cursed by their beauty.

Kaede in turn looked appraisingly at his clothes and remarked on how fine he looked. She indicated he should sit knee to knee with her, and dismissed everyone else.

The dog sat quietly at his side.

As soon as they were alone Kaede let her outward appearance of calm slip away and leaned forward to say quietly but urgently, 'This is the outcome I feared. A young man is dead and Masao cannot be found. A few of his companions were apprehended but they refuse to speak. It seems they take a vow of secrecy when they join him and they will not break it.'

'No one has given a report of what actually happened?'

'Some of my retainers have suggested torture but I will not resort to a practice my husband so steadfastly opposed. Yet without eyewitnesses, since Masao disappeared, he must be presumed guilty and must be punished. It is a challenge to my authority.'

'Maybe he did not mean it to be,' Sunaomi said. 'Maybe it was a situation that just got out of hand.'

'Whether it was his intention or not, it has resulted in riot and murder. He must be found and brought before me.'

She was studying Sunaomi's face intently. 'Do you know anything about this incident? I feel you are not as shocked as I would expect. You are not hiding something from me? Have you seen Masao?'

'He visited last night,' Sunaomi said, 'but I have not seen him since.' He did not want to tell his aunt about Kiyoko. There were subjects he would not dare discuss with her and the matter of the Tribe was one of them.

'So, where might he have gone?' she demanded.

'I'm afraid I know no more than anyone else.'

'I intend to send out guards in every direction. He will be tracked down.'

The idea of Masao being the object of a manhunt was distressing. 'I could go after him with Taro and Kaneda,' he suggested.

Kaede's gaze fell on the dog for a few moments while she considered this.

'Starting a manhunt will only cause more suspicion and unrest,' Sunaomi argued. 'And you risk leaving the city with too few guards.'

Kaede nodded. 'Sometimes it's better to damp down sparks rather than fight fire with fire. If you can find out which direction he might have fled in, you may follow him. We will say the death was a tragic accident and impose a curfew on the city. When Kahei arrives I'll review the situation with him. Till that time I leave Masao to you.'

'Thank you,' Sunaomi said, bowing.

'I'll prepare letters and permits for you to pass through the barriers. Kaneda can bring them to you later. You realise, though, after this, I will have no alternative but to send Masao into exile, as punishment for fighting and to put him beyond the reach of the Saga clan.'

•

'So it seems we must prepare for another journey,' Sunaomi said to Taro when they had returned to the house and were unsaddling Kiki. 'But how can we set out when we don't know where Masao has gone?'

Taro's face was sorrowful. He had always admired Masao deeply. 'I can't believe we are to pursue him like a criminal.'

'We are still his friends,' Sunaomi replied. 'Our intention is to prevent more harm either to him or to anyone else. Do you have any idea where he might be?'

'I can ask around. I'll go to the inn where I found him before. Someone must know.'

'Come back as quickly as you can. We will leave today.'

'I'll ask my mother to start making preparations,' Taro said.

'I'm sorry I'm taking you away from her again so soon.'

'It can't be helped. But I've one small request to make.'

'What is it?'

'I found a book among the ones we were moving from the old house. I don't know what made me pick it up. But I started reading it and I don't want to leave it behind. May I bring it with me?'

'You'd better show it to me. It might be valuable and you shouldn't risk losing it.'

'Come with me now, I'll show you before I speak to my

mother.'

Sunaomi was touched by the request and as they walked through the gate and into the garden he reflected how strange it was that a book should mean so much to Taro, who would have remained illiterate if Sunaomi had not taught him to read.

All the doors of the scribe's former house were open and the rooms were full of light. Saya had maintained it since her master's death; the matting was fresh and the polished floors gleamed. Minoru had been an austere and frugal man but he had had a restrained taste for works of art and this elegant place reflected it.

The adjoining house, which had been abandoned when it became haunted, could be made as beautiful, Sunaomi thought, and he decided to ask Saya to get the work started while he was away.

He followed Taro into the study where one small section in the corner was matted. A desk and writing materials stood there as though waiting for their owner to return. On the polished floor were chests and boxes that contained books in various bindings. Some stood in neat piles on the floor.

'Most of them are handwritten copies,' Taro said, kneeling down. 'Poems, warrior tales and histories, religious texts, all mixed up together. I was trying to arrange them in some sort of order. I look at the cover and inside each one to see if I can make out the title and the author. Sometimes, if that doesn't tell me the subject, I read a little—that's how this one pulled me in.'

He took a small volume from the top of one of the piles. It was stitched in a folded style with a dark indigo cover and two characters written on it in gold.

'I can't read this,' he said. 'But look, the same characters are inside. *The Hidden Wisdom of* ... is it a name? The author, perhaps?'

'I think it's read as Yoshimori,' Sunaomi said. 'Wasn't there an Emperor called Yoshimori, a long time ago?'

'I don't know,' Taro replied. 'You're the one who's studied all that history.'

'It looks almost as if it were meant to be a travel companion,' Sunaomi said, taking the book in his hand. 'It is so light and compact.'

'So, I can take it with me?'

'I don't see why not. It seems to be a copy; it's not hundreds of years old.'

'I'll guard it with my life,' Taro promised as he tucked the little book away inside his jacket.

Why had Taro asked his permission, Sunaomi wondered as they walked back through the house. Who did the books actually belong to or for that matter whose was the property, which contained the two houses, the shrine, the stable and the gardens? He had come back to it as if it were his home and Saya had greeted him as if he were its owner, but he was not. He had just lived there for a while with Hiroshi and Hisao. His aunt had already said she would bestow the house on him but why did he expect that when Taro obviously did not?

'You didn't have to ask me,' he said to Taro. 'I'm sure everything here is as much yours as mine. More, probably, as it is what Minoru would have wanted for you and your mother. Let the house and everything in it be yours. I'll restore the old place and we will be neighbours.'

Taro looked astonished. 'I asked for one book! You don't have to give me the whole house!'

'We'll make it legal when we return.'

'I won't tell Mother yet,' Taro said, 'in case you change your mind.'

'I won't,' Sunaomi promised.

•

Taro spoke briefly to his mother, explaining he was going out for a while, and that they hoped to set out on their journey within the next couple of hours. Then he left and Sunaomi told

Saya about his plans for the old house. She agreed somewhat reluctantly to bring in workmen and walked through the garden with him so he could explain what he wanted.

In the former tea room, she looked at the box. 'I took the books out of the study but I haven't opened this one,' she said. 'I don't know what's in it.'

Sunaomi thought of the doll lying inside. 'I think it's empty,' he said. 'Leave it here until I get back.'

After they had been through the other rooms and were out in the garden again she said, 'I don't really like coming here. It's always had such a sad atmosphere. I don't understand why you wanted to stay here.'

'It appeals to me,' Sunaomi said. 'It will be different when it's made new. Get a priest in to purify it. We will rebuild the shrine too and hold festivals again. The garden will also be restored. The old trees and shrubs can be saved and the cistern and the rest of the stonework are beautiful.'

Scarlet azaleas were blooming among the long grasses and weeks. Chin ran through the grass chasing lizards and grasshoppers. Only the plume of her tail was visible. In the warm sunshine of early summer Sunaomi could see many possibilities.

All the time, at the back of his mind, he was thinking of Utahime, longing to feel her icy touch and her cold breath. He could not leave the doll behind.

'I might take a look at that box now,' he said, 'while I am packing for the journey.'

'Let me help you,' Saya said at once.

'I can do it alone. You have plenty to do, preparing food for us to take.'

'Where will you be going?' she asked.

'I'm not sure yet. I hope Taro can bring back more information. I am sorry we are going away again so soon.'

'When he was a child I could determine his comings and goings,' Saya said with a hint of sorrow in her voice. 'He is an adult now, and he must choose his own path.'

He listened to her footsteps fade away, heard the horses whicker as she went past and her voice as she replied to them. The gate creaked as she opened and closed it.

Chin reappeared, panting. She sat next to him and he pulled grass seeds and burrs from her fur. Leaving her soaking up the morning sunshine he went back into the house.

Birds were singing and from the distance came the voices of street criers and other sounds of the town. Within the house all was silent.

Sliding the doors closed behind him, Sunaomi went to the end room. His travel garments hung on the rack. His belongings were set out on the floor: a flask of perfume, writing tools and a small light box to hold rice balls and other items of food. He knelt, unfastened his sash and slipped his robe from his shoulders. Against his chest, the bear hung on its silken cord, as always warmer than it should be. Sunlight slanted in, lighting up the floating motes of dust.

Sunaomi opened the box and lifted out the doll and the silver nail.

'Utahime,' he whispered.

The pale wistful face seemed to look away from him, gazing into the past. With trembling hands he thrust the nail into the doll's breast.

The air chilled. Utahime stood before him and then without hesitation was in his arms. She did not move like a physical being; she flowed with the speed of thought. But her body felt real as he embraced her. Her mouth, her hands on his skin were cold and hot at the same time, bringing intensity and delirium. His body ached and shivered as if gripped by fever.

'I was afraid you would not call me back,' she said. 'You won't leave me, will you?'

'I have to go away,' he said. 'I have to find Masao. But I will carry the doll so you are always with me and I will bring you to life whenever I can.'

'Masao? My brother?'

'Yes, he has fled. I have to go after him. If I can catch up with him I hope I can save his life.'

'He is riding west,' she said in her grave voice. 'I can see him. The crows are cawing round him. There are mountains in his path. He cannot go north, he cannot go south. He must go west, to Hofu.'

'Why is he going west? I expected him to flee to the northeast to the Saga ancestral lands.'

'He is not interested in the Saga family or their lands. He cares nothing for the past. He wants to escape from the Eight Islands. He seeks the foreigners with their strange ships and language.'

'The foreigners?' Sunaomi was astonished for a moment and then it seemed obvious. Masao had spoken of his fascination with the exotic goods and garments from the Southern Isles.

'I must follow him at once,' Sunaomi said and reached for the doll. Utahime clung to him. Icy cold tears fell from her eyes. He wiped them from her cheeks saying, helplessly, 'It's only for a little while.'

'I am so lonely there.'

He wanted to keep her with him forever. Her long black hair seemed to encircle him. He was drowning in her eyes.

Outside on the verandah Chin started barking excitedly.

'Someone's there,' Sunaomi said. 'I must conceal you.'

'No!' she begged.

Feeling as if he himself were being torn in two, he pulled the nail from the doll. Utahime slipped away from him like water, leaving only the trace of her tears on his skin. He was shaking.

He called to Chin and she quietened. He wrapped the doll and the nail in the silk cloth and placed them along with his other possessions in a pouch. He changed into his travelling clothes and packed his formal wear in a light bamboo basket.

When he walked outside he was aware of the sharp, sweet smell of jasmine. Kiyoko was sitting on the verandah, teasing Chin who continued to growl at her. The dog had her ears back and her eyes were round. She ran to Sunaomi and hid behind his legs.

'Your dog doesn't like me,' Kiyoko said. She was looking at Sunaomi in a curious way. He gazed back, challenging her. What had she seen, he wondered, or, more likely, heard.

'Why have you come back?' he demanded.

'Kichizo heard your servant inquiring about Masao.'

'Taro is not my servant,' Sunaomi replied.

'Whatever he is, then,' she said.

'He is more of a friend.'

Kiyoko gave him a look of contempt. 'You are as foolish and sentimental as ever. Call things what they are. His mother keeps house for you. He is your servant.'

He thought of telling her that the house was Taro's now but it would probably make her even angrier than she already seemed to be. Not wanting any more discussion he said, 'We're leaving soon, so I'll bid you goodbye.' He clicked his tongue to Chin and she followed close on his heels as he stepped past Kiyoko down into the garden. He could hear Kaneda's voice. Now the warrior had returned they could leave immediately. It was only just past midday. There were still many hours of daylight.

'Not *goodbye*,' Kiyoko said quietly. 'Kichizo and I are coming with you.'

Sunaomi stopped so abruptly the dog ran into him. 'You most certainly are not!'

'We are offering you our services, cousin,' Kiyoko said, looking up at him with a slight smile on her face. 'We want to work for you. I told you there are dangers and risks of which you are completely unaware. You need my brother and me to protect you.'

'I already have Kaneda and Taro, and anyway I think I can look after myself.'

Her smile grew broader but she said nothing.

Sunaomi went on. 'Why would you want to work for me? So you can take the first opportunity to turn on me?'

'No, we will swear to serve you. I'll vouch for my brother.

Don't you remember I promised once to always tell you the truth? I won't go back on that.'

It was impossible to know whether to believe her or not. The Tribe dealt in lies and deceit. She had to have some underlying motive.

As if reading his thoughts Kiyoko said, 'I can't pretend it would not be convenient to travel to the west with you. I'll make a deal with you. Take us to Hofu and we will forget that you almost killed me when you ran away.'

'Who said anything about Hofu?'

'Kichizo thinks that is where Masao would go.'

'We only have two horses,' Sunaomi argued. 'You will slow us down if you are on foot.'

'Kichizo has a horse,' Kiyoko said, adding with a sly look on her face, 'He stole it from Maruyama.' Then she said quickly, 'I'm teasing you. Of course he didn't. It's Jun's old horse, Hitare.'

'I suppose if I don't agree you will follow me anyway. I prefer to have you at my side where I can see you.'

The thought came to him that she was a witness to the street fight in which the Kono youth had been killed. When he found Masao he would hear the truth from both of them.

'We're leaving at once,' he said. 'Where's your brother?'

'He's waiting at the gate,' Kiyoko said.

•

It was years since Sunaomi had last seen Kichizo. Then he had been a precocious, good-looking boy, confident and gifted. The young man holding the reins of the dark bay, Hitare, looked less confident, almost self-effacing, and his good looks had diminished into a sort of flat anonymity. Sunaomi could see his father, Taku, in him, and remembered Taku's ability to disguise his features and pass unnoticed in any surroundings. Yet beneath this subdued demeanour Sunaomi sensed an unwavering self-belief, just as he sensed beneath the plain travelling clothes the supple limbs and strong muscles of his Muto cousin. Kichizo would be as swift and ruthless as an adder. Far better to keep him in plain sight.

The two young men nodded to each other but did not speak. Kiyoko did not say anything either but some hidden message must have passed between the siblings. Kichizo mounted the horse and held out his hand to his sister. She sprang lightly up behind him.

Kaneda was holding the reins of Kiki and his own roan, Baku, and as Sunaomi went to mount said under his breath, 'Who are they? Why are they coming with us?'

'They are my Muto cousins,' Sunaomi replied equally softly, using Kiki's body as a shield. 'Taku's children. They may be useful to us but don't take your eyes off them. And watch what you say. They both have far hearing and other skills.'

'Ah yes, I remember the girl now,' Kaneda said. 'And the horse. I never forget a horse.'

Sunaomi lifted Chin into the bamboo basket fastened to the saddle. 'Do you have my aunt's permits?' he asked as they prepared to move off.

Kaneda tapped the bamboo container slung across his shoulder on a red silk cord. 'In here!'

Saya called out farewell, and stood watching them until they had turned the corner. Taro walked between the horses guiding them through the crowded streets until they came to the city gates. Here the guards knew Sunaomi by sight and waved them through, shouting out greetings and wishes for a safe journey.

Temple bells sounded the midday chime. Taro leaped up behind Kaneda and the horses began to trot along the dusty road towards the west.

The mountains displayed the new green leaves of early summer in a hundred different shades. A warm breeze blew from the south. The horses were fresh and eager. Despite his anxieties Sunaomi could not help feeling a burst of excitement and anticipation for whatever lay ahead.

CHAPTER FIVE

Just after sunset they arrived at one of the large inns that had been established along the highways throughout the country. The guards outside wore the crest of the Miyoshi family on their jackets.

'Lord Kahei must be here,' Kaneda said.

'If he had been two days earlier I would have been able to have my coming-of-age ceremony,' Sunaomi said. 'Now I have to forgo being an adult until I return.'

Kaneda gave him a stern look as if to condemn his flippancy. 'Tell Lord Miyoshi that Arai Sunaomi is here,' he said to one of the guards and the man bowed and hurried inside.

Kichizo and Kiyoko had dismounted. As Sunaomi did the same and stood alongside them, Kichizo said, 'You should not wear perfume. It gives you away.'

'It's true,' Kiyoko added. 'Smell my brother. He smells of nothing at all. Not even your little dog could detect him. There is never any odour on him but the dust of the road or rain water.'

Kichizo had no discernible body smell. He opened his mouth in a wide grin and his breath did not smell either. 'How do you do that?' Sunaomi said, intrigued in spite of himself.

'It's a secret.' Kichizo grinned even more.

'There are herbs you bathe in or eat,' Kiyoko said. 'You should consider using them. Your perfume reveals your identity immediately.'

'If I ever need to conceal myself I'll remember that.'

The owner of the inn came out with his wife and welcomed them, apologising for the lack of space.

'Who would have expected it? Lord Miyoshi and his daughter just arrived and now Lord Arai is here.'

The maids hurried to wash the dust from their feet and then led them to a room, rather small but tastefully decorated with a pleasing arrangement in the alcove, a vase of irises beneath a scroll depicting a misty moon.

The maid apologised for the size of the room, adding, 'The view is pretty, however, and the bath house is just at the end of the garden.'

'It's perfectly adequate,' Sunaomi reassured her, remembering the many nights in his past when he had slept outside on the ground in all weathers.

'You had better bathe right away,' Kaneda suggested. 'Lord Miyoshi will no doubt send for you directly, once he knows you are here.'

Leaving Chin with Taro, who promised to find her something to eat, Sunaomi walked through the garden. Irises like the ones in the vase flanked a small pool, and the steam from the bath house made the garden misty. While he was soaking in the scalding water he heard distant flute music. It made his heart falter, recalling Utahime, but then he realised it must be Kinu, Lord Kahei's daughter. Kinu was a little older than he was and he had always thought of her as a sister. He was very fond of her and he looked forward to seeing her but he also dreaded the meeting, knowing her father hoped to arrange a betrothal.

The flute music made him long to see the ghost girl. He thought of the doll, so carefully wrapped, among his things. When would he be alone so he could bring her to life? He closed his eyes imagining her body next to his and, despite the heat of the water, shivered.

He heard footsteps on the boards outside and opened his eyes to see Kiyoko entering silently.

'I came to see if my lord needed anything,' she said, in a voice that was both submissive and provocative.

'You don't have to pretend to be my servant,' he replied.

'Your man, Kaneda, expects it of me. He thinks I am here to be a maid to the rest of you. It's hard for him to imagine a woman having any other purpose. I don't mind. It's a good enough disguise. Or I could pretend to be your lover. You know in the Tribe we can take on any role.' She slipped off her robe unselfconsciously. 'So, here I am!'

Sunaomi looked away. 'I don't need anything. And I'm not going to sleep with you.'

'How arrogant of you to think that was on offer! I said *pretend*.' Nevertheless she gave him a long appraising look that he thought held an invitation. To his annoyance he felt the colour rise in his face. He did not like being naked under her gaze.

Kiyoko squatted on the floor. 'There's something I want to tell you. Actually it's a confession. I lied to you before.'

'That didn't take long,' he said, showing his irritation.

'It was only partly a lie. I told you Kichizo thought Masao might go to Hofu, and he did think that. But I knew because I heard the girl tell you.'

He stared at her blankly.

'The girl, your lover. Don't get angry, I didn't look. I just heard her voice.'

He saw her curiosity and a touch of jealousy that angered him even more. 'You are mistaken,' he said coldly. 'There is no girl. I have no lover.'

'You should not lie to me, Kasho.'

'Don't call me that. It's not a question of lies or truth. You may have made a promise to me that it amuses you to keep, but I am not going to share my thoughts with you no matter how much you probe. My life does not concern you. We knew each other for one summer when we were children. I am a different person now.' He was aware he sounded distant and haughty.

Kiyoko gave him an ironic look. 'We are cousins,' she said. 'Nothing will change that.'

Sunaomi stood and stepped out of the water, wrapping his robe around him. As he prepared to leave, Kiyoko said, 'The strangest thing is, I heard her say *my brother*. Masao only had one sister and she is dead.'

♦

Chin greeted him effusively when he returned to the room, licking the mineral-smelling water off his feet.

'I fed her,' Taro said. He was holding the little book he had borrowed, his thumb marking his place.

'How's the book?' Sunaomi said casually, not really expecting a reply. He went inside and took out his carefully folded evening robe. He could not stop thinking of Utahime, and the doll hidden inside its silk wrapping. She was with him yet she was absent. It was almost unbearable. Kiyoko had unnerved him. She and everyone else were watching him all the time. He would never be alone.

Taro said, 'It's as if it was written for me—so many things I've vaguely thought about or wondered about, set out so clearly.'

For a moment Sunaomi had no idea what he was talking about. Then he remembered the book. 'What sort of things?' he said as he slipped into the robe and tied the sash.

Before Taro could answer Kaneda came though the garden and called from the verandah, 'Lord Miyoshi wants to see you right away. The evening meal is being served and he expects you to eat with him.'

'You had better come with me,' Sunaomi said. 'Taro can arrange for food for himself and the others. I'll take Chin—it will amuse Lady Kinu to meet her.'

With the dog at his heels he followed Kaneda along a winding gravel path between azalea bushes to the grand rooms, reserved for guests of the highest rank. The twilight had deepened and in the shadows around the stream the first fireflies flickered. Kaneda was so tall and Chin so tiny it made him smile to think of himself between them, supposedly their master.

The flute music began again. Every time he met Kinu and she played for him he recognised how much her skill and sensitivity had increased. She was truly gifted. It was a shame that so few people would ever hear her, just her family and a few carefully chosen friends. Perhaps she might join the court musicians around the Empress, but of course her father would prefer her to be married.

Miyoshi Kahei was at that time the most powerful man in the realm, Kaede's second in command and general of the Imperial army. He was around fifty years of age, his hair and beard beginning to grey, his face lined, his limbs sinewy.

Sunaomi had seen him as a captive, condemned to death, thrown into a bear pit, where he would have died if Sunaomi had not released a more powerful bear which had saved Kahei's life and his brother's. Yet the lord had never spoken of that time. He disliked, and so discounted, all that lay behind what he considered the real world. Closing his eyes to all hints of sorcery and magic, he put his trust in arms, military strategy, the way of the warrior. He was the author of several famous texts setting out his beliefs in precepts which Sunaomi had learned by heart as a child.

Sunaomi admired and respected the old warrior yet he had walked in *that other world* and he knew that, perilous as it might be, it was more dangerous to deny its existence. His hands still bore the faint scars of the bear's teeth and he wore the carving around his neck.

A wind chime tinkled and fireflies thronged beyond the verandah. Father and daughter both wore light summer robes, Kahei's blue, patterned all over with grey herons, Kinu's white, splashed with red and gold peonies. As Sunaomi knelt and bowed, Kahei said, speaking in a rather formal way, 'Ah, Arai Sunaomi is here.' He called to the maid hovering on the verandah. 'Bring the food now.'

The reception room was three times the size of Sunaomi's, its transoms carved with turtles and serpents, the matting fresh and green. It was lit by oil lamps in each corner. In the alcove stood a large mauve glazed vase holding a single sprig of magnolia with three perfect blossoms. Above the vase hung a black ink painting of two crows on a rock.

Sunaomi sat up and Kahei said, noticing his gaze, 'Lord Takeo drew it in the last year of his life. I carry it with me at all times.'

'It is very fine,' Sunaomi replied.

Kinu laid aside her flute and patted the dog who had run in after Sunaomi. Chin, usually wary of strangers, seemed to take to her immediately. 'Is Lord Sunaomi well?' the girl inquired, also in a formal tone.

'I am, thank you. And you? Are you quite recovered?'

When he had first met her Kinu had suffered from an inexplicable illness. Even now he thought she lacked the vibrant spirits of young women of her age. Her face was rather long and she was too tall to be considered beautiful. Her hair was thick, but short—he supposed it had been cut many times during her frequent bouts of sickness. Her eyes were well shaped and expressive and her skin unusually translucent.

Her father answered for her. 'She is, thank Heaven. But you, Sunaomi, are you sure you are in good health? You look very thin.'

'Father!' Kinu remonstrated.

'Well, he does. He is setting out on a long and difficult journey, from what Kaneda has told me. It won't do to fall ill on the way.'

Sunaomi was amused rather than offended by Kahei's bluntness. 'I am stronger than I look,' he said.

'Let's hope so. But what has prompted this unexpected journey to the west? I thought we were to meet in Miyako for your coming-of-age ceremony. I have been hurrying back for it.' Kahei poured wine and offered a cup to Sunaomi.

'I did not mean to leave so suddenly,' Sunaomi said. 'My aunt wanted me to catch up with Masao. He was involved in some trouble and instead of staying to explain, he ... departed.'

'You mean he ran away?' Kahei fixed Sunaomi with the gaze that had terrified many a soldier. 'He must have a guilty conscience.'

'I believe he saw an opportunity for change and adventure. He has been restless for some time. But my aunt wants him back and I must obey her.'

'I am fond of Masao,' Kahei said. 'His adoptive father, Mizuno, was the finest example of a staunch and loyal warrior I have ever met. For his sake I would like to help him. You think he's heading for Hofu and you will follow him there?'

Sunaomi bowed in affirmation.

'I hope you find him. But that's convenient for me. I might make use of you for my own purposes.'

'Lord Miyoshi knows I will serve him to the best of my capabilities.'

At that moment the maids arrived with trays of food.

Kahei gestured to Kaneda who was kneeling on the verandah. 'You may join us.'

'Lord Miyoshi,' the warrior said with deep respect and gratitude, and shuffled inside on his knees. Kahei nodded benevolently. Sunaomi knew he approved of Kaneda and his old-fashioned punctiliousness for the moral code of the warrior.

After they had eaten and the trays had been removed Kahei told his daughter she might enjoy a closer look at the fireflies under the moon, which had just become visible through the gnarled branches of the pine trees.

'We will join you shortly and you may play for us. But first I want to speak in private with Sunaomi.'

Kinu rose obediently, giving Sunaomi a quick amused look as though she knew all too well what her father wanted to talk about.

Kaneda also took Kahei's words as his cue to thank the lord profusely for the honour of sharing his food and retreat to the verandah.

Sunaomi was not looking forward to the coming conversation and had begun to rehearse all his arguments against an early betrothal. However, Kahei's first subject was not marriage but the current situation in Hofu.

'You will find Terada Fumio has become quite important in the city. I know he is supervising the construction of ships in the foreign style. I want you to question him about the foreigners, what their intentions are, what they want from us. I'm afraid the Nankoku lords, in particular Mizuta Yasunobu, are becoming very close to them, even, in Mizuta's case, converting to their religion. Only the strait separates the island from Hofu, which puts the port in considerable danger. Mizuta has been very busy defeating enemies and strengthening alliances. We need to make sure he remembers who rules the Eight Islands and to whom he owes allegiance. We cannot let him or anyone else break away, for if one part secedes the whole realm will fall.'

'I met Terada Fumio in Miyako,' Sunaomi said. 'He came to see Hiroshi.'

'He did?'

'It was a long time ago, before Lord Saga died. I just remember the night, their quiet conversation, a young woman with him whose name was Ame.'

'That's to be expected,' Kahei said. 'He is very fond, overfond, of young women.'

'In the morning they were gone. I haven't thought of that in years.'

'I believe Terada is loyal.' Kahei sighed. 'He was prepared to join my sons in the struggle against Lord Saga. But he was very angry with Lady Kaede, as were many in the Middle Country. And he was always easily beguiled by the new and the exotic. His family were pirates and he still has a pirate's heart. He is restless, as you say Masao is. They would probably get on well.' He refilled his wine cup and emptied it at one gulp. 'Fumio has a daughter, the same age as Lady Shigeko. But she has never married. So many young men died at the battle of Takahara, there were not enough survivors to go round. It is sad to think of all those young women never to have children and so many old people with no one to look after them. We live for war and think it is glorious. We must never forget its ongoing rippling effects.'

Now he will speak of marriage, Sunaomi thought, bracing himself. But there was something else on the lord's mind. The wine was making him loquacious.

'I spoke just now of religion and converts like Mizuta. Lord Takeo believed matters of religion were no concern of the state. He used to say, "I will believe in nothing so others may believe as they please." Lord Saga was very different, as was Iida Sadamu and indeed most other warlords and warriors. They hated sects and cults and sought to eradicate them. I won't make a judgement as to whether they were right or wrong. But since Lord Saga's death there's been a resurgence in previously prohibited beliefs. Who knows why? In particular the so-called Hidden. They have become very bold. You know what I am talking about?'

Sunaomi nodded, remembering the victims he had seen hanging from crosses, the incessant blood-chilling drone of their prayers. And hadn't Ame, Terada's young woman, prayed with the same words that long-ago night in Miyako?

'I've been looking into the matter,' Kahei said, leaning forward and lowering his voice. 'It seems the creed of the Hidden and the foreigners' religion are one and the same thing at heart. They share the same beliefs and worship the same god. Yet one strand has been in our country for many hundreds of years and the other arrived with the foreigners. I find that intriguing.'

'Perhaps belief is like a precious metal,' Sunaomi observed. 'It is found underground and mined in one region and then, like silver or gold, crafted into something else in another.'

'So, the Hidden are the raw material and the foreigners the refined artefact?' Kahei said. The concept seemed to amuse him.

'I don't know enough about either of them to judge,' Sunaomi replied.

'Well, I want you to remedy that and educate yourself about them. Find out all you can: if you consider them harmless, if the foreigners seek to gain the allegiance of their converts, if there are any signs of subversion or rebellion.'

'I will do all I can, lord,' Sunaomi promised.

CHAPTER SIX

Kahei nodded vigorously several times and took another gulp of wine. His voice became more warm and fatherly. 'I think you know how fond I am of you, Sunaomi. I have been like a parent to you for years now, you who were orphaned so young.'

'Ever since you plucked me from Terayama,' Sunaomi said, smiling. 'I am deeply grateful to you.'

'I will officiate at your coming-of-age ceremony and it is to me that you will swear allegiance as well as to your aunt. I am fortunate to have three sons of my own, losing none in the wars. My older children are all married or betrothed. Just my youngest, Kinu, my heart's chick, remains. She is only a little older than you and she has always liked you. When you first met I was astonished at how quickly she took to you and how easily she confided in you.

'She says she has no desire to marry, that her music and her spiritual practice are everything to her but I will have failed in my duty if I do not find her a husband. She will be like Terada's poor daughter.'

He gave Sunaomi a look that was both hopeful and affectionate. 'You will, of course, with your quick wits, have guessed my intention. It is my desire that you and Kinu be married. When I learned you had arrived here it was like a sign from heaven. We will seize this opportunity to conduct the betrothal, and the wedding will take place on your coming-of-age day.'

Sunaomi was silent. The way Kahei spoke did not leave much room for discussion, let alone refusal.

'I can do nothing without my aunt's permission,' he said finally. 'You may not know that it was Lord Takeo's desire that I should marry their daughter, Miki. Of course it is far too great an honour, as is your offer, but ...'

'I did not know that,' Kahei said. 'But Miki is years older, surely?'

'Only five years.'

'I shall discuss it with Lady Kaede when I arrive in the capital. But I suppose it would be better to delay any announcement.' Kahei frowned, annoyed. 'Otherwise, you would accept?'

'I feel I am too young to marry,' Sunaomi said diffidently. What excuse could he make that would not offend Kahei or irritate him further?

'Nonsense! At seventeen you are quite old enough. Better to marry young than get embroiled with some unsuitable woman.' Kahei gave him a piercing look. 'There isn't such a woman already, is there?'

There is, but one I can never tell you about. Sunaomi said nothing.

'Very good.' Kahei gave one more decisive nod as if the matter had been settled. 'Now can I suggest a stroll in the garden with—we won't call her your betrothed yet, but you and I know, and you may share the secret with her. The moon and the fireflies are so beautiful.'

As Sunaomi stood to leave Kahei added, 'Send your man in here to share a drink with me.'

While they had been talking Chin had kept watch for a while and then settled down to sleep. She awoke when Sunaomi stepped into his sandals and followed him into the evening garden. A bell frog was trilling, but the fireflies pulsed with no sound.

He was grateful for the dog's presence, for Kinu bent to pat her and they were able to talk about her—Kinu to marvel at her silky fur, Sunaomi to praise her intelligence and devotion—until the new awkwardness between them eased.

'I suppose my father talked to you about marriage,' Kinu said eventually. 'I'm sorry, I wish I could have spared you that.'

'It's a great honour,' he said sincerely.

'Thank you for pretending,' she said, with a spark of wit that animated her face. 'I've told him over and again that I don't want to marry. If I have to marry I would like it to be you, Sunaomi. We've been friends for a long time. But I don't believe I could make you happy.'

'I am sure you could,' he said, touched by her honesty. 'The truth is, I don't want to be married yet.'

'Do you love someone else?' It had grown so dark he could barely see her face.

'I don't know. Maybe.'

'Love has little to do with marriage,' she said wistfully. 'My mother has told my sisters and me that ever since I can remember. I know myself. I know that I will never fall in love and I will never desire …' Her voice trembled a little. 'What men and women do together. I will never, ever do that. So, I cannot make you happy. But if you had a lover who would satisfy you, and we could just continue to be friends.' She did not lower her gaze but stared at him directly.

'You sound so certain!' he said.

'I've had a lot of time to think about it. I have to be honest with you. It's strange that I could not talk like this to anyone but you. When I was so sick only music saved me. It was the only thread that tied me to this world. Do you remember how I thought I saw the girl, playing the flute that took away my senses? I feel I owe my life to her spirit and I must devote myself to her service.'

Sunaomi was silenced by her words, unable to tell her that the girl with the flute was the ghost he was enthralled by.

'I wish I could live like a hermit,' Kinu said, 'in a cave or a mountain hut. I simply want to exist alone with my music, entering ever more deeply into that other world, understanding myself and other people, what is our purpose, why we were born, what happens to us after death.'

'Would your father allow you to become a nun? Have you told him how you feel?'

'I've tried to, and I've made that suggestion, but he dismisses it. He does not seem to be capable of truly hearing what I am saying to him. Yet he is my father, I respect him deeply and I have to obey him.'

'We both have to,' Sunaomi said.

'I am so glad to hear you say that. For if you refuse to entertain the idea my father will decide on someone else, some man who will be a stranger and far less understanding than you. But you would honour and respect my decisions, wouldn't you? You would not force me into anything?'

He had heard older men boasting of overcoming a woman's reluctance or coldness, instructing them in the pleasures of the body and igniting their desire. Or of simply forcing their participation. He was too inexperienced for the first and the second filled him with revulsion.

Kinu said urgently, 'Can we agree to be betrothed, to satisfy Father's demands?'

He could see no way of refusing her.

Kinu seized his hand at the same moment as her father approached.

Neither of them said anything as they turned to face Kahei. He looked at their joined hands and drew his own conclusions. A smile broke out on his face.

'My beloved daughter! My new son! Nothing could make me happier!'

Escorting them back to the room he called for more wine, and though he kept his promise not to announce the betrothal he could not resist making barely veiled references as he drank.

The moon had set and the inn was silent when Sunaomi finally managed to get away. His head was swimming from too much wine since his discomfort with the situation had made him drink unwisely.

Kaneda held his elbow to make sure he did not trip over, and whispered in his ear, 'I understand the need for discretion but let me tell you I am glad. Lord Miyoshi is a powerful ally and now I know you intend to take up the Arai inheritance. No more of this nonsense of handing it over to your brother. You are Zenko's eldest son.'

His assumption was misguided, Sunaomi thought. For if he married Kinu, according to the agreement they had made, they would never have children. He tried to explain this to Kaneda, then recalled she had told him in confidence and found he was babbling.

Kaneda smiled and said indulgently, 'The wine has made you incomprehensible!'

When they entered their room Sunaomi saw to his surprise that the other three were all still awake. Taro sat next to the flickering oil lamp, the book in his hands. Kichizo and Kiyoko knelt in the shadows in the watchful attitude of the Tribe. They struck him as comical.

'Why are you not asleep?' he said, laughing.

'We are on guard, of course,' Kiyoko said. 'Taro's not sleeping, so we won't either. We work for you, so to keep watch is part of our duty.'

'You can sleep now,' Kaneda said immediately. 'I'll take over.'

'I'll stay up with you,' Taro said.

'There's no need,' Kichizo remarked. 'We can go without sleep.'

'There's no point everyone staying awake,' Sunaomi said, exasperated. 'What danger is there anyway? The Miyoshi guards are outside.'

The four of them stared at him sullenly, none wanting to give in first.

'Kaneda and Kichizo take the first half of the night—what's left of it. Taro and Kiyoko, the second. That's an order!'

He lay down. Chin crawled into the crook of his arm. He fell asleep almost immediately but woke a couple of hours later to hear Kaneda rousing Taro. Kiyoko must have already been awake. She said something to Taro but he did not respond.

When Sunaomi next woke it was dawn and the birds were

singing loudly. He went to the privy and then walked to the end of the garden with Chin. She barked at the sounds of the Miyoshi men preparing the horses for the lord's departure.

So, he was now betrothed to be married. But what curious agreement had he entered into?

Taro came down to join him. He looked tired but, more than that, he had an air of preoccupation, a distant look in his eyes.

'You can't have got much sleep,' Sunaomi said.

'I wouldn't sleep before them,' Taro replied. 'I don't trust either of them. And I was thinking about the book. There's so much I don't understand. Can we talk about it sometime?'

'Tonight, perhaps, when we stop, wherever that's going to be. We should get on the road as soon as possible.'

Did Masao waste time in sleeping and drinking or did he ride all night? How far ahead of them was he now?

CHAPTER SEVEN

The dog rode in a bamboo carrier that Kaneda had made for her, her fawn head looking out, her red–brown eyes alert. Her black ears with their silky fringes twitched in response to every sound. Occasionally she let out a flurry of loud barks at a passing dog or some strange shape, a man carrying a hoddle laden with yams on his back, a priest in a mushroom-shaped hat. At those times Sunaomi held her with one hand to prevent her jumping out. He felt the rapid beat of her heart and her excited breath. Under the silky coat she was all muscle.

The rare dog and the striking horse drew people's attention. Sunaomi recalled Kiyoko's remarks and wondered if he was too flamboyant, too noticeable. But what could he do about it? He didn't want to give up Chin or Kiki. He didn't want to change the way he looked.

Kaneda took advantage of the attention and made sure everyone knew this was Arai Sunaomi, riding on the orders of Lady Otori Kaede, the Empress's favourite.

'You no longer have to hide who you are,' Kaneda said when Sunaomi expressed his misgivings. 'You must be proud of it and enjoy your inheritance and its benefits. You suffered greatly as a child—I know that better than anyone—and no doubt more sacrifices will be demanded of you before your life's journey is over. Make the most of these days of peace and pleasure.'

Sunaomi saw Kiyoko tighten her grip on her brother's waist and whisper in his ear. Kichizo gave his soundless laugh. Kaneda amused the siblings greatly though they treated him with an ironic deference. Next to them the old warrior seemed rigid and humourless. They rode with easy grace, vaulting on and off Hitare's back as the mood took them, sometimes running alongside for many miles, apparently tireless.

Kichizo was extremely competitive. Often in the evenings while it was still light Kaneda and Sunaomi practised sword fighting. Kichizo joined in, eager to prove he was their equal in martial arts, and their superior in other ways. He was strong and swift, his moves unorthodox and unpredictable. Kaneda disapproved of them but had to admit they were effective. Kichizo rarely used his Tribe skills, only when he saw an opportunity to goad Kaneda or outwit Sunaomi.

Sunaomi suspected that both Kaneda and Kichizo were half-hoping for an attack so they might prove their superiority by being the one to rescue him.

On previous journeys Taro had also taken part in these practice sessions but now he spent the time studying his book. He remained quiet and thoughtful. Once or twice he seemed about to approach Sunaomi to discuss his reading, but the time was never right. They rode all day, bathed, ate, slept, and Kaneda made sure any spare moments were filled with practice.

The days went by with no trace of Masao, despite Kichizo and Kiyoko using all their skills of infiltration and information gathering. No officials in Sanda and the other towns they passed through had seen him or anyone resembling him.

'He is covering his tracks,' Kiyoko said. 'Using forest paths, avoiding towns.'

'So, is he eating nothing and talking to no one?' Sunaomi asked.

'It is strange to find no sign at all,' Kichizo said. 'Maybe he never intended to go to Hofu.'

'Maybe you deliberately misled us and still do,' Kaneda said accusingly.

Kichizo did not reply but he and Kiyoko exchanged a smile.

'Lord Miyoshi gave me other tasks to accomplish in Hofu,' Sunaomi said. 'It will not be a wasted journey.'

He did not know if he wanted to catch up with Masao or not. He hoped for it and dreaded it, waking each morning with the same mix of anticipation and fear.

Every night he longed to awaken Utahime but he hardly dared even to unwrap the doll, only in the rare moments when he was alone snatching a glimpse of her face. It seemed to him that each time she was more beautiful. Day and night he held her in his heart.

Once he said casually to Kiyoko, who was riding alongside him while Kichizo ran ahead, 'Do you still have the dolls you and your mother made?'

'When we came of age we presented them to the shrine in the village,' she replied. After the horses had trotted a little further she said suddenly, 'Ours never came to life in the way yours did.'

When Sunaomi gave her a sharp look she went on. 'Don't think I didn't notice you talking to it. You called it Moritsugi, didn't you? Ours never had any name but our own and they never moved or spoke. They were not without power but it was a different kind of power. You would never have thought to throw Moritsugi into the fire if the doll itself had not told you to. I'd never known anyone with that ability to bring things to life. I wondered if you were a ghostmaster, like Hisao, and that was why there was a bond between you.'

'I am nothing like Hisao! If I had any ability like that, it's gone now. It was something childish, linked to a child's imagination, and now I am an adult.'

'Not quite, not officially,' Kiyoko said with a mocking look.

Sunaomi could feel the carved bear beneath his robe. It was warm but still, as if it were in deep hibernation. What would cause it to wake?

Kiyoko leaned towards him and whispered, 'And your lover, the ghost girl? That's what she is, isn't she? A doll that you bring to life?'

'There is no lover, no ghost,' Sunaomi replied, as he urged Kiki into a canter. Kiyoko saw and heard too much. She knew him through and through.

Kiki was much faster than the other two horses and he left them far behind. Sunaomi made him gallop, holding Chin with one hand so she would not fall. For a short while he was alone, revelling in the sense of freedom, the speed of the horse, the warm, fragrant air in his face.

Kiki began to tire and Sunaomi let him slow to a walk. The air around him had changed, made more humid by the flooded rice fields he was now riding between, and smelling of manure and woodsmoke. He passed a few farmhouses, and then rode into a small town.

It was strangely silent, no shops or marketplace and no living beings apart from a skinny dog which slunk away when Chin growled at it. Sunaomi did not want to go further into the deserted town and came to a halt, waiting for the others to catch up.

Chin growled again, pointing her nose towards a house along the street, and Sunaomi saw the shadow of a boy disappear between the buildings. He thought at once he must be a thief, stealing while the townspeople were all elsewhere.

'Hey!' he shouted, outraged on their behalf. 'Come back!'

Kiyoko caught up with him. Hitare was breathing heavily, showing his age. Kiki snorted at him.

'Where is everyone?' Kiyoko said, looking around.

'There was a boy up ahead, but he vanished.'

'Vanished?' She gazed in the direction he indicated. Her face took on an alert, concentrated expression. Before she could say anything else, Kaneda arrived, Taro clinging on behind him. As soon as the roan, Baku, stopped Taro slid down, clasping his stomach.

'My insides have been churned to mush,' he complained.

Kaneda was more interested in scolding Sunaomi. 'You should not gallop ahead like that! Who knows what danger you might be heading into?' He too glanced around. 'I don't like the feel of this place. Something's wrong. Let's ride through quickly.'

Kichizo loped up, hardly panting at all. He stood motionless, sniffing the air and listening.

'I can smell incense. Priests are chanting and people crying and wailing.'

'It's a funeral,' Kiyoko said.

After they had ridden a little further, Sunaomi could hear the sound too, the desperate wailing of the bereaved, underpinned by the deep voices of priests or monks reminding them vainly that all life is impermanent, that everything born must die, that all beginnings lead to endings.

His skin tingled on his neck. The chanting voices faded and were replaced by gongs and drums. Chin put her nose in the air and howled.

The horses jigged, their ears laid back, their eyes rolling.

'We should not interrupt their grieving,' Kaneda said. 'All the more reason to ride straight on.'

But as they passed the entrance to the approach to the temple, a group of men emerged, carrying staves and poles, shouting in incoherent rage. After them came women, their faces ugly with tears, stones in their hands.

Kaneda drew his sword, moving Baku quickly so the horse stood between the crowd and Sunaomi, and called out, 'Stay back! We are envoys from the capital. We serve the Empress. Any attack on us will be severely punished.'

His composure as much as the long shining blade made the men pause for a moment.

A stone flew through the air narrowly missing Hitare, making him rear a little. Kichizo grabbed the reins and soothed him.

Sunaomi urged Kiki forward and spoke to the closest man who seemed to be the leader of the group. 'What has happened? Have you suffered some terrible loss? I am Lady Otori's messenger. I swear, if a crime has been committed or some other wrong done to you I will do all I can to put it right and punish those responsible.'

'What?' the man replied scornfully. 'What do you imagine you can do, you, barely out of boyhood, with your pretty dog and horse? Our bravest lads are dead. We have just buried them.' He turned away with a derisive gesture. Behind him the men tightened their grip on their weapons and shuffled forward.

'On your knees,' Kaneda ordered. 'No one insults my lord, Arai Sunaomi.' He raised his sword and was about to cut the man down.

'No!' Sunaomi cried. 'There will be no more bloodshed. Only fools take words spoken in grief as insults.'

He slid quickly from Kiki's back, thrust the reins to Taro, and went towards the man.

'I will not draw my sword,' he said. 'I must know what happened. Let us sit down together and I will listen to you.'

For a moment he felt the surge of emotion among the crowd and he thought they would overcome him and beat him to death but he gazed unflinchingly at them and something about his demeanour must have calmed them. Their leader held up his hand and they began to back away. At that moment their ranks parted and a priest in black garments hurried through.

Casting a quick look over the strangers, the priest said, 'Three men wearing the crest of the Empress, and a woman? What justice can you bring us?'

Three men? Sunaomi turned to look behind him. Kichizo was no longer there. He did not know whether to feel reassured or dismayed. Kiyoko's eyes were lowered and she had assumed a submissive appearance. If she had seen her brother go she was not saying anything.

'I am Arai Sunaomi and I ride on the orders of the Empress,' he said, trying to sound authoritative but not too challenging. 'Tell us what happened and how we can help you.'

The priest addressed the leader of the crowd. 'Genjiro, I'll take them to my house and we'll talk there. Make sure there are no disturbances. Please stay calm.'

'Someone must pay,' Genjiro replied. 'The Empress must give us justice or we'll seek it ourselves.'

'But these travellers had nothing to do with the murder.

Their sympathies are all with you,' said the priest. 'Don't do anything to incite the people further or you will have blood on your hands too.'

His tone was conciliatory, his words persuasive. Genjiro's anger subsided but in its wake grief returned. He nodded, his lips pressed together, his eyes suddenly wet.

The priest bowed to Sunaomi. 'Follow me, Lord Arai.'

Kaneda dismounted to walk with Sunaomi, while Taro led their two horses, and Kiyoko followed close behind on Hitare.

The crowd parted to let them through. Sunaomi sensed their mood had changed, like Genjiro's, but they were still volatile, still seeking some consolation for their corrosive pain.

'Genjiro is a good man, really, a strong leader,' the priest said. 'But he tends to let himself get carried away.'

At the end of the street stood a small temple with walls of faded and weathered wood and a shingled roof. It was neat and well kept but there were signs of decay, missing tiles, water stains, a broken step. The garden was lush with the new green leaves and brilliant flowers of early summer but the grass had grown high and there were many weeds.

'There is always so much to do,' the priest said apologetically, as if seeing the place anew through their eyes. 'We have been so busy with the spring planting, and now this disaster has befallen us. The great wheel turns and crushes us beneath it.'

Without looking directly at Kiyoko, the priest indicated she should stay outside. Sunaomi and Kaneda followed him into the house beside the temple hall while Taro waited at the gate with the three horses and Chin. The animals were still restless. Sunaomi could hear Chin yelping, the horses' sudden shrill neighs and Taro's voice as he soothed them.

'Please sit here.' The priest went out to the back of the house and spoke to someone there. He returned and sat down opposite Sunaomi, wiping his eyes on his sleeve.

'I try to cling to the teachings of the Enlightened One,' he said. 'I should not be so attached to the things of this world. But they were such fine young men, our best, and their mothers are inconsolable. None of my words can ease their grief.'

His face crumpled and his shoulders shook with emotion. For many moments no one said anything. Then an ancient man in monk's robes shuffled in with a tray, a tea kettle and bowls. He poured each one slowly and carefully, and then shuffled out again.

After they drank Kaneda prompted, 'These young men, how did they die?'

'A stranger came, on horseback. He was not old, maybe a little older than Lord Arai. He was dishevelled, his clothes and hair unkempt. I don't think he had bathed in a long time. Yet he carried a fine sword, his horse was a good one, and he had money to buy wine. He drank a great deal, though it did not seem to affect him: we cannot blame the wine. He attracted our young men around him. They were curious about him, and his silence, broken only by outrageous statements, provoked them. They were not completely blameless, I can see that.' He sniffed and wiped his eyes again.

'What sort of statements?' Sunaomi asked.

'That they would not believe who he was, that he was the best swordsman in the realm, that he had already sent ten men to the next world.'

'Who did he claim to be?' Kaneda said, glancing at Sunaomi.

'I did not hear,' the priest replied but Sunaomi did not need confirmation to know it was Masao.

'So a fight broke out?' he said, a mixture of sorrow and dread making his voice break a little.

'It was not a brawl,' the priest said. 'He was not attacked, apparently. But somehow two of our lads, best friends since childhood, one of them Genjiro's son, found themselves challenging him. I imagine they wanted both to impress him and to teach him a lesson. They have been practising fighting with poles at our school, one of those set up by Lord Miyoshi. They thought they would knock the arrogance out of him.'

'Fighting with poles?' Kaneda questioned, frowning. 'Did they end up using swords?'

'The stranger taunted them,' the priest said. 'It got to the stage where they could not back down. They went to the school and came back armed with swords. He fought them both at the same time and killed them within minutes.'

'And what happened to the stranger?' Sunaomi asked.

'He mounted his horse and rode away.'

'Was he alone?'

'When he first arrived, I'm told, a young boy was with him. He held the horse while his master drank, and then during the fight. But in the shock and confusion afterwards no one saw what happened to him. Presumably they left together.'

'How long ago was it?' Kaneda asked. 'A day? Two days?'

'Two days.' The priest gave a deep sigh. 'Already two days. Soon it will be seven days, then seven weeks, seven years, but the parents' grief will be as sharp as ever until they too pass over into that other world.' He stared bleakly into the distance, finding no consolation anywhere.

'Grief does pass,' Sunaomi said diffidently, hesitating to offer comfort to one so much more advanced in years and wisdom.

'When you are young, maybe that is true. But as you grow older each loss is harder to bear.' He looked at Sunaomi as if remembering something. 'It is the natural way for parents to die before their children, not for children to be taken first.'

Sunaomi wondered if the man knew something of his history. His parents had been condemned to kill themselves and were considered traitors, yet he thought of them every day and would for the rest of his life, honouring their courage and their pride. His youngest brother's face floated now into his mind, and his tiny hands, marked with the sign of the Kikuta. Hiromasa had been only two years old. Their mother, Sunaomi had been told, could not bear to leave him behind and had killed him herself. Tears came into his own eyes, for his family, for Utahime, his beloved, who had also died with her parents in a similar fashion. Her brother, Masao, had been spared by an unthinkable sacrifice, when his father's retainer had substituted his own son ...

Sunaomi had never known this boy's name. Perhaps it had also been Masao. He would be a young man now if his father had not taken his life.

Maybe the price paid for Masao's life had been too high. Maybe the spirit of the son who had been slain in his place had possessed him and was driving him mad. Sunaomi had not wanted to believe Masao had killed the Kono boy but now he had to face the fact that his old friend was not only a murderer but one who took pleasure in killing.

He was all the more determined to find Masao, confront him and, if possible, save him. 'We should go on at once,' he said to Kaneda.

'I am sorry we cannot offer you anything more,' the priest said. 'No one has gathered food, cooked or eaten since the murders.'

Kaneda said sternly, 'It is your role to encourage others. Have food prepared, invite everyone. People must eat and drink. Life must go on. Grief cannot be avoided but it must not be indulged.'

The warrior's bracing words seemed to invigorate the old man a little. He nodded, smoothed his robe and prepared to stand.

'It seems this murderer is the same one we are pursuing,' Kaneda said. 'He will be arrested and brought to justice before the Empress and Lady Kaede.'

The priest was on his feet. 'I will tell Genjiro and the others that.' As he went out onto the verandah he said something under his breath. Sunaomi did not catch it but Kiyoko, still kneeling patiently, looked up at him and he knew she had.

There was no sign of Kichizo when they came to the temple gate. The horses whinnied at them and Chin nearly fell out of her basket in excitement.

'Where's the next town?' Kaneda said, glancing up at the sun. It was well into the afternoon.

'Taguchi is an hour's walk away but it has no inn,' the priest said. 'Beyond that, since you have horses, you might get to Kara-sumachi before sunset. That's a big place, on the river.'

'Then we will head there, if you agree, lord.'

Sunaomi nodded and mounted Kiki. Crowds were still in the streets but they did not trouble the travellers as they rode away.

'Where's your brother?' Sunaomi asked Kiyoko.

'He went after the boy.' She brought Hitare alongside Kiki. 'I caught a glimpse of him and I'm sure it was the same boy who was with Masao in Miyako, the night I was attacked.'

'So, they didn't leave together? I wonder why not.'

'You'll be able to ask him yourself.'

'Kichizo will be left far behind,' Sunaomi said. 'We must travel fast to make Karasumachi before sunset.'

'He'll find a way,' she replied.

The town's buildings quickly gave way to rice fields and then to open country, wild and uncultivated. The road became narrower, at times no more than a stony track. There were no bridges but the rivers were shallow and the horses splashed through them.

Sunaomi was happy to ride without speaking. He had many things to turn over in his mind, and beneath his confusion his longing for Utahime pulsed as steadily as his heartbeat. He felt he would die if he were not soon alone with her again. But he did not see how he would ever get away from his companions.

Once they were past Taguchi they saw few other travellers. It was only then that Sunaomi recalled the muttered words of the priest. He asked Kiyoko what she had heard.

'Something about the rule of females bringing disasters. He doesn't care much for women, as you may have noticed.'

'Do many people share his opinion, do you think?'

'It's one of the reasons I was attacked,' she reminded him.

'I know about those young men. I meant ordinary people, in the provinces. What else have you heard?'

'A few comments here and there. From men, of course, who

can't see what's under their noses. They ignore the years of peace and the country's prosperity. They blame every flood and earthquake, every untimely death such as we just witnessed, on Lady Kaede and her unnatural rule. False stories and rumours circulate. People believe what they want.'

'You seem remarkably cheerful about it!' Sunaomi said.

'Oh, you know, in the Tribe, peace and prosperity don't count for much. We prefer discord and suspicion, for then we find employment.'

'I suppose you are behind many of the false stories and lying rumours.'

'Maybe some are started and spread by the Tribe, but not by Kichizo and me, not at the moment. For we serve you and you serve Lady Kaede.'

'But, we are talking about the Tribe,' he said, amused in spite of himself. 'How can I believe anything you say?'

She rode so close their knees touched. A picture of her naked body came into his mind with such force it made the blood rise to his cheeks.

'Trust me, Sunaomi. You know you can.'

They came to Karasumachi a little before sunset. In the deep shadow of the mountains the town had a dreamlike, melancholy air. Rice fields surrounded it and there were the usual smells of manure and cooking fires. The slopes of the foothills had been cleared of trees in many places, revealing curious outcrops of black rock which rose higher than the remaining trees. The tallest was large enough to have a shrine on top of it. Sunaomi could just make out a path and steps.

The innkeeper had a scarred, pockmarked face as though he had been stricken by smallpox not long ago. He was not rude but not effusively welcoming either. The rooms were adequate, the food plain.

While the others were eating, Taro went out into the town. It was around dusk when he returned. He had found meat for Chin, and gave it to her in a small bowl.

'So, Taro, what can you tell us about this place?' Kaneda asked.

'They have the same complaints as everywhere. They even grumble about the new roads which offer more opportunities for trade but bring more strangers who cause trouble and allow them to escape more quickly.'

'Anyone in particular?' Kaneda said.

'No, it is just a general resentment. And as well as itinerant troubles, there is a residential one.' Chin had finished eating and gave Taro a lick in thanks. He patted her head and went on. 'A restless ghost apparently has put a curse on the district. There's been an epidemic of smallpox, crops are blighted, animals and infants don't thrive. Several people suggested that if Lady Kaede really wanted to do some good for them she should send someone to placate it.'

'We don't have time for that,' Kaneda said. 'We must sleep and rise before dawn to ride on. The moon is still bright.'

Sunaomi finished eating and pushed his bowl to one side. 'Where is this ghost?'

'In the shrine we saw as we rode in, on top of the huge rock. No one dares go near it now. Last year some young men went to climb the path, with drums, for that used to be the tradition, but as soon as they started playing, thunder began to echo them and a storm broke out with lightning and huge hailstones that damaged the drums and badly bruised the men.'

'I will take a look for myself,' Sunaomi said. It was a chance to be alone. He would take the doll with him and awaken Utahime, certain not to be disturbed. He could feel her calling to him, as desperate as he was to be together. The thought made him dizzy with excitement.

'That's a ridiculous suggestion,' Kaneda said. 'This is nothing to do with us. We have a different and more important mission. Even supposing there is such a ghost, what can you do to calm it?'

'It will show the townspeople that Lady Kaede does care for them and will help them.'

'You need to sleep,' the warrior protested. 'We have a long journey ahead of us. Besides, there might be unexpected dangers.'

Sunaomi could see that if he persisted Kaneda would offer to accompany him.

'I will go alone,' he said. 'You will remain here.' Before Kaneda could argue any further he said curtly, 'It is my command.'

He did not like using his status to get his own way. Yet his desire to be alone was now so great he would stick at nothing.

'I'm just going to look,' he said, more gently. 'Maybe I can do something, maybe not. At least it will show we are concerned.'

'Let Taro go with you,' Kaneda begged. 'And you must go armed.'

'Very well.' Taro could keep watch and look after Chin. Sunaomi went to the room to get his sword and the bundle with the doll wrapped inside it. As he returned to the front of the inn, Kiyoko brushed up against him. He wondered if she suspected his hidden reason, if she could sense his desire.

She whispered, 'The innkeeper is a man who is hiding something.'

He nodded. 'Keep an eye on him. Your brother has not arrived yet?'

'Don't worry. He'll be here soon.'

As Sunaomi and Taro walked away from the inn, the innkeeper came after them, calling out.

'I heard you say you were going to the old shrine. You must not. It is dangerous.'

'I want to see it for myself,' Sunaomi returned. 'Maybe my visit will calm whatever evil has taken up residence there.'

'There is nothing to see. You're wasting your time.' The man's tone was insolent.

Taro said, 'Do not address the lord in such a manner. He is seeking to help you.'

'We do not need your help. We manage our own affairs.'

He has become a warlord, Sunaomi thought. *He rules this town and does not want any interference. He's afraid of what we might turn up.* He looked up at the bare hills. It was unusual to see such indiscriminate logging. He guessed the innkeeper was involved in the illegal sale of timber. He would not want strangers from the capital wandering around.

It made him all the more determined to go to the shrine. He did not think the man would dare to stop them physically. He gave him a cool look and walked on without saying anything.

'Be it on your own heads!' the innkeeper shouted. 'I've warned you.'

'What was that about?' Taro asked, when they were beyond being overheard.

'He has committed crimes that he doesn't want uncovered.'

'Selling timber?' Taro said, looking up at the clearing.

'That, certainly, and maybe other things,' Sunaomi replied.

Chin was glad to have the chance to run and was delighted by the myriad smells of the town and then the rice fields. They followed the river for a little way. A mist was rising from the water, frogs croaked from the reeds but there were no fireflies. They could see the dark mass of the rock rising up to their right. Once they had turned onto a narrow track that led towards it, Sunaomi noticed that the fields on either side had been neglected. Where there should have been green seedlings there were only the bare stalks of a long-ago harvest. The banks of the dykes were crumbling. Broken tools lay here and there as if thrown down and abandoned. An old straw rain cape slumped on the ground like a dead animal.

Chin approached it, growling, and sniffed at it for a long time. Sunaomi called her to follow them.

Taro said suddenly, 'Lord Sunaomi.'

'You know you don't have to call me *lord* when we are alone.'

Taro nodded. 'That's partly what I wanted to talk to you about. The book, the one I brought with me, says we are all equal in the eyes of the Secret One. It seems so right, and yet so wrong. There's a lot like that—I seem to be on the verge of understanding, and yet not getting it. I don't want to talk about it in front of Lord Kaneda. I'm afraid of offending him. But you tell me not to call you *lord*. You offered the house to my mother and me. I feel you understand and will explain it to me.'

'I would have to read it myself,' Sunaomi said. 'I will, I promise you.'

All he could think of at that moment was the doll he held so closely and how soon he would be able to wake her.

'I can't do it tonight, though. It will be too dark and I must be alone.' He added, to soothe any hurt feelings. 'You can read while you wait, by the light of fireflies and the moon, like the scholars of old.'

The long twilight was fading. The mountains in the east were rimmed in silver as the moon, one week past full, rose behind them. The track became more overgrown with grass that came up to their knees and hid Chin completely. The grass gave way to a bamboo grove, the trunks gleaming as if polished, the fronds rustling in the slight breeze. The path was soft with dead leaves, muting their footsteps. Next, a few immense trees rose around them, Sunaomi recognised them as cedars by their smell. Beneath them he and Taro looked tiny, and Chin as small as an ant. He could hear the high squeaking of bats. Before them loomed the dark basalt rock.

An owl hooted overhead, making them jump. Chin gave a mournful howl in response. Sunaomi picked her up and handed her to Taro. She was quivering and her heart was beating fast.

Taro said, 'She's scared, and I don't blame her.'

Sunaomi sensed the dark atmosphere that flowed from the shadows of the trees and the rock but he was even more aware of Utahime's insistent pleading. She was not afraid of restless spirits. She already dwelled in *that other world* and she was calling to him to join her.

'Wait here with Chin. Don't let her bark and don't come any further.'

'What if you need help?' Taro said.

'I won't.'

'Leave the bundle you're carrying, at least.'

'I need it,' Sunaomi replied shortly, gripping it more tightly.

As he had seen from afar, there was a path up the face of the rock with rough steps hewn out. It was hard to see, the steps were slippery and the moon cast treacherous shadows. His sword and the bundle were hindering him. A little way up a small ledge allowed him to pause. He took the doll from the bundle and tucked her with the nail inside his jacket. He left the wrapping cloth with his sword on the ledge and climbed on.

From the ground the shrine had not looked very high but now the ascent seemed endless. He looked down once and could see neither Taro nor the dog. The darkness closed around him, impenetrable and heavy, pushing back against him with a warm, suffocating weight. He felt he was at the level of the treetops. The wind had risen with the moon and he could hear it surging through the branches. An owl floated silently past, making him almost lose his footing. Something was trying to prevent him going any further.

He stopped for a moment with a pang of unease. How would he ever climb down again? At the same time his longing intensified. He felt for the doll. 'Utahime,' he whispered. 'Help me.' His fingers grazed the carving of the bear. It felt warm, soft, its fur thick and silky. He recalled the authority with which he had awakened it as a child and then returned it to the wood it was carved from. Suddenly he was seeing with those other childhood eyes. They penetrated the darkness and saw the shrine clearly, not far above him.

A gate of weathered wood stood before it. Sunaomi stepped through it and onto the verandah. It was covered with dead leaves which rustled beneath his tread. Cobwebs brushed against his face. A board cracked under his weight and he jumped forward lest he fall through it. A creature scuttled past his feet. Somewhere a shutter was banging.

The doors were open. Sunaomi stepped inside, holding his breath, letting his eyes adjust to the new darkness. He could not see anyone, dead or living, nor could he hear breathing. He unlooped the bear from round his neck and placed it near the door.

'Keep watch,' he whispered, his excitement making him playful.

Then he drew Utahime out and pierced her to bring her to life.

'Sunaomi,' she said. 'My beloved.' Then with the same flowing swiftness she was in his arms.

After the cloying humid warmth he had climbed through, her cold touch was as reviving as ice in summer. She smelled fresh like water and when he touched her throat he could feel no blood.

'I am healing,' she whispered. 'Every time we are together

my wounds close. I am becoming what I was before, a young girl full of hope and beauty.'

In the glow that shone from her eyes he could see that it was true. His heart opened to her.

'I miss you,' she said. 'I want to be with you all the time. I wish I were not dead, yet I embrace my death for if I had lived we would never have met and never been together. But I don't want to waste time in talking. Let us lie together while we can. Let me feel your skin against mine so your heart burns me.'

It was all he wanted, with a reckless urgency that did not heed the suffocating darkness or the malevolent spirit that had cursed the town. All that mattered was that they were alone and could become one.

CHAPTER NINE

Sunaomi awoke, as he had before, to feel Utahime's icy fingers caressing his neck.

'There is a woman here,' she said, 'with a dead child.'

Through his own perfume he could smell the stench of decay.

'Leave now, and take me with you,' Utahime begged, her hand closing over his arm.

He loosened her fingers, and stood. He felt curiously disembodied, as if his essence had been consumed and absorbed by her. The only light was the glow from her eyes.

He could just make out a mass, vaguely human in shape yet not human, something ancient that had emerged from the earth or from the trees. Perhaps it had been a woman, as Utahime had said. The child lay in the curve of its massive lap. The child's eyes were open and unseeing. It was human and it was dead. He could see its small face was encrusted with pox.

Moved by pity, he knelt and said, 'Ah, the poor thing.'

A voice emerged like a deep groan. 'What man are you that dares to come here?'

'I am Arai Sunaomi,' he replied.

'Prepare to die, Arai Sunaomi. All men are my enemies and I have vowed to kill any that climb up to this place.'

'It may be my fate to die here,' he replied, half in love with the idea. Then as if someone, Utahime perhaps, were guiding him he went on. 'But first I will listen to you and then I will bury your child.'

A long silence followed. When the voice spoke again it had become gentler and more human. 'That is all I desire, to be heard and have my grief recognised. I do not pray to have it taken from me, for into all lives trouble must come and no one is spared. But cruelty must be spoken of and exposed.'

'For some years I lived in the world of women,' Sunaomi heard himself say. 'I know their insight and wisdom. I know how to listen. Let me take the child. I will dig a grave at the base of the rock.'

'I am not ready yet.' The voice was again deep and dark. 'I have other desires that must be fulfilled.'

'Who are you?' Sunaomi dared to ask.

'I am the spirit of this place, the guardian of the trees, and I am the woman who tried to save them, who was raped and murdered, along with her sick child.'

Sunaomi could guess who the culprit was: the innkeeper, given away by his scarred face.

'Her spirit and mine became one. She serves me and I protect her and we feed each other's desire for revenge.' All traces of humanity had disappeared from the voice. Suddenly Sunaomi was afraid. *I am a fly who has blundered into a spider's web. This is far beyond my powers. I must get out.*

He edged backwards, feeling behind him for the doll. Where was it and where was Utahime? The being reached out with its bulbous shapes where a human arm would have been and pressed down on Sunaomi's knees with the weight of the whole world. It recalled the heavy smothering power of the black fox that had trapped Kaneda and had nearly overcome Sunaomi himself.

A terror greater than he had ever known swept over him. He was going to die here, his spirit imprisoned forever.

'Utahime,' he gasped. 'Help me!'

There was no reply from her and the glow of her face had faded. Complete darkness enveloped him.

He thought of Chin and Taro far below. The dog would wait for him endlessly, starting at every footfall, but he would never return to her.

And Utahime? He had kept her with him for his own pleasure. She also would be trapped here for all eternity, punished for his desires.

He could no longer move the lower part of his body. The massive weight held him down. He fell backwards, his hands behind his head.

His fingers grazed something hot, almost burning. It was the bear. He tried to seize it with his right hand but it slithered away from his grasp. He twisted his body and grabbed it with his other hand. The weight was moving up his body, slowly paralysing him. His legs had turned to stone.

His shoulders aching, he worked his fingers into the bear's shape. He felt its stern will, its stubborn resistance, its animal intractability. It wanted to obey him and resisted him like a half-tamed horse. The wood was solid. Had it ever come alive or had he dreamed it? It was just a carving. It could not help him.

Then his fingers touched the silver band that had joined the two broken pieces together. He called on the bear, shouting out loud, and felt the silver become soft and dissolve into fur.

The neck swelled beneath his fingers. It was far too big to hold. He felt its massive shape emerge and tower above him. In the darkness its eyes shone red. Its hot breath swept over his face. It growled, the sound echoing through the building.

Far in the distance he thought he heard Chin barking.

The being that weighed him down was recoiling. Feeling returned to his limbs and he realised he could move again. He rolled over and pushed himself up, sick and dizzy.

He could just make out the mass of the bear as it rose onto its back legs.

'What have you unleashed?' the being said. 'I will let you go for I see you have brought to life the creature that will avenge me. And you will bury my child as you promised.'

Sunaomi heard Chin bark again, a shrill desperate sound, and heard Taro shouting. Something was happening below. Had they been attacked?

He took the small corpse in his arms. It was unbelievably heavy.

Tears came rushing through the air like drops of winter rain. The being wept with a grief that encompassed the whole world. Sunaomi wept too. The sorrow swelled like a thunder cloud, the tears turned to driving hail.

Sunaomi had to retreat, bowing his head to protect his face. He could not see the doll and he would not have been able to pick it up with the child in his arms. He knew he should hurry back down to rescue Taro, and he longed to breathe fresh air.

'Utahime,' he called. 'Wait here! I will come back for you.'

No reply came from the ghost girl.

The bear's enormous presence filled the shrine and then it burst through the doors.

Sunaomi followed, holding the child's corpse up against his shoulder. He wondered if he would be able to carry its great weight but the further he went down from the shrine the lighter it became. Out in the moonlight he could see the flesh was dissolving, the hair falling away, as the laws of the natural world reclaimed it. Briefly the stench of decay almost overwhelmed him, but it passed, and by the time he came to the ledge where he had left his things the corpse was no more than bones. He found the cloth that had held the doll and wrapped the bones in it, steadfastly repeating the words of the sutras that he had chanted so many times at Terayama.

He took up his sword and, holding it and the bundle, continued his descent. The bear was crashing ahead of him and, as Sunaomi neared the bottom of the rocky path he could hear its fierce growling, mingled with screams of pain and fear.

The moon disappeared, swallowed up by a mass of clouds. Rain drove against his face and a flash of lightning lit up Chin at his feet. She was almost shrieking in her relief to see him. Her eyes were huge with alarm and her ears flat against her head.

Sunaomi laid the bundle down and leaped down the remaining steps.

It was growing light. Taro was kneeling beside a man. When Sunaomi approached he saw the man was dying. Near them another lay on his back, his throat ripped out.

Axes and spades were abandoned on the ground, Taro's sword next to them.

'They wanted to climb up after you,' Taro said, looking up at Sunaomi. His forehead was grazed with a long shallow wound. 'I was trying not to harm them, just stop them from passing. But then a bear came and killed them both in an instance. One is the innkeeper.' He looked pale with shock.

'Where did the bear go?' Sunaomi asked, half-dazed, aware that he should pursue it and take control of it, returning it to the wood as he had done before.

'It ran off. Did you see it? It was enormous.'

The rain was soaking. A crash of thunder set Chin barking again.

Sunaomi said, 'There is a child here that we must dig a grave for.'

They found a patch of soft ground where kingcups and dandelions grew profusely. Taro took one of the spades and dug a hole deep enough for the small bundle of bones. Sunaomi laid the child to rest, repeating the verses of the sutra, and adding silently, *Your mother had her revenge.*

Taro knelt and said a quiet prayer. Sunaomi recognised the words. He had heard them long ago and had never forgotten them—they were spoken by the Hidden at the moment of death.

They covered the earth with rocks and replanted the flowers between them.

'Let's go,' Taro said, picking up Chin.

'I have to climb back up,' Sunaomi said. 'I left something up there.'

Taro said something in reply but Sunaomi could not hear it for at that moment the world lit up as lightning flashed directly overhead. They heard the bolt crack and immediately thunder split the sky making the ground tremble.

'That must have struck the shrine,' Taro said, looking upwards.

Strange colours swept over them as though a brilliant dawn was breaking. Sunaomi ran past the bodies on the ground to where he could see to the peak. The shrine was ablaze.

'Utahime!' he screamed but his voice could hardly be heard against the wind and the rain.

Hailstones were crashing around them, bouncing and rolling on the ground. Chin yelped as they struck her, and Taro gasped. Sunaomi welcomed the icy blows. He picked up one large stone, his fingers numb as if under Utahime's touch. Was she in each piece of ice, was she dissolving as they did, slipping away like melted water, or like the smoke that wafted around them and dissipated into the fresh morning air? He had lost her.

The idea was unbearable. He could not leave her. He turned to climb up.

'You can't go up there now,' Taro cried, holding Sunaomi firmly by the arm. 'Everything will be burned. Whatever you left there is gone.' He pulled Sunaomi away roughly, making him stumble. 'We have to report what's happened. We must get back to Lord Kaneda as quickly as possible.'

The hail turned to rain, dimpling the surface of the rice fields, as they approached the town.

It is nearly the fifth month. The plum rains are beginning, Sunaomi thought as he saw horses coming towards them in the dawn light. Kaneda rode in front, leading Kiki while Hitare followed, carrying Kichizo and, he thought, Kiyoko. But as they came nearer he saw it was not Kiyoko. The girl was running behind. Sitting in front of Kichizo, his hands tied, his face angry, was the boy he had seen before.

'You are here! You are safe!' Kaneda exclaimed. 'Mount quickly. I packed your things, they are on the horse.'

'You found him,' Sunaomi said to Kichizo. Once on Kiki's back he took Chin from Taro and placed the dog in the basket. 'Did you find out who he is?'

'He won't say anything. But he has Kikuta hands. He's from the Tribe.'

Kaneda pulled Taro up behind him, asking, 'What happened?'

Sunaomi could not begin to explain the night's events. He chose one part.

'A bear came and killed two men. One was the innkeeper.'

'A bear?' Kaneda gave him a sharp look. 'This is not bear country.'

'Taro saw it,' Sunaomi replied but said no more.

'The whole town is alarmed by his disappearance,' Kaneda said. 'Swarming like bees who have lost their queen.'

'He was a murderer and a rapist. He has been clearing forests and selling timber illegally. We should go back to the town, explain his death and punish his accomplices.'

'We are too few,' Kaneda said. 'I don't trust the townspeople, given the mood they are in. My first duty is to protect you. We will ride on.'

'Definitely the best plan,' Kichizo agreed. He held out his hand to Kiyoko.

'Hitare cannot carry three,' she said. 'I will ride with Sunaomi.'

Without waiting for his permission, she leaped up onto the horse. Her arms clasped him round his waist. He was aware of her strong compact body pressing against his.

He took another look at the captured boy. He had only caught a glimpse of him back in the town but now he felt there was something familiar about his face. Where had he seen him before?

CHAPTER TEN

The rain continued all day. Sunaomi rode in silence, wrapped in regret and grief. In the trickle of water, the splash of the horses' hooves, he thought he heard music, a flute playing, and his heart lifted but when he turned his head he saw nothing. No one followed. Utahime was lost to him.

He should never have gone to the shrine; he should have kept the doll with him all the time. What good had he done? He had buried the child and the murderer had died, but the destruction of the land had been carried out by humans, not by angry spirits. It would have to be restored by human effort and will. Trees were not going to sprout magically overnight.

And he had unleashed the bear and let it escape. Where had it gone and what would happen to it? He missed its warm weight around his neck. He did not know if he could summon it back or if it would return to him of its own free will.

Kiyoko spoke behind him, interrupting his thoughts. 'At least we found the boy. That means we are on the right road and Masao is not far ahead of us.'

Sunaomi forced himself to concentrate on his mission. 'We'll find out how much he knows about Masao when we stop.' He called to Kaneda, 'What's the next town?'

'We must be close to Sasaki,' Kaneda replied. 'We will stay there overnight.'

Sasaki was the domain capital, much larger than Karasumachi with many dwellings clustered around a small castle on a hill overlooking the valley along which they were riding. The river was flowing strongly, its waters level with the road, spilling across it in many places. The horses quickened their pace, sensing food and shelter ahead. Their coats were soaked, their hocks coated with mud.

The town was fortified, with guards at the gate. Kaneda presented their documents of passage, and after the captain had read them he ordered one of his men to take the travellers to the castle.

'Our lord will want to receive Lord Arai himself,' he said with grudging deference.

Sasaki Tsunenaga was a middle-aged man, so lean he looked taller than he was, with a face made up of sharp planes like an axe, and a bony nose.

Kaneda towered over him. Sasaki looked him up and down, remarking, 'You are indeed a tall man.' It seemed to displease him.

Otherwise his greetings were courteous enough, though not warm. He seemed eager to hear news from the capital and of Kahei, who had passed through the town not long before and whom Sasaki admired.

'We fought against each other at Takahara, and then as allies against your father,' he said to Sunaomi. 'But I should not bring up the past. All that is forgotten now we all serve the Empress and Lady Kaede.'

'They can't help bringing it up,' Sunaomi complained later to Kaneda, after they had been escorted to the guest rooms. 'Will they ever let me forget my father was a traitor?'

'Don't dwell on it,' Kaneda said. 'You have more than redeemed his memory and yourself.'

But Sunaomi did not feel redeemed. He felt belittled and inadequate for the task that lay ahead of him. The loss of Utahime had thrown him into a black pit. He questioned what he was doing, why he was pursuing his best friend, and what he was going to do with Masao when he caught up with him.

'Sasaki speaks glibly,' he continued. 'I don't believe he is sincere.'

'He seems honest enough,' Kaneda replied. 'We only need his hospitality for one night. There's no need to antagonise him.

This time tomorrow we'll be far away.'

Kichizo and Kiyoko remained in the guest room with the boy. Taro had stayed with the horses, keeping Chin with him. Suna-omi and Kaneda had been invited to Lord Sasaki's residence to share the evening meal.

Like the rooms and furnishings the food was sparse and austere, the main dish being small bony birds, taken by hawks.

'I am very fond of hunting,' Sasaki said. 'The deer have their fawns now, but come back later in the year and we will hunt together and eat venison.'

He questioned them about their journey and what they had seen on the road. Kaneda mentioned briefly the grumbling and unrest they had encountered. He spoke in his usual direct manner and Sunaomi saw that Sasaki was offended.

'I don't believe it is anything,' the lord said. 'And if it is I will deal with it.' He was silent for a while and then explained, 'It is hard for men to adjust. It will take time. But Lady Kaede has my complete loyalty.'

They have had seven years to adjust, Sunaomi thought. *They are slow learners.* He said mildly, 'I would like to write to my aunt while I am here. I would be grateful if you would arrange for a messenger.'

'Of course,' Sasaki said. 'I will also write and report on our meeting.'

'I will have to tell Lady Kaede about the forest clearances at Karasumachi,' Sunaomi said, alert to Sasaki's reaction. 'She will want to send inspectors.'

Sasaki was frowning. 'There is such a demand for timber for buildings and ships. It's a sign of our magnificent prosperity. You may have met the man behind it, Shinzaemon. He's the innkeeper, among other things. He's a reasonable, honest man. I'm sure he has a replanting plan.'

So, Sasaki has either given his consent or tacitly allowed it. Suna-omi decided not to reveal that Shinzaemon was dead. It meant too many explanations and would certainly delay them.

He retired early with the excuse that he had to write the letter. Kaneda produced ink and paper from his pack. Taro had returned with Chin and sat by the lamp, reading. Sunaomi wrote swiftly, telling his aunt about the journey, the grievances they had heard, the destruction of the forests. He only mentioned the killings briefly, adding that he thought Masao was not far ahead. By now Kahei would already be in the capital so there was no need to describe their meeting. He simply sent greetings to Lord Miyoshi and his daughter.

When the letter was finished and sealed in a bamboo tube he gave it to Kaneda, who said he would take it immediately to Lord Sasaki, to be dispatched at daybreak.

Sunaomi went into the adjoining room where Kichizo and Kiyoko waited with the boy. Chin had been sleeping alongside him; she woke, stretched and followed him.

The boy's hands were untied and his face seemed a little less sullen. Kichizo showed Sunaomi his palms. 'See, Kikuta hands. Just like mine, hey?'

He gave the boy an affectionate punch, producing a reluctant smile.

'You have established a bond with him,' Sunaomi said.

The boy's eyes turned to Chin. He stared at her for a moment then looked back at Kichizo.

'I think we are cousins,' Kichizo said.

'In the way everyone in the Tribe is a cousin to everyone else?'

'Even closer than that,' Kiyoko said, laughing. 'Don't you think he has that Shirakawa look, the same as you?'

Sunaomi was silent. He had thought the boy looked familiar. He was about nine years old. But it was not possible.

'We think he is your brother,' Kichizo said.

'Hiromasa died with my parents,' Sunaomi said.

'Maybe your mother could not bear to kill him. Maybe she gave him to the Tribe,' Kiyoko said. 'It must have been kept a complete secret. Even our mother did not know.'

'Where did you grow up?' Sunaomi said to the boy. 'What do

you remember?'

The blank sullen expression returned. Chin was sniffing at his feet. The boy stretched out and patted her but he did not reply.

'It will take a while to gain his trust,' Kichizo said.

'I don't believe he is my brother,' Sunaomi said. As soon as he spoke he saw it could be possible. In the next moment he was sure it was not.

'I'm not,' the boy muttered, keeping his face turned away from Sunaomi. 'I don't want to be.'

Fine, Sunaomi thought, *we are in agreement on that.* 'More important,' he said, 'is if he knows anything about Masao.'

'He was with him in Miyako,' Kichizo replied. 'He was the one whom Kiyoko saw. They were together until the town where we saw the funeral. Then it seems Masao abandoned him. Perhaps he thought he was an unnecessary burden or perhaps he did not want to endanger him. Hiromasa was hard to capture.'

'He is not Hiromasa,' Sunaomi said.

'I'll call him that for the time being. He won't tell me his name. He has many skills, all innate and uncontrolled. He doesn't seem to have had any training.'

'I did,' the boy interrupted. 'I hated it. That's why I ran away.' He looked up at Kichizo. 'They weren't like you.'

'You don't know me,' Kichizo replied. 'I can make your life a misery. And my sister is even worse. However, I'll permit you to stay with me if you promise not to try to escape. I don't want to waste any more time running after you.'

'I promise,' the boy said.

'Then I won't tie you up again.'

Chin's ears stood up. She turned her head towards the door.

Kiyoko was listening too. 'Someone has arrived on horseback,' she said quietly. 'The horse is gasping as if it's galloped a long way.'

'From Karasumachi presumably,' Kichizo said.

They sat in silence for a few moments, all aware that some

new threat might have arisen. Sunaomi heard Kaneda enter the adjoining room and speak to Taro, asking where he was.

'I am in here,' he called.

Kaneda came in swiftly. 'Lord Sasaki invited me to share a flask of wine with him. While we were drinking, a messenger arrived with news of Shinzaemon's death. His body was discovered after the storm, apparently attacked by a wild animal. The lord wants to question you. You and Taro were seen walking to the shrine the previous evening. An eyewitness described the dog.'

'I suppose I must tell him what I saw,' Sunaomi said, still confused by his thoughts. How could it be true that this boy was his brother? He had thought Hiromasa dead for years. He could not accept that he was alive. Yet there was a possibility, enough to make him doubt his own reason. He made an effort to concentrate on the new problem. 'It's what I told you: the men were killed by a bear.' He felt suddenly exhausted.

'He may find that hard to believe.' Kaneda frowned, thinking for a moment. 'We are his guests here but we might as well be his prisoners.'

'He will not dare lay hands on me or prevent me from travelling on,' Sunaomi replied. 'I am an envoy from the Empress. I will go to him now.'

Kaneda followed silently behind as Sunaomi walked to the lord's residence in the lower floor of the castle. It was still raining and the air was dank and oppressive. Although it was nearly the fifth month, inside the castle it was chilly. He thought how cold and cheerless it must be in winter.

The main hall was dim, lit only with a few lamps in the corners. Lord Sasaki was pacing up and down, his shadow looming behind him. He stopped when Sunaomi came in and sat down abruptly, indicating that Sunaomi should sit too.

Sunaomi gave the older man a slight bow. Kaneda knelt to one side.

'It seems Shinzaemon is dead, along with one of his friends.'

Sasaki spoke with barely contained fury, the anger that men used to intimidate and control.

Immediately Lord Saga and Okuda Tadaie leaped into Sunaomi's mind. Both had terrified him as a child; both had died violently in front of his eyes. Sasaki's rage invigorated him, driving away his tiredness, making him determined not to be cowed into evasion or compromise.

'Shinzaemon was a murderer,' he said. 'He was killed by a bear, but the bear was driven by the spirit of the mountain whom Shinzaemon had deeply offended.'

'This fanciful account and the fact that you said nothing of this earlier leads me to believe that you were somehow complicit.' Sasaki leant towards Sunaomi. His hot breath smelled of meat.

'I was not present when the deaths occurred. I saw the bodies afterwards, and next to them the weapons with which the men had attacked my servant. They were afraid of what I would discover at the shrine, and with reason, for what I found there disclosed their crimes.'

'Your servant killed them and made up the story of the bear. He will pay with his life. Give him up to me and I'll send you on your way.'

'Certainly not,' Sunaomi replied. 'He was attacked; he defended himself but he killed no one.'

Sasaki regarded him closely. 'Bears are only seen here rarely and they are timid, more likely to run away than to turn on a man.'

Sunaomi felt a strange mixture of pity and contempt for the man in front of him who understood nothing of *that other world*. 'The bear was merely an instrument,' he said, striving to speak calmly and truthfully. 'The anger of the goddess incited it. I mentioned earlier the depletion of the forests. The land is suffering. Perhaps you have not seen its degradation? People spoke of a curse. The source of that curse has been removed and justice has been carried out. Bury the dead with respect, replant the forests and hold ceremonies to calm the goddess.'

'You are very young to sit there and give me such advice on how to conduct the affairs of my own domain!' Sasaki said, his fury intensifying. 'It's too easy to blame goddesses and spirit animals for crimes committed by oneself or one's men.'

'I have written a report in my letter to Lady Kaede. She will send inspectors and the matter will be dealt with. But I must ride on as soon as possible or the man I am pursuing will outpace us and we will lose him.'

Sunaomi bowed again and made to stand up. But Sasaki leaped to his feet, shouting, 'I will not let you depart unless you leave your servant, or this man here.' He gestured at Kaneda, who had also stood. 'One or the other. He will be my hostage to make sure those inspectors come. If they never arrive he'll be executed.'

When Sunaomi did not reply at once, Sasaki said tauntingly, 'You know you are outnumbered. I could imprison or kill you all. But I respect Lady Kaede's rule and you are her nephew, so I will let you go on this condition. Choose who it will be.'

Sunaomi felt his own anger rise. It was an intolerable request. He would not give up either Taro or Kaneda to become the helpless victims of Sasaki's cruelty. Moreover, he could not hide from himself the fact that the deaths were his fault. Maybe the innkeeper deserved to die but if Sunaomi had not gone to the shrine, driven by his desire to be with Utahime, if he had not released the bear, Shinzaemon would still be alive.

He spoke out boldly. 'I will stay here with Lord Sasaki. I can tell Lady Kaede's inspectors exactly what happened. I will spend the time until they arrive overseeing the reparations and inspecting the forests.'

Sasaki stared at him, biting his lip.

'Perhaps you will be good enough to provide another horse,' Sunaomi said. 'For I will, of course, keep my horse with me, and my companions will be hard pressed without him.'

'Very well,' Sasaki conceded. 'But they must leave now. I am not extending my hospitality to them any longer.'

'Now, at night, in the rain?' Sunaomi did not try to hide his astonishment at the man's incivility.

'Lord Sunaomi,' Kaneda began, controlling his emotion.

Sunaomi turned to his warrior, saying, 'We must prepare our companions. I will talk with you before you leave.'

Sasaki sent a guard after them. Sunaomi ordered him to wait outside the guest residence while he told the others of his decision. Taro and Kaneda both argued heatedly against it but Sunaomi convinced them it was the only solution.

'Sasaki will not dare harm me,' he said quietly. 'And each of you has a task to perform. Taro must look after Chin, Kaneda must catch up with Masao, Kiyoko and Kichizo must take care of the boy.'

He had had no time to discuss who the boy might be with Kaneda. Now he said, 'Tell me your honest opinion. Does he look like me?'

Kaneda's expression was puzzled. 'I suppose he does, now you mention it. But why do you ask?'

'Kiyoko and Kichizo will explain while you ride. If you think there's the slightest chance they are right, you must guard Hiromasa with your life.'

Maybe he is my brother, maybe not, but they will keep him safe for now.

Despite his brave words he could not help feeling lonely when the others departed. He could hear Chin yelping, and Kiki neighed in alarm at being left behind. He wondered if he should stay awake but he had barely slept in two days and once he was lying down the sound of rain pattering on the roof and trickling through the gutters sent him into the deep sleep of exhaustion.

CHAPTER ELEVEN

Sunaomi dreamed of music in his sleep and woke thinking he was in Terayama listening to the Abbot play. He remembered where he was and wondered where his companions were, how far they had travelled during the night, and what this day would bring.

Lord Sasaki seemed in a better mood. He chatted pleasantly while they shared the morning meal and then suggested they ride out so Sunaomi could see the forests for himself.

'We might find this bear,' he said with a chuckle. 'Or perhaps get a boar. I will lend you one of my hunting bows.'

Sunaomi declined the offer. He had studied archery since childhood but was out of practice. 'I will watch Lord Sasaki,' he said.

'Perhaps that is the role that suits you best,' Sasaki said, looking him up and down. 'You don't have the appearance of a fighting man.'

The tone was insolent and the men sniggered but Sunaomi let it pass, saying only, 'Looks can be deceiving.'

Six warriors rode with Lord Sasaki, as well as servants and beaters on foot and a falconer carrying a pair of hawks. The rain had ceased but the air was full of moisture and mist covered the mountains, hanging beneath the trees, muffling the horses' tread, turning the men on foot into shadowy shapes.

From time to time these men shouted hoarsely and banged together their poles. Deer leaped out of the mist, their coats dark from the rain, their fawns springing after them on fragile legs, but they were allowed to escape. Their turn would come in the autumn.

The forest trees were in blossom, chestnuts, oak and beech,

along with cypress and cedar. In the dank air their fragrance was heavy, almost rotting.

Kiki had been relieved to see Sunaomi but the horse remained restless and anxious, holding his head high and turning back often, ears pricked as if searching for Baku and Hitare.

They rode slowly on an uphill track while Sasaki pointed out aspects of the forest and various landmarks, a pool at the foot of a waterfall, a rock outcrop that resembled a dragon. The trees gave way to a more open plain. From here, Sasaki said, they would have been able to see as far as Karasumachi but a sea of clouds covered everything, apart from the black columns of rock that emerged abruptly from the cloud surface. Sunaomi could just make out the tallest one where the shrine had stood. A plume of smoke still hovered over it. He thought of Utahime and wondered if the doll's ashes lay there, soaked by the rain, or if they had already blown away in the wind.

Sasaki said nothing, just glanced at Sunaomi's face and then stared out over the valley.

Kiki was fussing, dancing and jigging. When they rode on Sasaki said, 'That looks like a good horse. Is he fast?'

'Quite fast,' Sunaomi replied. 'He is still young, so he can be flighty. He was a gift from Maruyama.'

'Maruyama, eh? You are fortunate. We may not have your advantages but we still have good horses.'

What a proud, prickly man he is, framing everything as an insult, Sunaomi thought.

'You should let him have his head, give him a gallop. There's some grassland ahead. We'll see if we can put up a pheasant or two.'

'Or a bear,' one of the men said under his breath, making the others laugh.

They came to the high plain. Animal tracks cut through the grass but there was no road nor any sign of human habitation. The mist hung over it, every blade of grass beaded with moisture. It crossed Sunaomi's mind that the place Sasaki had brought him to was isolated but he did not feel afraid. He had his horse and his sword and he still did not believe Sasaki would harm him. He might insult him obliquely and allow his men to tease him but these things could be endured with patience and good humour.

'Off you go!' Sasaki said and gave Kiki a whack on the rump.

The horse shot forward, bucking from surprise and then from high spirits and nervousness. Sunaomi was not unseated; he brought him back under control and then allowed Kiki to stretch his legs, but he could hardly see ahead and did not like galloping blind across unknown terrain. There were many burrows and rabbit holes and Kiki might put a foot in one at any moment. He was bringing the horse back to a canter when something bright and glossy whirred up under the horse's hoofs.

Kiki shied at the pheasant, gave a huge leap forward and then began to gallop in earnest.

The hawks had been released and they swooped overhead. An arrow went thrumming past.

They are shooting at the pheasant, Sunaomi told himself. But he knew they were not.

Several thoughts flashed through his mind. His letter would never reach Kaede. The envoys would never come. A hunting accident would be reported. How regrettable. Never to see Chin again, or Kaneda or Taro.

But maybe Utahime waited for him in *that other world.*

Kiki stumbled and Sunaomi flew over his head.

He landed on his shoulder, rolled, found his feet. Kiki circled round him, trotting with high steps, whinnying at the approaching horses. Sunaomi noted, as he drew his sword, that the horse did not seem to be lame and he felt relieved, then smiled at himself for he did not think he would need a horse again after this day, this hour.

All his upbringing had been to this end, to meet death without fear, and now it had come for him. It waited in the staves and swords of the men who dismounted and came to surround him, it looked at him through Sasaki's cold eyes, it smiled with his cruel lips.

'You are going to fight?' said the lord, sitting on his horse, his bow in one hand, an arrow in the other. 'How entertaining. I will be the one who watches now.'

Sunaomi said nothing, tightening his grip on the sword's hilt, watching for the first movement from the men around him. The blade kept them at bay for a few moments. Then one of them raised his own sword, another came from behind with a stave, trying to disable Sunaomi's right arm. Sunaomi sensed him there, slashed out and caught the man's arm between wrist and elbow. He felt the jar as the sword hit bone, saw the blood spurt, came back and met the swordsman's forward thrust, parrying it, and with the returning stroke piercing the man's groin.

Two down, but there were still eight or more, warier of him now and angrier.

The ground grew slippery beneath his feet. He was tiring. He did not have the brawn and muscle to sustain a drawn-out fight. He saw Sasaki raise his bow and feared the arrow which if it did not kill him outright would signal the beginning of the end, slowing him down so the men on foot could finish him off.

The arrow flew and struck him in the shoulder. His arm went weak. He gripped the sword more tightly with his other hand, staggering from shock and then pain. He felt fury that his body should be treated in this way and pity for the wounds it was going to endure. Till this moment he had been silent, determined not to give Sasaki the satisfaction of hearing him grovel or plead for his life but now a cry burst from him, a howl of rage and despair.

It was answered by another cry that came echoing out of the mist, a roar like nothing he had heard before. It made the men pause and lower their weapons for an instant. Then came the sound of wild neighing from the horses, as they broke away from the men holding them, and stampeded towards Sunaomi and the circle around him.

The men struggled to get out of their way. Sunaomi was knocked to the ground. He saw a horse's shaggy belly as it leaped over him and, as he tried to stand, another. Something offensive and unnatural was sticking out of his shoulder. He realised it was the shaft of the arrow, and pulled vainly at it, only causing so much pain it made him dizzy.

He could not understand why the circle was not reforming, why someone did not deal the death blow while he lay helpless on the ground. He turned his head and saw two men lying not far from him, their throats torn out. He saw Sasaki's horse go wild with terror, saw the lord's face contort with disbelief and fear, and then he saw the bear.

It was larger than he remembered. The silver fur encircled its neck like a collar and the red cord dangled at its throat. It stood on its hind legs, lashing out with its huge paws.

At least Sasaki will believe me now, he thought, smiling at his own foolishness.

Sasaki was clinging to his horse's neck as it bolted. The remaining men hesitated, then scattered as the bear dropped to all fours and loped after them. How swiftly and effortlessly swiftly it ran! Two more men fell beneath its blows. The rest managed to get away and call to their horses. He heard the trample of hoofs as they galloped away.

Silence returned, broken only by the distant mewing of kites. Sunaomi sat up, his mind blank with shock, and looked around. Apart from the dead he was alone.

He saw Kiki in the distance, stood shakily and whistled to him. The horse's head went up and he pawed the ground.

Sunaomi whistled again, his mouth drying. *If Kiki comes to me I might live but if he leaves me I'll die here.*

Kiki turned and slowly began to pick his way across the rough ground. Sunaomi licked his lips and tried to whistle once more to encourage him, but barely any sound came out.

Something responded with a gentle roar like a cat greeting its master. He turned to see the huge shape of the bear appear over the crest of the plain.

Despite its bulk its movements were lithe and graceful and its tread light. It padded closer on its huge paws. Its muzzle was streaked with blood and foam. Its flanks heaved as it panted. Its brown eyes shone with a reddish glow like Chin's.

The paw was the symbol of his clan and he was the bear's master. Yet he could not find within himself the strength to dominate this huge creature. *I will let it go,* he thought.

Kiki whinnied to him nervously. The horse wanted to approach him but was frightened of the bear.

'It's all right,' Sunaomi said aloud to soothe him. 'Everything's all right.'

The bear thrust its massive head towards him, its teeth bared. Its jaws fastened on to the arrow shaft and snapped it. Fainting, Sunaomi fell to his knees, and felt the bear pull out the arrow head. The bear's tongue was hot on the wound and he could sense blood oozing from it. He vomited several times and then his vision cleared and he realised he could move his arm. The arrow must have missed bone and artery and just pierced the flesh at the top of the shoulder.

He held out his hand and the bear lowered its head and breathed on his palm.

'Thank you,' Sunaomi said and bowed to it. For a few moments they stayed without moving.

I can't do this, Sunaomi thought. *But I must.*

He placed his other hand on the bear's head, felt the thick fur and began to summon back the wood from which it had been carved.

The bear growled as it resisted. Sunaomi's fingers found the silver fur at its neck and gripped it, bringing back the metal that had joined body and head together. He knew it had to obey him and sensed that it wanted to with its deepest essence, but it was divided. Its bloody rampage had awakened some other part of its nature, one that craved men's terror, and relished their blood and their death.

His fingers probed and caressed with steady insistence and gradually the bear began to diminish. The whole time Sunaomi did not stop staring into its eyes, reaching for the wood and the metal, even as he regretted the loss of the living creature. Finally the glow left its eyes and the carving lay inert in his hands. He slipped the cord round his neck. The wood was warm against his skin.

Kiki came up to him. Sunaomi leaned against the horse's shoulder, trying to stop his body's trembling. Kiki was quivering too.

The mist became heavier until it was almost rain. Sunaomi held his face up, mouth open, licking the drops as they fell. He had no idea how much time had passed. There was no sun to indicate what hour of day it was or which direction to go in. If he went back he would almost certainly run into Sasaki and his men returning to finish him off. If he went on he risked losing his way in the mountains. He had neither food nor drink with him nor did he have a bow for hunting.

He looked at the dead men. Already crows were circling above them. He felt regret for their deaths and the chain of events that had led them to this place. Maybe they had done their best to kill him but they were only obeying their lord. Asking forgiveness of their spirits, he checked their clothes.

He found a pack containing rice balls wrapped in young oak leaves and a small flask of some sort of alcohol. Sunaomi ate two of the rice balls and drained the flask in two mouthfuls. It gave him enough energy to get up on Kiki's back. He noticed the flattened grass that showed the way the horses had come, and then fled, and set out in the opposite direction.

He feared most riding round in circles for the mist had barely thinned, but Kiki found a fox track and followed it. It wound its way between huge boulders which loomed up suddenly, dark and massive like animals. Occasionally Sunaomi stopped and wiped their dripping surfaces with his hand, taking the moisture to his mouth. Each time his skin seemed hotter. He burned, then shivered and knew that wound fever was taking hold.

He heard kites and crows but no other birdsong until after a long time the grass of the plain gave way to copses of small trees and thickets and then larger trees. Here he thought he heard trills of musical song, a robin perhaps or flycatchers. Now and then it sounded like flute music. Just as he realised it was flute music the track widened into a real path, the slope turned downhill and he passed a small statue of the wayside god, decorated with a red bib.

I am not lost, he thought and saw a figure ahead of him. It moved so lightly it barely touched the ground and it wore a white robe that shone through the misty twilight of the forest. It—she—was playing a flute, the music haunting and tender.

'Utahime,' Sunaomi said in wonder. 'Can it be you?'

She turned and he saw it was her. She lowered the flute and waited for him to draw near. Kiki came to a halt, eyes rolling, breathing hard.

'Sunaomi,' she said in her deep, grave voice and held out her hand. He bent and lifted her up onto the horse's back.

She sat in front of him, encircled by his arms, as cool as ice against his burning body, her hair like silk against his lips.

Kiki stepped forward and for a long time they rode through the forest as though they were enchanted, neither of them speaking. Occasionally the girl set the flute to her lips and played, bringing tears to his eyes, for the music spoke of partings and endings.

The rain stopped and the mist cleared. Rays of sunshine set the forest sparkling, drops on leaves and grass reflecting tiny rainbows of fractured light.

'You know I must leave you,' Utahime said.

'Why? Why can't you stay with me?'

'Sunaomi,' she chided him. 'It's wrong. You are alive and I have been dead for years.'

'I am barely alive,' he said through chattering teeth. 'I will die and follow you.'

'It's not yet your time.' She leaned back against him, chilling him to the bone. She whispered, 'It was not right to use the doll to keep me tied to this world. When the fire destroyed it I was free. Your love had healed me and mended my broken heart. My rage and my desire for revenge were quenched. Now we must say farewell. Maybe we will meet in another life under a different fate. We will recognise each other and remember that we loved each other.'

'No one will ever mean to me what you do,' he said, hearing his voice break.

'You will meet living girls and love them,' she said wistfully.

'No!' he protested.

'I will leave you my flute,' she said. 'Play it and remember me in the music.'

'I will never forget you.'

She played a few soft notes, then took the flute from her lips to say, 'Let us ride like this for a little while longer.'

The music wove its magic around them, recalling all that bound them together. Kiki moved with the lightest of treads, head lowered docilely, through a forest that seemed endless.

Eventually the music faded away. Utahime gave the flute to Sunaomi. 'I know you acted from love but it was not right to use the doll. You should not do it again. I was captured by it, but now I am free.'

The flute was solid in his hand but Utahime no longer was. Her hair became as soft as gossamer and then transparent. He saw the trees, the leaves and the raindrops through her form. He felt her body dissolve leaving only a cold waft of air and then that too passed and the humidity of the forest enveloped him.

It seemed Kiki took only a few more steps and the forest ended. The trees vanished abruptly as though he had ridden back into a different world. The track beneath the horse's feet was no longer soft with leaf mould but rutted and muddy. Puddles reflected the sky. Frogs were croaking and a heron startled up with its harsh cry.

The sky rose high above him, white clouds breaking up to show blue beyond. Sunaomi came to a wide road and realised it was the highway. To his left, the sun was about to set behind the mountains, its light spilling brilliant and lavish over the cultivated fields, the trees planted neatly on either side of the road, the stone markers.

Grief and pain almost overwhelmed him. Tears were pouring down his cheeks but he did not look back. He tucked the flute into his sash and began to ride towards the west.

CHAPTER TWELVE

Sunaomi kept riding through the twilight, not knowing what else to do. The fever was rising and he feared that if he dismounted from Kiki's back he would never get back on. He had nothing apart from the horse and his sword, the bear and the flute. He did not know where he was. Kiki walked slowly, now and then grazing, and Sunaomi half-dozed, strange snatches of dreams appearing behind his closed eyelids.

Chin was yelping as she had when Taro had carried her away. She was running towards him, her wide mouth gaping with the effort, her ears back. His eyes opened and he saw there was a small dog on the road ahead, barking with excitement and joy.

He blinked in disbelief. Then she was under the horse's feet, making Kiki snort and spin. Sunaomi slid down, his legs crumpling under him, and found himself sitting on the ground while Chin leaped all over him. She licked away the salty tears from his cheeks, nipped at his hands, yelped in delight.

He gripped her solid form, muscled beneath the silky fur. What a brave heart she had! But why was she here alone? Were his companions nearby? They should have been a long way ahead by now. If they had been delayed they would surely lose track of Masao completely.

He tried to stand, and eventually pulled himself up by leaning on Kiki. The road ahead was deserted, as far as he could see. He did not have the strength to remount. His shoulder blazed with pain. Kiki began to walk slowly forward and Sunaomi went with him, Chin limping behind.

He recalled their proud ride through the city when he, the horse and the dog had attracted so many admiring looks.

'We are not so fine now.'

He did not realise he had spoken the words aloud but Chin gave a small yap in response to his voice. She sounded reproachful. She must be hungry and tired. He remembered the rice balls and, stopping by the side of the road, he half-sat, half-fell down onto a grassy patch. He took the balls out, gave one to Chin and forced himself to eat the other. It stuck in his throat, reminding him how thirsty he was.

Night was approaching, the light fading. Kiki grazed steadily. Chin crept into Sunaomi's lap, giving a deep sigh.

I suppose I may as well see out the night here, he thought, and was relieved he had come to a decision.

He had fallen into a restless sleep when a shrill whinny from Kiki woke him. The horse had flung up his head and was gazing down the road.

An answering neigh echoed back. A horseman was approaching.

Chin began to bark excitedly, in welcome, not warning.

Sunaomi did not recognise the horse. It was small, almost like a pack animal. But he knew the voice that called out.

The fever cut the passing of time into segments. One moment Taro was riding towards him, the next he was kneeling beside him, Chin yapping and trying to lick his face.

'She ran away,' Taro said. 'At midday when we stopped and I put her down for a moment.'

Sunaomi nodded although nothing made sense to him.

'What happened?' Taro put his hand on Sunaomi's brow. 'You are burning!'

'Someone shot an arrow into my shoulder.' He could not remember who or why.

'Is it still in there?' Taro felt the wound with gentle fingers. 'You pulled it out?'

It seemed like a dream now, impossible to describe. Sunaomi said, 'I'm thirsty.'

'Lord Kaneda was afraid of this,' Taro said. 'All day he's been in two minds whether to turn back or ride on. I don't know who felt worse about leaving you, he or Chin. Chin didn't stop whining since we left.'

Then his voice faded. He must have gone away for a bit, for suddenly he had a wet cloth in his hands. He wiped Sunaomi's face and lips.

'I'll help you up. You can ride the horse Sasaki lent us. It's not as tall as Kiki and it's old and quiet. I'll put Chin in the basket. Can you hold on to the reins?'

For a moment it all seemed beyond him, then Sunaomi clenched his teeth together and nodded. But when he was up on the horse's back faintness overcame him.

Taro caught him, steadying him.

'I'll sit behind you and hold you,' he said. 'Kiki will follow us. The others are a few hours ahead but they will have stopped to rest, after riding all the night before.'

The horse turned reluctantly. Perhaps it had thought it was going home. It did not want to go back into the darkness. In his fever Sunaomi fancied he could see into its mind, read all its thought and feelings. He spoke to encourage it. He could just make out its head and saw one of its ears flick back.

'What did you say?' asked Taro.

'I was talking to the horse.'

'Sasaki gave us the worst one he could find,' Taro said.

Sunaomi saw the years of service, the constant ill treatment, the wearing down of the horse's spirit. Once it had been a foal, joyful at being alive and young. He felt his heart would break with sadness. His soul ached for the horse, for the men who had died, even for Sasaki who had behaved like a coward and a traitor, for Masao, for Utahime.

He had been hot but now he was so cold he could not stop shivering.

Taro pressed him close, saying, 'Let me warm you.'

Beneath Taro's jacket Sunaomi could feel the firm square shape of the book. Taro carried it everywhere with him, reading at every opportunity. He had wanted to talk to Sunaomi about it, and there had never been time. Now the book seemed to exude a steady heat as if it were hot charcoal.

'I think you may have saved my life,' Sunaomi said, in a moment of lucidity. 'If you had not come back for me ...' He could not find words for the gratitude that was flowing from his heart, bringing tears to his eyes.

'Love your friends like your own soul,' Taro said. 'That is one of the teachings Yoshimori wrote in his book. It's one of the things I wanted to talk to you about. You told me not to call you lord and you speak of me as your friend. I know your heart is open to many things. Of course I am your servant, but I love you like a friend. I would give my life for you. I can say this now we are alone together; you are not yourself, you are out of your mind from fever and pain and will probably forget every word. For the moment our roles are reversed. You are weak and I am strong. I am the one supporting you, you who have always supported me, who gave me every opportunity in my life, above all the gift of reading. I would be nothing without you. But another teaching comes to mind: that many of the first will be last and that children will show the way into the kingdom.

'I read these words every day. They are hard to understand but they nourish me as if they were food. I feel I could live on them alone. I don't need anything else. Yoshimori wrote, "I must keep my beliefs hidden as if in a secret village for I have become the embodiment of the Divine for the whole realm." He was the Emperor. He could not speak of these things but he wrote them down.

'You promised before, will you help me understand when you are recovered?'

If I recover, Sunaomi thought, for the veil between this world and the next had become as thin as gossamer and he longed to slip through it. But Chin would pine terribly and he had promised to help Taro. These two kept him tethered. He owed them that duty.

He heard Lord Kahei's voice speak of duty and thought he

was riding alongside or behind, but only the riderless Kiki followed them.

'Yoshimori distilled what he believed and what he could do,' Taro went on. 'He called it the Luminous Way. It is so simple yet so profound. All are born into this world through the suffering and devotion of women. Everyone must be treated with the same respect and solicitude. In the eyes of the Secret One the lowest servant is as worthy as the greatest lord. Life is the delight the Secret One takes in creation, where it reveals itself for it is neither male nor female, yet it is both.

'"Split a piece of wood and I am there. Life up the stone and you will find me."

'No one should ever take the life of another being, for whatever you kill you kill the creator within it. Revenge must be left to heaven.'

It is what they teach at Terayama, Sunaomi thought, recalling the solicitude with which insects were removed and carried outside. Even fleas, which made him laugh. The sound that came out was more like a groan.

'Are you all right?' Taro asked.

Sunaomi nodded, sending a shaft of pain through his shoulder and head. He was about to say he had never killed anyone, but he remembered Sasaki's men and a heavy weight settled over him. His own life was branded by death and he had seen many die. In some cases he had wept whereas in others he had been glad and relieved that they were no longer in this world.

'Should I have died myself?'

He must have spoken aloud for Taro answered, 'Rather than take another's life? It is better. But there is no death, only existence in the light.'

Taro spoke confidently, but then he said with less assurance, 'This is another part I don't understand. Our images come into being before us and neither die nor are visible. I think it means we have within us a part of the light, our spirit, that existed before we were born and will never die. Am I right?'

The sky had cleared and the land was lit by a starlight more intense than any Sunaomi had ever seen. The stars appeared so close he could almost touch them. He was in the arms of an angel being transported into the light. A sense of awe came over him as if that light were all around him and within him and death was no more than allowing himself to flow into it.

His eyes closed. His breathing that had been so rapid slowed. The pain faded away.

Taro was shaking him. 'Lord—Sunaomi—wake up! Don't leave me! Stay with me!'

His grip on Sunaomi's shoulder was agonising. Sunaomi could not help crying out, and realised where he was, back in the world with all its hardship and pain.

'You must not die yet,' Taro said. 'I will not allow it!' There was a note of authority in his voice that Sunaomi had not heard before, as if he were rebuking death, as if he were indeed an angel.

The horse went slowly on. The ecstasy faded away. The night and the journey seemed endless. Sunaomi longed to lie down, his throat rasped with thirst. He dozed and woke and still the horse was plodding on, still it was dark.

Finally the horse came to a halt. There were lights from flaming torches. He heard a shout and recognised Kaneda's voice. He was lifted down and carried inside.

'I was waiting outside,' he heard Kaneda say to Taro. 'Hoping against hope that you would return. And here you are with our lord, the dog, and even the horse. Well done, well done, you are a brave lad.'

It pleased Sunaomi to hear such high praise for Taro from the old warrior.

'Our lord is wounded,' Taro said.

'How bad? He's not going to die?'

'No, he will live,' Taro replied with the same quiet authority.

Sunaomi drank at last, gulping the lukewarm liquid, and at last lay down, falling immediately into a deep sleep. The fever had broken.

The following morning he woke to find Chin lying close to him. The bear hung on its red cord round his neck and the flute lay next to him on the floor. He gazed at it in wonder, thinking he had dreamed it.

He sat up, his back naked, while Kaneda inspected the wound.

'It is quite clean. Did you pull out the shaft yourself?'

'I must have. I don't remember.'

'Well, you were lucky.' The warrior was silent for a moment, then burst out, 'I should never have left you.'

'It was my decision,' Sunaomi said. 'Don't blame yourself.'

'Sasaki will pay for this, if I have to return and bring him to justice myself!'

Sunaomi glanced at Taro, hearing an echo of his voice: *Revenge must be left to heaven.* Taro sat, his eyes lowered. He looked as he always had, an ordinary boy but last night he had been an angel.

CHAPTER THIRTEEN

'What happened to you?' Kiyoko asked a few days later when Kaneda judged Sunaomi well enough to ride on. 'You are changed in some way. And where did the flute come from?'

Sunaomi had been aware of her watching him. She had brought food, bathed the arrow wound, her shrewd glance penetrating into his soul. Now she sat behind him on Kiki, close enough for him to feel her breath and her heartbeat.

The flute was tucked into his sash. He was tempted to play it but also felt a lingering fear.

'Was it something concerning ghosts?' Kiyoko whispered.

'Maybe one day I will tell you. But I don't want to talk about it now.' To change the subject he said, 'We have lost Masao, I'm afraid. He will be days ahead of us.'

'According to Hiromasa he was heading for Hofu. He may still be there, he may have already left on a ship. Either way, I'll catch up with him.'

He rode in silence for a while, pondering her meaning. His own feelings were ambivalent. Masao had to be brought to justice, on his aunt's orders, but Sunaomi hoped to save his friend from the worst consequences.

'He and his friends attacked me,' Kiyoko said. 'They were going to rape me, until they started to fight among themselves.' She drew a breath as if she was going to say more, but she apparently changed her mind.

Sunaomi suddenly thought of the night she had come to him after the attack. She had been covered in blood, she had wiped her blade clean. How could he have overlooked that? Why had he believed her when she said she would not lie to him? What was her real purpose now? It was convenient for the siblings to travel with him, protected by his letters of passage, receiving free lodging as part of his retinue. So far they had done little to earn it. And presumably everything would change once they reached Hofu.

The fever had left him unusually sensitive. He saw everything with extreme clarity. Kiyoko's words suggested she would never forgive Masao, but what about Sunaomi himself? He had fought with her when they were children, had overcome her and left her, even though she was his elder and in Tribe law he should have obeyed her. She had vowed to make him pay for that. What rancour did she still hold, hidden beneath her teasing and her promises?

He glanced behind him at the boy they all now called Hiromasa. Sunaomi and Kaneda had discussed him briefly, both wanting to believe he was the youngest of the Arai brothers, both unable to convince themselves beyond doubt.

Hiromasa rode behind Kichizo on Hitare. He had become devoted to the young man and followed him everywhere. He was shy and wary with everyone else, though he liked Chin.

'I wish he could tell us more about his time with Masao,' Sunaomi said.

'Hiromasa?' Kiyoko replied. 'Maybe he will in time. You have to win his trust. But he is a child of the Tribe, as well as being your brother.'

In other words a liar, just as you are, Sunaomi thought.

♦

The weather was unfavourable. It was a bad time of year to travel while the plum rains swept over the country bringing mud outside and mildew within. Sunaomi made notes of everything he saw, spoke each night to farmers, townsfolk and other travellers, sent Kichizo and Kiyoko out into the streets to glean information. Every few days he wrote a report to dispatch to Kaede whenever they passed through a town large enough to have messengers. This work helped to alleviate the tedium and hardship of the journey and distracted him from his obsessive thought about Kiyoko and Hiromasa, and his grief for Utahime.

Mostly the condition of the land was good and towns seemed to be thriving though people all grumbled in the same way. But the amount of tree felling was alarming. The forests were disappearing. Sasaki had said it was a sign of prosperity, an increase in construction and ship building. Sunaomi remembered from childhood the strict laws of the Three Countries that had been put in place to protect the forests. Now it seemed no one obeyed them.

He saw the truth behind Sasaki's claim when they arrived in Hofu. The town had new gates and walls and was far larger than he remembered, with many expensive and luxurious merchants' houses and in the port area a forest of ships under construction. Anchored in the harbour were several carracks such as the foreigners sailed, yet newly built, flying the black and white banners of the Terada family, as well as the Otori heron.

Through the roofs and the masts of the ships, overlooking the port, Sunaomi saw the red walls of the temple which had seemed such a safe haven to him as a child.

'Let's go to Daifukuji,' he said to Kaneda.

'You have a residence here,' Kaneda said. 'The Arai mansion. That is where you should stay.'

But Sunaomi dreaded seeing it, fearing the memories that would linger there.

'You go and see what condition it's in. Maybe it is derelict, maybe it has passed into other hands. I'll go to the temple and talk to the Abbot.'

'Very well,' Kaneda said. 'I'll join you there.'

Kichizo and Hiromasa followed Kaneda, while Sunaomi rode on, Kiyoko sitting behind him, with Taro on the old horse alongside. A brisk westerly wind blew off the water. Sunaomi remembered that this was the wind everyone waited and prayed for, the one that brought ships from Nankoku and the Southern

Isles and sent them on through the Encircled Sea to Akashi. It had shaken the port town into life. The streets thronged with people, many dressed in outlandish styles and colours, porters carrying huge loads, elaborate palanquins in which mysterious figures hid behind oiled blinds. Sunaomi heard many different tongues spoken. Dogs roamed everywhere. Chin felt obliged to bark at each one, making Kiki startle.

The way narrowed and the old horse fell behind. Sunaomi glanced back at it and saw it looked calm and contented, its eyes half-closed as if it walked in its sleep. It had become fond of Taro, like all animals. He became aware that a small crowd had followed them. It filled the temple way, growing every minute as more people clustered around them.

'Have they come to welcome you?' Kiyoko said, mocking.

Can it be that they remember the Arai? Sunaomi thought, feeling strangely moved. He was about to speak to the crowd when he realised he was not the object of their attention.

Kiyoko said, 'It's not you and your pretty pets! It's your servant, Taro.'

Some, their faces alight with hope and devotion, pressed forward to touch the horse or Taro's garments, others, murmuring in quiet voices, dropped to their knees, their hands folded in prayer. They were common people, workmen, porters, sailors, their clothes faded and mended many times, their hands rough from hard work, toughened by ropes and tools.

The gates to the temple were open. As Sunaomi dismounted, a young woman pushed through the crowd and stood in the entrance. She looked familiar though Sunaomi could not remember where he might have seen her before. She did not speak to him but gazed intently at Taro.

Sunaomi was about to address her when a monk came out to greet them, looking penetratingly at Sunaomi when he said his name.

'I remember you. You came years ago, with Lord Miyoshi.'

'You have a good memory.'

'I never forget a face, though names escape me more and more. I did not know then that you were Lord Zenko's son.'

'You remember my father?'

'Many do, in Hofu, though not always favourably. Are you hoping to stay? We are very crowded.'

Sunaomi recalled him saying the same sort of thing, all those years ago. At Daifukuji nothing changed, year after year. The tides rose and fell each day, the seasons followed each other, travellers came, and waited, and left again. Daifukuji welcomed them and sent them on their way, refreshed and protected.

'Maybe I could go to my old house,' he said.

'Hmm, I don't know about that,' the monk replied with a wry smile. 'We'll find a space for you here. How many are you?'

Sunaomi looked for Kiyoko, but she had vanished. 'Myself, and a couple of my men,' he replied.

'I don't know why this throng is here,' the monk grumbled quietly. He called to the young woman who was still standing at the gate. 'What is this gathering? What do you all want?'

'We have been waiting for him,' she replied.

'For Lord Arai?'

'No, not for Lord Arai.' She smiled and said to Sunaomi, 'So, it is you? I thought so. He is your servant, isn't he?'

She gestured towards Taro who still sat on the old horse, surrounded by eager hands reaching up to him. He did not seem in the least disturbed or surprised. His face was calm, almost illuminated.

'I suppose so,' Sunaomi said, 'though I think of him more as a ...'

'Servant of the World,' she interrupted, 'who brings the ancient teachings written down.'

'He carries a book which contains the writings of the Emperor Yoshimori,' Sunaomi said.

'Of course. He is the one we are expecting. Farewell, Lord Arai. We will meet again soon. I am Ame. I met you in Miyako once, a long time ago.'

He remembered now, the silent girl and her defiant prayer.

She took the reins of Taro's horse and began to lead it back down the temple way. The crowd followed. Sunaomi could see Taro's head above the throng. Chin gave an indignant bark but Taro did not look back.

The monk clicked his tongue, annoyed. 'There are many sects in Hofu now,' he said. 'People talk of end times and the last days of the law. They pray and prophesy and see miracles in everything. Well, let's go inside. Is anyone else coming?'

'Maybe one,' Sunaomi said, 'and one more horse.' He felt lost without Taro to look after Kiki and Chin. How could he just ride away like that? He had wanted Taro to feel his equal but he had not seriously expected him to leave whenever he felt like it.

The monk called to one of the novices to hold the horse. 'You can bring your dog with you. It's a temple dog, isn't it? Our Abbot has one of his own, a gift from Silla.'

◆

The dogs sniffed each other in their own greeting. The Abbot's was a male, larger than Chin and with darker fur. Chin seemed to like and admire him instantly, licking his face, making play bows, her tail wagging furiously. The older dog was more reserved but Sunaomi thought he would make a good mate for Chin. She was nearly old enough. Would they stay in Hofu long enough for her to carry and raise a litter of puppies?

The Abbot petted and admired her, talking about his own dog which he had had for some time, and then remarked, 'There are envoys from Silla in Hofu at the moment. I believe they are waiting for a response from Lady Kaede and the Empress.'

'I must try to meet them. Chin was a gift for my aunt but the dog became very attached to me. You could say I am her guardian now.'

'They are devoted dogs and single minded. Shishi serves only me. He tolerates some, but ignores or dislikes most others.

It is flattering and in return I am very fond of him, perhaps more than I should be, for it threatens my aim of serene non-attachment. But I feel he is an incarnation of the guardian dogs that you see in temples like this. We have two statues of them at the steps to the main hall.'

'I remember them,' Sunaomi said. 'My brothers and I used to like to stroke them.'

'And they are the symbol of the light that is in everything, as the Enlightened One teaches us.' The Abbot stroked the dog's head. It had taken up position in the folds of his robe, alert to every sound.

The shutters rattled in the wind. From the garden came the trickle of water. Seagulls mewed like cats above the slap of waves against the sea wall. Sunaomi had not been in Hofu since the days he had spent there with Masao and Lord Miyoshi, when Hisao had been put on trial by the Tribe, and Sunaomi had cast the deciding vote to spare his life.

But the Tribe had punished Hisao in the end. Sunaomi had watched them poison him and had done nothing.

'When you were last here you were just a child,' the Abbot said, as if reading his thoughts. 'You must let go of remorse and regret. No one escapes being sullied by the dust of the world. It is the human condition. But look at you now. You must be nearly at your coming-of-age.'

'The ceremony was to have been held in Miyako,' Sunaomi said. 'But then I had to leave on an urgent matter, and Lord Miyoshi gave me other instructions for my time here, and so it was put off until my return.'

And then I will marry Kinu, I suppose, he thought, remembering his commitment to her and her father's wishes, and he thought of Utahime, with the by now customary mixture of regret and relief.

He looked up, caught the Abbot's shrewd glance and smiled at him. 'I don't feel very grown up,' he admitted. 'Will I ever stop making mistakes and acting foolishly?'

He immediately regretted speaking so openly.

'The danger, if I may be honest,' said the Abbot, 'is more in not acting at all. You are in a position of authority as Lady Kaede's nephew, and leader of an ancient, once very powerful clan. But I sense a certain passivity in your nature, and I remember thinking the same thing when you were a child. You were so different from the other boy who came with you. What was his name?'

'Masao,' Sunaomi replied. The Abbot's criticism stung, though Sunaomi had to admit others had said the same. Hiroshi in particular had often pointed it out to him. It was true he preferred to be a witness rather than an actor, to defend rather than attack, to avoid provocation. But his outer self, the one who liked fine clothes and perfumes, who rode a pale black-maned horse with a matching dog, was to a certain extent something he cultivated to hide what truly lay within.

He thought of Masao, who was all action and little reflection. It had been good growing up together. Their characters had complemented each other. Masao had always been the leader and he the follower.

'Of course it's possible that you disguise your true nature,' the Abbot said, surprising Sunaomi again with his acuity.

'It is because of Masao that I am here,' he said. 'I believe he is in Hofu. Several weeks ago there was an ugly brawl in the streets of the capital. A young nobleman died. Instead of staying to clear his name Masao fled. My aunt had many concerns, chief among them the need to suppress street fighting and other unrest, and Masao's safety. She sent me to bring him back. He has become a sort of masterless warrior, an itinerant swordsman. He has killed several young men in fights, he openly flouts Lady Kaede's authority, and, you may not have known this, he is Saga Hideki's grandson.'

The Abbot nodded several times but did not speak.

'I have to report to Lord Miyoshi,' Sunaomi went on, 'on the state of affairs here in Hofu, the foreigners' intentions, what the

Nankoku lords are up to. So, I need to be an onlooker and an investigator. I must gain the trust of all these disparate groups and they must see me as harmless.'

'Like a fawn among tigers,' the Abbot said half to himself.

'I am not quite as defenceless as a fawn,' Sunaomi replied.

'I haven't heard of anyone like Masao arriving recently,' the Abbot said. 'But that means little. Hofu has grown so large and has so many new people streaming in every day I can no longer keep up. Terada Fumio will be able to tell you more. To be honest, he is the chief of the city now. He has a hand in everything and nothing happens without him hearing of it. He is close to the foreigners too, both from Silla and the West, and speaks many languages. He is building ships for trade and defence, as well as continuing his ways of piracy when it suits him.'

'Then I will speak with him first. Where will I find him?'

The Abbot looked slightly embarrassed. 'You did not know? Of course not, it is so long since you have been here. Terada took over the old Arai mansion, your former house.'

Sunaomi hardly had time to absorb this revelation before he heard footsteps and a monk just beyond the door said quietly, 'Kaneda Sunamori is here.'

The old warrior hurried in, knelt and bowed to the Abbot and then burst out, 'Your house has been stolen!'

'*Stolen* is a harsh word,' Sunaomi replied. 'Let's just say Terada is living there temporarily. He has borrowed the house.'

Kaneda hardly heard him. 'I did not go inside. I was not sure how I would react seeing that pirate in the place that belongs to you. I left a message with the guards at the gate. They were like no human I'd ever seen: huge men who spoke among themselves in unintelligible words and carried wide, curved swords.'

Sunaomi had never seen him so flustered.

'The gates have been replaced. The Arai symbol, the bear's paw, is no longer carved over the lintel. The house and garden have been restored, from what I could see, to how they looked in the old days. It was always a beautiful place.' Kaneda stopped abruptly for which Sunaomi was grateful. He did not want to be reminded of the past, of his childhood when his parents were alive.

'We cannot stay there,' he said. 'We will find somewhere else.'

'What do you mean?' Kaneda looked astonished. 'You must demand Terada leave at once. Not only is it your clan's mansion, you are an envoy from the Empress. You must have suitable lodgings that reflect your status. Otherwise no one will respect you or your role.'

'You are welcome to stay here,' the Abbot offered.

'That would be best,' Sunaomi said. 'Thank you—but there may be three or four of us, including a young woman.'

The Abbot tried to hide a smile.

'Nothing like that,' Sunaomi hastened to explain. 'She is my cousin, my uncle Taku's daughter. She is travelling with her brother, and another young boy.'

'Taku's children?' the Abbot said. 'Well, well. I would like to meet them some time.'

'They've gone elsewhere for now,' Kaneda said. 'Kichizo said to tell you they'll be in touch. But what about Taro? Where is he?'

'He also went elsewhere,' Sunaomi replied. 'I am not sure if he will come back or not.'

'What?' Kaneda scowled. 'He cannot just leave you. You need him now more than ever.'

'So, it is just the two of you?' the Abbot said. 'We can easily make room for you. Many people will leave today with this favourable wind. Go and bathe and rest after the journey, then we will eat together.'

Hot water seemed like a good remedy for his state of mind as well as his body. The shoulder wound had healed cleanly though it still ached sand he had other bruises from the fall and the fight that he hardly remembered getting. They had faded from deep purple to a greenish yellow stain.

Kaneda announced he would bathe later. Sunaomi sensed

he wanted to stand guard though it hardly seemed necessary within the walls of Daifukuji. Still, the bath, a large natural one with stone sides, overlooking the harbour, was quite open and monks came and went, indistinguishable one from another in their naked state, though they had no place to conceal weapons.

Sunaomi was half-smiling at the idea that one of them would be an assassin, his eyes were closing and he was slipping into a dream when he was awakened by the sound of voices from the garden.

Kaneda was almost shouting. 'You must wait a few moments. Lord Arai will receive you directly.'

The other replied, 'No, no, we will bathe together. I often take a bath here, everyone knows me.'

'I insist you wait.' Kaneda appeared on the edge of the pool, his form misty in the steam. 'Get out and get dressed,' he said quietly. 'Terada is here but you must meet formally.' He dropped his voice further. 'What an outrageous suggestion!'

Returning to the guest room Sunaomi thought, *Being clothed is not going to make me more impressive!* His formal wear had been left behind at Sasaki, along with all his other belongings, apart from the bear. *I must get new clothes made. I wish Terada had waited until I had something better to wear.*

When he was dressed he walked through the garden, Chin at his heels. Kaneda came to meet him.

'I persuaded Terada to join the Abbot. They are drinking together,' he said.

'*Lord* Terada,' Sunaomi corrected him. 'Let us treat him with courtesy.'

Kaneda muttered, 'I will not call him *Lord*.'

'At least try not to antagonise him.'

But from the first exchange Sunaomi saw that Terada Fumio was already hostile towards him.

Fumio was still plump and prosperous looking, his hair black and, as Sunaomi had feared, his clothes magnificent. He was accompanied by another man, dark skinned, his head shaven like a monk's, showing his blueish scalp and the fine shape of his skull. He was also sumptuously dressed and wore a chain of gold around his neck.

They both carried themselves with a swaggering confidence. Fumio spoke familiarly to the Abbot, accepting what must have been a second or third bowl of rice wine and emptying it at a gulp. His face had taken on a reddish hue. The other man drank in a more restrained manner.

Sunaomi had his bowl filled by the Abbot, and drank a little, feeling the alcohol rush through his veins. He began by conveying greetings from his aunt and Lord Miyoshi but Fumio cut him short.

'That all goes without saying. What is your purpose in coming here and what do you intend to do?'

'I am hoping for your assistance,' Sunaomi said mildly. 'I have been told no one knows as much as you about the foreigners in Hofu and the Nankoku lords.'

'Whose business is that other than mine?'

'There are activities that have not gone unnoticed. The ship building, the ever-increasing number of foreigners, these things have come to the attention of Lord Miyoshi.'

'We are breaking no laws,' Fumio said.

'Trade and diplomacy should all be conducted with the permission and knowledge of Miyako, now we are one country. I am here as the representative of the Empress and Lady Kaede.'

Fumio gave him a long challenging stare. 'The last time I saw you, you were a fugitive child, hiding in a deserted house. You don't look much older now, to be honest. Your father and mother were traitors. Together with Lady Kaede they caused the death of my dearest friend. I will never forgive her and I want nothing to do with you.'

He spoke so boldly and loudly it made Chin growl. Sunaomi flinched inwardly though he tried to maintain an expressionless face. He had heard such attacks on his parents for years and they no longer had the power to wound him, but Fumio's open defiance of Kaede could not go unchallenged.

'We must leave the past behind us,' he said. 'Let Lady Kaede's achievements speak for themselves: peace throughout the realm, no children starving, no aged parents turned out to die in the forest.'

Fumio listened with an expression of contempt. The other man smiled into his wine bowl as he took a small sip.

Fumio said, 'You can tell Shirakawa Kaede that we are equally prosperous here, thanks to our own efforts—nothing to do with her. Go back to Miyako with that news and don't poke your nose into my affairs.'

'I intend to stay in Hofu a little longer,' Sunaomi said, certain that Fumio had a great deal to hide and determined to uncover it. 'I will meet with the foreigners and travel to Nankoku if necessary. And there are other matters that I've been asked to investigate, on which perhaps you will cooperate. We have been told that there have been converts, including Lord Mizuta and his retainers, to a new religion, together with an increase in activity of all sorts of different sects. I need to know that none of this will threaten the fabric of our society.'

The dark-skinned man listened with a new degree of alertness. He was watching Fumio, his lips pressed together.

'In this port town people of all beliefs have always mingled freely,' the Abbot said. 'Iida Sadamu and Saga Hideki both tried to eradicate anything they considered subversive, but they only drove believers into hiding.'

'There is no call for persecution,' Sunaomi said. 'Only for knowledge. I would like to know more, for example, about the young woman called Ame. She came to that deserted house with you. I saw her again earlier today when I arrived. She and a crowd carried away my servant, Taro.'

'He is your servant?' the dark-skinned man questioned, speaking for the first time. He had a slight accent but otherwise his speech seemed perfect.

'Renzo,' Fumio said, gesturing to him. 'He is my interpreter.

He is an expert in many things, including the foreigners' beliefs. You can talk to him whenever you like, as long as you stick to religion.'

Renzo made a small bow.

'Have you seen Taro?' Sunaomi asked. 'Maybe you can tell me where he is.'

'He is with Lady Ame. He is showing her the teachings. It is a blessed day.'

'I look forward to hearing more from you,' Sunaomi said. 'The last matter concerns Lord Saga's grandson, Masao. I believe he is in Hofu and I need to find him.'

'I wouldn't know him if I saw him,' Fumio replied dismissively.

'But you or your men may hear of him. He is a talented swordsman who seeks out opponents.'

'If I find his corpse I'll let you know.' Fumio drained his bowl and stood. 'My lord Abbot, it's always a pleasure to share a drink with you.' He nodded at Sunaomi. 'Arai. I'll send Renzo to you sometime soon.'

Renzo followed him out.

Kaneda exhaled, a furious expression on his face. He stood and began pacing the room, looking as if he wanted to kill someone. Sunaomi sat for a few moments breathing slowly to calm himself, one hand on Chin who was growling quietly. He had not expected such outright hostility nor to be so insulted. It had thrown up a huge obstacle in his path. Without Fumio's cooperation what could he hope to achieve? He would be told lies or varying versions of the truth, he would be blocked and hindered, threatened and even harmed. Yet the more hostile Fumio was the more it confirmed his suspicions.

Sunaomi took another sip of wine, vowing to himself that he would put up with the insults, he would allow Fumio and everyone else to think he was a weakling. The more they underestimated him the more they would reveal.

Kaneda stopped his pacing and knelt next to him. 'What are you going to do, lord?'

'Well, tomorrow I must arrange to have new clothes made so you must find a tailor and have him come here with patterns.'

Kaneda struggled to control himself in the face of this new frivolity. 'I mean about Terada and your house!'

'He can stay there for the time being. I am quite comfortable here.'

'You are, of course, welcome to stay as long as you like,' the Abbot said, with what seemed like his usual jovial sincerity.

At that moment monks came in with trays of food, raw fish and seafood, grilled sea bream, eggplant and summer greens.

'We usually eat more frugally,' the Abbot said, though his size made this hard to believe. 'But since you are here we can indulge ourselves with the bounty of the sea.'

When Sunaomi returned to the guest room it was almost night. The red walls of the temple were losing their glow and a few raindrops spattered on his face. He hastened his step and found Kiyoko sitting outside on the verandah.

'I was afraid you would disappear into the tangled alleys of Hofu and I would never see you again,' he said, sitting down next to her.

'You're pleased to see me? That's nice.' She must have moved a little closer for he became aware of the touch of her body on his.

'Kichizo and I think you're going to need our help,' she said.

'I'm going to need someone's,' he confessed.

'We talked about it. You're our cousin, and we don't like Terada Fumio.'

'You don't? Why not?'

'Old Tribe stuff. And he had no reason to be so rude.'

'Did you overhear? Where were you?'

'Just outside. Kichizo went after them to catch what they said when they were alone.'

'Where's Hiromasa?'

'Somewhere. I'm going back there now, unless you'd like me to stay?' She pressed against him even more closely.

Kaneda was approaching. Sunaomi stood up. 'Goodnight,' he said and went inside.

He lay down, thinking he had at least some allies, wondering if he could really trust them. He fell asleep to the sound of the rain and the waves.

CHAPTER FOURTEEN

By morning the sky had cleared. The sun was very hot, making the roofs and paths steam. Kaneda went out early on various errands, and a little after midday a merchant arrived with two servants bearing armfuls of cloth samples, the finest silk from Shin, cotton gauzes for the hot days of summer and other luxury fabrics Sunaomi had never seen, velvet and satin, brought, the man said, on the foreign ships.

Sunaomi spent an hour in the guest room going through the materials and ordering sets of clothes that would reflect his status. The merchant was flattering and praised his choice, at the end offering him a string of prayer beads, pearls set in silver, saying, 'Everyone wears them now. They are the height of fashion.'

Sunaomi took the necklace. The pearls held the cool freshness of the ocean. He liked the feel of them on his palm and against his fingers. He found himself counting the beads, one by one. It was calming. *A very useful accessory,* he thought as he put it round his neck.

Chin had wandered off in search of Shishi, the Abbot's dog, and now Sunaomi heard her yelp excitedly. A few moments later Taro appeared carrying her. He put her down on the verandah and at once began to apologise while she jumped around him in pleasure at his return.

She is probably hungry, Sunaomi thought, for she had only had a little rice and fish the night before. Taro had always been the provider of meat.

'I don't know what happened,' Taro said. 'It was as if I was bewitched. The woman, Ame, took me to a place called the Temple of the Poor. There were crowds of people there and they kept saying strange things about me. They wanted to hear about the book.'

The merchant stopped in the middle of his jotting and stared at the young man.

'It was you who arrived yesterday? The whole town is talking about you. You have brought the secret teachings of Yoshimori.'

Taro nodded, his face puzzled.

'You should have new clothes,' the man said, appraising him. 'Choose some fabric. There will be no charge for you.'

'I don't need anything,' Taro replied. 'I am just Lord Arai's servant.'

The man's face softened. 'Servant of the World,' he said, his eyes glowing. 'That's who we were told would come. I will make something befitting.' He bowed deeply, showing even greater respect than he had to Sunaomi. 'I will make the garments as quickly as possible,' he promised.

When he had left Taro sat down opposite Sunaomi. For a moment neither of them spoke.

'So, who do they think you are?' Sunaomi said finally, trying not to sound irritated or mocking.

'There was a prophesy,' Taro said awkwardly. 'Among these people called the Hidden. Ame is one of their elders. She was shown a dream in which a servant came riding on an old broken-down horse, bearing teachings that everyone thought were lost. He would heal the sick, among other things.' He glanced sideways at Sunaomi. 'I told them about your recovery when you were on the brink of death.'

'Was I really dying? I don't remember.'

'I would not let death take you,' Taro said. 'They said it was a miracle and proof that I really was the Servant of the World.'

'Do you believe that's what you are?' Sunaomi said, trying to choose his words carefully.

'I don't know. I did feel something when I held you in my arms. I knew you were dying and that it was up to me to save you. And the words in the book speak to me in a special way as if they reveal to me secrets of the divine.'

Sunaomi rubbed his temples. Taro spoke hesitantly and humbly yet something had changed in his demeanour. Something had touched his spirit and called to him.

'What do they want from you?' he asked. 'What do they want you to do?'

'It's said that the Servant of the World will establish the kingdom of heaven here on earth where all men and women will live in peace.'

'But that challenges the authority of the Empress,' Sunaomi said, a little alarmed.

'No,' Taro replied. 'The kingdom will be in this world but not of this world. It threatens no one. It is already within everything and everyone. It is up to me to reveal it. I wish I could stay with you and continue to look after Kiki and Chin but ...'

'But you have another allegiance now that takes precedence over me?' It was painful to say it.

'Yes,' Taro said quietly. 'I serve the Secret One and must obey it. I need all my time to study the writings and pray. I'm asking you to release me from your service.'

Sunaomi said nothing.

Taro went on, 'You said we were friends rather than master and servant.'

It had been easy to speak the words but it was hard to live by them. No doubt Kaneda would think Taro was being ridiculous, would give him a cuff round his head and tell him to get back to work, and part of Sunaomi felt he should do this, that he would save himself a great deal of trouble and heartache if he put Taro in his place and refused to tolerate his delusions. But he had offered him his freedom and he had to keep his word and live with Taro's choices.

'Chin will miss you,' he said.

'You should ask Hiromasa to take over my role. It will strengthen the bond between you.'

'Is he my brother?' Sunaomi asked. 'If you are some kind of

prophet can you discern the truth?'

'Only you can know if he is or not,' Taro replied. 'Maybe if you treat him as if he is he will be.'

Sunaomi nodded but said only, 'Where will you go?'

'Back to the Temple of the Poor.'

'I'll come and see you in a few days,' Sunaomi said. 'I'll bring the new clothes and see for myself what you have chosen.'

'You will always be welcome,' Taro said. 'I just ask that you don't come to mock.'

'I would never mock you!' Yet he was half-laughing as he said it.

Taro regarded him unsmiling. 'You have a mocking nature that treats everything lightly and dismisses those around you by laughing at them.'

Was this really how he appeared to others? He cultivated an outward frivolity and maybe it was true that he did not take the world too seriously for he knew the other reality that lay behind it. He did not like the feeling that Taro was admonishing him but Taro's earnestness touched his heart.

'I promise I will come with an open mind,' he said. 'I will respect your beliefs though I don't think I will ever share them. Moreover, you know, if there is anything subversive behind them I will have to report it to Lord Miyoshi.'

Taro hesitated as though he wanted to say something more.

'What is it?' Sunaomi asked.

'The bear,' Taro said. 'I see you are wearing it round your neck again. I know it is some kind of spirit. You should burn it and anything else like it. Otherwise they will come to possess you. You are in great danger.'

Sunaomi touched the red cord round his neck, and thought of Utahime's flute which he carried in his sash. He would never destroy either of them.

'Thank you for your concern for me,' he replied. 'No doubt there are many dangers around me, but this carving is not one of them.'

After Taro had left, Sunaomi sat for a while thinking of what he had to accomplish: meet with the foreigners and the Nankoku lords—were any in Hofu or would he have to sail across the strait to Utsu? Inspect the boat building and check the source of the lumber; find Masao; come to a decision about Hiromasa.

Kaneda returned and asked if the cloth merchant had visited.

'Indeed he has and I've ordered some very fine garments,' Sunaomi replied. 'They have beautiful fabrics here, rivalling anything in Miyako.'

'They think they are more than equal to the capital in every way,' Kaneda remarked. 'And they are very happy to look after their own affairs without any interference.'

'Is it just provincial pride or is it more rebellious?'

'That's what we hope to find out,' Kaneda said.

'Let's go down to the port. I can't meet any of the people I need to talk to until I am dressed appropriately, but this old robe will do fine for walking around before too many people recognise me or know I am here.'

◆

Flashes of childhood memories assailed him, awakened by the smells of the harbour, the feel of the westerly on his skin, the way the afternoon light fell on the water, the creaking of boats on the rising tide.

'Apparently high tide is around midnight,' Kaneda said. 'So, many travellers will be leaving then. I don't think the sea allows anyone to sleep here.'

'Have you ever been to sea?' Sunaomi asked.

'No, I don't care for boats or water,' Kaneda admitted, adding swiftly, 'Though of course if you decide to go further south I will accompany you.'

They both gazed out towards Nankoku whose mountains could just be seen above the clouds.

'It's closer than I thought,' Sunaomi said. 'Close enough to transport men and horses across without any difficulty.' He wondered what forces Lord Mizuta was assembling out of sight on the further side.

Fishing boats were returning on the incoming tide, weaving their way between the carracks and skiffs of all sizes ferrying passengers to and fro.

Chin was climbing among the ropes coiled on the dock, sniffing around, transfixed by so many different smells. She was right on the edge and Sunaomi was about to call her back when someone came from behind and casually kicked her over into the water. Sunaomi did not see who it was, just noted the dark head covering, the swift deliberate movement. He heard Chin give one sharp yelp and then the splash. He ran to the edge; she was paddling desperately, trying to scramble up the wall.

Without thinking Sunaomi dropped straight into the water, feet first. He surfaced next to her and she scrabbled to him, her eyes bulging in alarm.

'I've got you,' he said, spitting out a mouthful of foul-tasting sea water, and looked up to where Kaneda stood above them, waving his arms and yelling. Sunaomi turned his head and saw a boat bearing down on him, driven by the tide. It was a medium-size skiff with a triangular sail and a man behind skulling with a single oar. In the front were a handful of passengers, shouting out in warning.

He tried to swim out of its way but the struggling dog hampered him. The green slimed stones of the harbour wall were right against his head. He was going to be crushed between them and the bows of the boat.

A rope dangled next to him. He grabbed it with one hand. It held taut. His feet found the cracks between the stones and he half-climbed and was half-pulled back up, as the boat thudded against the wall behind him.

As he sank down on the wharf, he realised Kaneda had been helped by Kichizo. Hiromasa took Chin from his arms.

'I thought she was going to drown!' the boy cried.

'What about me? Weren't you worried about me?'

'You saved her,' Hiromasa said, looking directly at Sunaomi above Chin's bedraggled body. She looked as thin as a rat. 'You didn't hesitate.'

'Yes, I'm a hero,' Sunaomi said, getting to his feet. 'It's a good thing you turned up,' he said to Kichizo.

'We were following you,' his cousin said. 'It was likely there would be a quick attack on you before anyone else knows you're here. I didn't expect them to use the dog, though.'

His voice sounded almost admiring.

'Who was it?' Sunaomi said. 'Did you see him?'

'No, I was watching you. But who else knows you are here apart from Terada?'

'It could have been just a random occurrence,' Sunaomi said. 'Someone took a dislike to my dog.'

'Get used to the idea that nothing is random where you are concerned. Someone wants you out of the way. Someone who knows you well.'

'I'm glad you foiled them, this time. Thank you. Lucky for me they are not employing you.'

'If they were you'd be dead already,' Kichizo said, grinning. 'I'll see if I can track that man down. Someone must have seen something. Keep an eye on the boy. I'll be back later.'

Sunaomi crouched down beside Hiromasa who was cradling Chin, trying to dry her on the sleeve of his jacket. She was shivering. Sunaomi felt her flanks and belly gently, which made her whimper. He hoped the kick had not broken a rib or caused internal injuries. The foetid water of the harbour was heavy in his throat and belly, and he found himself retching. Behind him the boat creaked against the wall. He imagined briefly the weight of it, crushing him, the murky water rushing into his lungs.

A small crowd had gathered round them, watching curiously but mostly indifferently. Sunaomi was embarrassed. He had hoped to make his first walk round the town inconspicuous so he might gather his own first impressions. Now he had become the centre of attention. And not only of the townspeople. The passengers from the boat had also disembarked, and one of them was making anxious enquiries.

He heard Kaneda say, 'Don't concern yourselves. My lord is fine. The dog fell in and he jumped after it. No one was hurt.'

'It could have been terrible,' the stranger said, his speech slightly accented.

Sunaomi stood up. So much for his hope to meet the foreigners in fine clothes as the Empress's envoy. For the two men in front of him were definitely foreigners, one in the dark robes of a priest, the other also in black: short puffed trousers and a long-sleeved tight fitting jacket. A thin sword hung at his side. Sunaomi could not be sure but he thought they were the men he had met as a child. The memory was engraved in his mind, the large wooden chairs his father had had made for the tall stiff-kneed visitors, the odd phrases of greeting he and his mother had practised together. Of course they would not recognise him after so many years.

'We live nearby,' the priest said. 'Let us give you dry clothes.'

'Thank you, but there is no need,' Sunaomi said. 'I am staying at Daifukuji, only minutes away.'

'Praise Deus you are unhurt,' the priest said, fingering the beads that hung around his neck. The two men bowed their heads and walked on, followed by servants carrying bundles and baskets.

'They must have arrived on one of the carracks,' Sunaomi said to Kaneda as they walked home. 'I wonder if they have been in Utsu.'

'Lord Saga banished all foreigners,' Kaneda said. 'But since Lady Kaede has been ruling in the name of the Empress they have been allowed in a small number of ports, like Hofu and Utsu, though they are not permitted to travel into the interior or to Miyako.'

'What do they do? How do they spend their time?'

'They trade goods. When I was looking for your merchant I asked about what kind: fabrics, of course, furs from the north, glassware, maps, time-telling devices like sundials and hour glasses, rouge to brighten your cheeks and other such unnecessary luxury items, and of course firearms.'

'Do the Nankoku lords buy such weapons, enough to arm many men?' Sunaomi asked.

'Something we'll have to find out.' Kaneda turned to address Hiromasa who trailed behind them, still carrying Chin. 'Hurry up if you are coming with us. Give me the dog if she's too heavy for you.'

'She's not too heavy,' the boy said, quickening his step.

Kaneda went on, 'The other way they pass their time is in worship and proselytising. They are very devout and strive always to make new converts. You may have heard the priest exclaim *Praise Deus. Deus* is their god, a sole authority who dwells in the sky and knows, sees and hears everything.'

'This is what Lord Kahei wants to know about,' Sunaomi said. 'Is it true that Mizuta is one of their converts?'

'It would seem to be.'

'And Terada Fumio?'

'People don't dare talk much about him,' Kaneda said. 'But I gather he pretends to be a believer in order to get his hand on ships and firearms.'

'That's about what I would expect of him,' Sunaomi said.

When they arrived back at the temple Shishi came out to meet them. The sight of the dog seemed to revive Chin and she struggled out of Hiromasa's arms to run up to him. He had not barked at them, but now he gave a yelp of surprise at her appearance and sniffed at her warily, his tail quivering. Chin rolled over and showed her belly.

'She's all right, isn't she?' Hiromasa said, crouching next to her.

'It looks like it. We'll wash her and give her some fresh water, maybe not feed her till tomorrow, when you can see if you can find a source of meat. I hope you will take Taro's place and look after her now.'

'I could steal it for her,' Hiromasa suggested.

'There's no need to steal. Tell them who you are, and that Kaneda will make sure they are paid.'

Sunaomi lifted Chin carefully and they walked towards the spring where he filled a bucket with water.

'But who am I?' Hiromasa said. 'Who am I to be?' Again he looked directly at Sunaomi. It was like looking into his own face, the same shaped eyes, the same high brow, the same small fine features: the Shirakawa look.

'You are my brother,' Sunaomi said. 'The third son of Arai Zenko and Shirakawa Hana.' He looked down at Chin as he sponged her with warm water. The moment had become unbearably heavy with emotion and to lighten it he said, 'I will have our tailor make you new, suitable clothes.'

Hiromasa picked up some rags and began rubbing the dog gently. 'I'm glad I am your brother. I'll never forget how you jumped straight into the water without hesitating. I don't need new things, though. I don't want people looking at me like they look at you. I would rather go unnoticed like Kichizo. Maybe that could be useful to you?'

Sunaomi smiled. 'Maybe. Look after Chin now while I bathe and then we will talk further.'

So, just like that I have won my brother's admiration and trust, Sunaomi thought as he soaked in the hot water. He now had to endeavour not to lose them. Hiromasa might be useful in all sorts of ways, but Sunaomi's first duty as his older brother was to keep him out of danger and then to give him an education. Thoughts about this new responsibility floated through his head, interrupted by sharper memories: the kick that had sent Chin flying into the harbour, the smack of the water as he plunged in, the shouts of the sailors as the skiff bore down on him.

Kaneda's voice woke him from a short doze. The warrior had

taken the soaked and dirty clothes to be washed and had borrowed a dark purple garment for him to wear. Holding it out for Sunaomi to slip into he tied the sash and then combed and refastened Sunaomi's hair.

'You have now lost or ruined all your robes,' he said sternly. 'It's a good thing the merchant will have replacements this week.'

Sunaomi would have felt rebuked like a child, but wearing the monk's clothing, faded and soft from years of use, made him feel invulnerable as if the many different bodies it had covered had imbued it with patience and endurance. He fell into something of a daydream, thinking of the hands which had woven, dyed and sewn the fabric, had washed and mended it over the years, all rendering service to others, like the haunted hands of maids who had dressed him when he was a child.

Servant of the World, Ame had said of Taro. At that moment, clad in the monk's robe, he wished he too could devote his life to the service of others.

'You are very quiet.' Kaneda was peering at him. 'Are you feeling all right?'

'I'm fine. The bath just made me a little sleepy.'

'Do you want to rest? I can spread out the bedding.'

'No, it is still early. And there is something we need to talk about. We have not had the opportunity until now. It is about Hiromasa.'

Kaneda waited, saying nothing.

'He does look like me, doesn't he? I am not imagining it?'

'He is the image of you as a child,' Kaneda replied.

'My cousins believe he is my brother. I was not convinced at first, but now I am.'

'I must follow your judgement in this, Lord Sunaomi.' Kaneda's face was creased with emotion. 'Let me just say, I am more than happy to.'

Sunaomi clasped his hand. 'Then we will treat him as Arai Hiromasa from now on. Now I need to talk to him. You may check on the horses, take Kiki out to stretch his legs. Give me some time alone with my brother.'

'I don't like leaving you with no other guard here,' Kaneda said.

'No one's going to attack me in Daifukuji,' Sunaomi said. 'Dressed like this no one's going to know who I am. Just take Kiki out down the road. You can come straight back. I only need a short time.'

Kaneda finally left and Sunaomi walked back to the guest room. Hiromasa sat on the verandah with Chin on his lap. A small bowl of water rested next to them on the floor.

'You remembered the water,' Sunaomi said as he sat down. 'Thank you.'

Chin's tail stirred at the sound of his voice.

'She only drank a little.'

'Rest is the best thing for her now.'

They sat in silence for a short time while the dog sank into a deeper sleep.

Slowly evening was approaching. Doves crooned from the temple roof and swallows twittered as they swooped and circled. Now and then the footsteps of monks could be heard as they crossed the courtyard or walked through the cloisters, but no one came to disturb them.

Sunaomi felt instinctively that he should not question Hiromasa directly but wait for him to speak first.

Eventually the boy said, 'Kichizo said someone who knew you well must have kicked Chin into the water.'

Sunaomi nodded.

'So, who could that be? Who do you know here?'

'No one, apart from Terada, the Abbot here, and our companions on the road.'

He wondered if it could have been someone from the Tribe, for Kichizo and Kiyoko must have already met up with their relatives in Hofu. But Kichizo had helped rescue him.

'What about the one you are looking for?' Hiromasa asked.

'The one Kiyoko told me about.'

'Masao? He would not hurt my dog, or me.'

'He has hurt a lot of men, killed them,' Hiromasa said in a low voice.

'Did you see that?' Sunaomi felt a wave of pity.

Hiromasa nodded. His face was closed and sad. Speaking even more quietly, he said, 'I can talk to you, can't I? I can tell you things I wouldn't talk about to anyone else?'

'I am your older brother,' Sunaomi replied. 'You can tell me anything.'

'He enjoyed having a witness. He made me hold his horse and watch. And afterwards ... he takes what he wants from people. They like him at first. I did. I thought he was kind and that he liked me. No one else ever had.'

His voice was so soft Sunaomi had to strain to hear. 'But then he forces people to do what they don't want to do. Even if they cry out he forces them. He is very strong. Then he shows you a little affection, he is kind again, so you crave more from him, but he won't give it to you.'

'Is that why you ran away?' Sunaomi said, his heart twisting.

Hiromasa nodded. Sunaomi did not think he would say anymore but after a long silence the boy said, 'Nobody owns me.'

Sunaomi sensed his deep buried rage and wondered what had happened to him during the lost years and if he would ever learn the whole story. The episode with Masao was still fresh but there must have been many other instances of abuse and ill treatment. He felt helpless, not knowing how to deal with such damage. And angry on Hiromasa's behalf. He wanted to protect him against the world.

'It's strange,' Hiromasa said slowly, as if he was having difficulty finding the words. 'Men like him act as if everything belongs to them. They take and they break and ride on, leaving everything in pieces behind them. Is it because they are warriors?'

'It is because they are men,' Sunaomi replied. He thought of Masao's wildness, his intense animal energy, so attractive until it turned lethal. He was like a predator; if you did not run from him or fight him you became his prey.

'Was our father like that? Tell me about him.'

'I wish I remembered more,' Sunaomi said. His father had become a dim memory. It saddened him that what he remembered most clearly was his angry voice. 'You and I look like our mother, but our brother, Chikara, takes after our father, they say.'

'*Chikara?* I feel as if that name is familiar.' Hiromasa frowned as if recalling the past. 'Where is Chikara?'

'He is in our home town, Kumamoto, with our grandmother.'

'So, I have a grandmother as well as two brothers? Can we go and see her?'

'I hope so. I'll write to her and tell her you are alive. She won't believe it.'

Hiromasa's face softened. 'Will she be happy?'

'Of course she will, just as I am,' Sunaomi said gently.

'You are not like most men,' Hiromasa said. 'Nor is Kaneda, for all his stern appearance.'

'Kaneda is the most honourable man I know,' Sunaomi said. 'He will be your servant for life now he knows who you are.'

'What about Kichizo? I liked him at first but now I think he is dangerous.'

'Well, the Tribe have different rules. But you are right. Kichizo and Kiyoko are both very dangerous.'

'Am I still part of the Tribe?' Hiromasa asked.

'That's for you to decide when you are older. In the meantime you need to have a warrior's education. Starting tomorrow, we'll find a teacher because you must learn to read and write.'

'Tomorrow I'm going to find meat for Chin.' Hiromasa stroked the dog in his lap. She moved a little, her eyelids fluttered, her legs twitched as if she were running in a dream.

'You find meat and I'll find a teacher,' Sunaomi said.

CHAPTER FIFTEEN

Chin slept without moving all night but woke needing to go out. It was already light. The monks had been up since before dawn, rising to pray while it was still dark. Sunaomi had heard the bell that woke them in his dreams, as if deep underwater.

He walked a little stiffly, and so did Chin, but otherwise she seemed unhurt. She squatted to relieve herself, then saw Shishi on the steps and ran to greet him, her tail wagging, her ears flat against her head. Shishi sniffed her all over while she tried to lick his face.

Sunaomi went to the privy and when he came back they were sitting side by side looking like statues. Male and female, they complemented each other.

The light was pale pink and pearly. A slight mist hung above the sea. The wind had dropped and the water was very calm. Boats hovered over their reflections, their sails golden. Seagulls were calling. It seemed so peaceful, yet beyond in the maze of alleys and further, across the straits, who knew what intrigues were brewing?

Kiyoko returned while they were eating the morning meal.

'I hear you went for a swim,' she said. 'And my brother had to pull you out. Fancy risking your life for a dog!'

Her voice was teasing but affectionate.

'Perhaps you can help Hiromasa find some meat for the dog,' Sunaomi said. 'I don't want to lose her to starvation, just after saving her life.'

'I think I know of a place,' Kiyoko said, calling to Hiromasa to come with her.

After they left Kaneda strolled about the garden, pretending he was simply enjoying the view, while Sunaomi consulted the

Abbot about a teacher for his brother. He was directed to the library, which he had not known existed.

It was in a small room on the south side, behind the main hall. The sunlight poured in along with the smell of lamp oil and incense and the sound of men chanting, mingling with the library's own smell of old paper and ink. Books and texts lay everywhere, beautifully coloured scrolls of all sizes, fastened with braided cords, and folded books with board covers. In their midst at a small desk sat a thin man whose age was hard to determine. His head was shaved, his skin unlined, his eyes, when he looked up at Sunaomi, bright and shrewd, though a little red rimmed from peering at the old writings.

When Sunaomi made his request, the monk frowned. 'I would like to help you. I don't mind teaching, and if our Abbot suggested me I suppose I must, but I am already falling behind on my task.'

'May I ask what it is?' Sunaomi knelt next to him. 'I am Arai Sunaomi. My brother, who would be your student, is called Hiromasa.'

'Yes, I know who you are.' The man's voice was neutral. 'I am known as Shomei. I am copying the older texts. They don't survive well here because of the salt air and the damp, and then there are mice and insects that feed on them. Once this was a fine collection, but the library has been neglected and now many texts are in very poor condition. There are valuable teachings here that lie unread. To tell you the truth, not many of our monks can read. They have good memories, they learn by heart, but I wonder if they know the meaning of what they are chanting.'

He pushed the brush and the inkstone towards Sunaomi. 'I suppose you were taught to write. Show me. Copy this passage here.'

Sunaomi looked carefully at the scroll. Some of the characters were unfamiliar to him, but he could understand the way they were written well enough to copy, and the meaning was clear. He took up the brush and wrote, *Split a piece of wood and I am there.*

It reminded him of something. Hadn't Taro spoken those words? Sunaomi's memory of that time was blurred; he had been half-delirious.

'What is this text?' he asked as he wrote the next line. *Lift up the stone and you will find me there.*

'Ancient teachings of the Enlightened One, brought from the mainland centuries ago,' Shomei replied.

'It wasn't written by the Emperor, Yoshimori?'

Shomei narrowed his eyes. 'Texts by Yoshimori are rumoured to exist. Occasionally I find references to them, but I've never seen one.' He looked at Sunaomi's writing. 'It's not bad,' he conceded. 'If you will take over the copying, I will teach your brother.'

'I'm afraid I'll be too busy,' Sunaomi said. 'I have many tasks to accomplish while I'm in Hofu.'

'You will find it relaxing and it will clear your mind,' the monk said decisively. 'It is nearly midsummer, the days are long. We will start now, and continue from tomorrow at first light.'

Sunaomi felt as if he'd been tricked into the agreement. Shomei had acted so swiftly, like a Go player, calculating many moves ahead. He was only partly mollified when the monk looked at his writing and murmured again, 'Not bad. Not bad at all.' He showed Sunaomi the pile of texts that were awaiting copying. 'As I said, you can start now.'

It will be good for Hiromasa to see me writing alongside him, Sunaomi told himself. *It will encourage him.* He took one of the texts and began to copy it carefully.

◆

Outside the guest room Chin was happily eating from a bowl of strong-smelling meat. Hiromasa sat next to her, Kiyoko beside him. Kaneda had moved to the gate, where he stood without moving.

'You are back so soon,' Sunaomi said. He had been unaware of time passing while he was in the library.

'We found some people who have lots of dead horses,' Hiromasa said, looking as pleased as Chin.

Sunaomi raised his eyebrows at Kiyoko.

'There's a small village just up the river,' she explained. 'Some outcasts have settled there. They deal with horses: the slaughter, skinning and tanning of the hides.'

'So close to town?' Sunaomi said, a little surprised.

'I talked to their headman for quite a while. They were protected by Lord Otori under the Jo-An laws, but Saga began persecuting them, despite the fact that they perform an essential role. Now they feel more secure, but they want more than that. They want to be fully accepted by society.'

'I suppose people find that proximity to death unpleasant, and they fear pollution.'

'People are such hypocrites,' Kiyoko retorted. 'Where do they think leather for armour and harness comes from? Anyway, I got the impression that these fellows will not allow themselves to be pushed around. They have come to the limits of their forbearance and since Saga's iron fist has been removed they have become emboldened. They have some formidable weapons: cleavers, knives, axes.'

'Yet another group that I need to be concerned with,' Sunaomi said.

'It's best that you know about these things. Kichizo is busy gathering information. If Masao is here my brother will find him.'

'Where is Kichizo staying?'

'There's a Muto house here. It would be impolite if neither of us stayed there, so Kichizo volunteered. You may remember Muto Yoshio and Kuroda Yasu.'

'Rather too well,' Sunaomi said, reluctant to recall the months spent in the secret Tribe village with the two men and slightly apprehensive that they might still resent the fact that he had run away, stealing, in their eyes, the horse, Ashige. He had no desire to meet them again.

'Muto Mai is also here and wants to see you.' Kiyoko said. She was studying his face carefully, alert to his reaction. Mai was another ghostlike memory from his childhood. He had not seen her since the day she had committed murder to avenge her sister and his uncle, Taku, Kiyoko's father. He wondered if Kiyoko knew this, if the girls shared their secrets, chatting about the men they had killed, the weapons they used, their Tribe skills, as other girls might discuss music and poetry.

And then Kinu's face, her delicate features, her translucent skin, floated unbidden into his mind and he was seized by a longing to see her.

'What are you thinking about?' Kiyoko asked.

'Nothing.' To change the subject he said quietly, 'Did you take my brother to this Muto house?'

'It's no good whispering,' she replied. 'Hiromasa has extreme far hearing, you know.'

I had forgotten that, Sunaomi thought. *Am I refusing to recognise his skills so he will never return to the Tribe? But denying they exist isn't going to make them go away.*

'She did take me, but I don't want to go back there,' Hiromasa said, stroking Chin, who had finished eating and was licking his fingers. 'I'd rather stay here with you.'

'You don't have to go back,' Sunaomi said, hoping it was true. It worried him that Yoshio and Yasu now knew of Hiromasa's existence. 'But you do have to have some education. It will start today. Your teacher's name is Shomei.'

Hiromasa looked surprised but only asked if Chin could come with him.

'Yes, since I have to accompany you. I have to make some recompense to Master Shomei. I hope you won't disappoint either of us.'

He spoke briefly to Kaneda about these new arrangements

and then he and Hiromasa went to the library with Chin at their heels. The pile of texts had grown even higher. Sunaomi knelt at the desk while the monk took Hiromasa onto the verandah.

Sunaomi could hear his patient instruction and it made him remember his own education at Terayama and then less formally with Hiroshi in the deserted house. The work was calming and, as Shomei had said, his mind slowly emptied of everything but the text in front of him and the process of transcribing it perfectly. It demanded complete concentration. One mis-stroke changed the whole meaning. Meanwhile the wisdom of the words passed into his brain almost without him noticing.

Time slipped away. The sun rose higher and moved across the sky, leaving the room in shadow. His meditation was broken by a voice calling, 'Visitors have come to see Lord Arai.'

Shomei appeared at the door. 'We have done enough for today. Your brother can practise on his own.' He looked at the passage Sunaomi had just completed and nodded. 'It's all right,' he conceded, making Sunaomi feel ridiculously pleased.

Kaneda stood by the gate with the foreign priest in his black robes and the man who had accompanied Terada Fumio, Renzo the interpreter. Chin barked at them and Renzo clicked his tongue at her and bent to stroke her, but she ran back to Sunaomi, still growling. He picked her up, noting Renzo was dressed in different, even more splendid garments and regretting that he was still in the borrowed monk's robes.

The two visitors made a slight bow as he approached and Renzo said, 'Don Carlo wanted to make sure you were all right.' He looked at Chin and added, 'It's amazing that you risked your life to save a dog. You must be excessively fond of it.'

Sunaomi did not reply directly but simply said, 'It's very kind of you. Let's sit in the garden. Kaneda, please arrange for tea to be brought to our guests, or perhaps they would prefer wine.'

'We will have tea, thank you,' Don Carlo said. His speech was fluent though his accent was clearly foreign.

'Don Carlo understands most things,' Renzo said, 'but he

likes me to translate his more complex thoughts.'

As they made their way through the garden he added, 'I hope you did not suffer any ill effects from your immersion.'

'I seem to be fine, thank you,' Sunaomi replied.

'We only saw the splash,' Don Carlo said. 'I thought a child had fallen in.'

'It was just a pet dog,' Renzo said in his deep smooth voice. 'The child jumped in afterwards.' He laughed and tried to pat Chin again but she showed her teeth, growling deep in her throat.

They went to a small wooden platform beneath a wisteria arbour overlooking the harbour and the Encircled Sea. On the far side the mountains of Nankoku could just be seen through the violet haze. A red carpet and firm round cushions had been placed on the floor.

'Please sit down,' Sunaomi said with careful politeness. He felt Renzo had been trying to belittle him. 'Or does Don Carlo need a stool?'

The temple had several wooden stools for elderly arthritic monks who could no longer bend their knees. Kaneda must have had the same thought for he appeared with one and placed it so the priest could enjoy the view.

Don Carlo thanked him and said to Sunaomi, 'You have hardly changed since I met you many years ago. You probably don't remember. You had learned a few words of our language. I thought it was enchanting. And your little brother, such a delightful child, came to Hagi with us by ship.'

'I do remember you, though I have forgotten any words I ever knew.'

'I was very saddened by the death of your parents,' Don Carlo went on. 'Your father was a fine man and your mother ... I did not think a beautiful woman could be so intelligent, until I met her sister of course, your aunt, Lady Kaede.' He touched the beads at his breast. 'I often thought about you and prayed for you. I felt sorry for you, orphaned in such a terrible way, so young. It gives me great joy to see you, a fine young man, entrusted with such an important mission. Deus be praised!'

The priest's flattery left Sunaomi speechless. Luckily at that moment one of the kitchen monks arrived with bowls of tea and sweet bean-paste cakes. While the guests ate and drank, Sunaomi was able to compose himself. He had hardly given the foreigners a thought in the intervening years. It was disconcerting to realise Don Carlo had been praying for him.

'Renzo tells me you have been sent by Lady Kaede,' Don Carlo said, placing his tea bowl on the tray. He refused the sweet cake. Renzo ate two, surprisingly delicately for such a big man.

'That is correct,' Sunaomi replied, and was about to explain more of his mission, but Don Carlo went on, musing, 'How I wish I could see her again. Unfortunately we are not permitted to travel freely through the country. Would she ever come to Hofu?'

'Lady Kaede rarely travels,' Sunaomi said. 'She went to Maruyama when her first grandchild was born, but other than that she has not left the capital in seven years.'

'She has grandchildren?'

'Two girls, Lady Shigeko's daughters with Sugita Hiroshi. They are still very young.'

A pensive expression crossed the priest's face. 'When I first met her, when we studied together, she herself was carrying a child. I thought she was like Our Lady, a Madonna of the Orient. What would it take to acquire permission to travel to see her? There is so much we can offer: trade with our country, gold, techniques of building ships, weapons.'

He had moved so smoothly and swiftly from his gentle reminiscences to diplomacy that Sunaomi was a little taken aback. A smile hovered on Renzo's lips. Sunaomi wondered briefly where the man had been born, how he had come to be with the foreigners. Surely at heart he was Terada Fumio's man and everything they discussed this day would be reported to Terada.

Renzo said something to the priest and they both chuckled.

'Tell me what amuses you,' Sunaomi said. He felt at such a disadvantage when they could converse in a language he did not understand.

'Forgive us,' Renzo said. 'I told the priest you have the gift of silence. It's a joke—he has a teaching about the gift of tongues.'

His tone was familiar, on the verge of insolence. Sunaomi felt his temper rise and fought to control it. He was aware of the flush on his skin, not only due to the summer heat, and of the sweat trickling down his chest. Once he had thought of his own sweat, he could smell the others', meaty and spicy.

'I will be writing to my aunt,' he said. 'I will convey your request. But we need to know specifically what you can offer and what you expect in return. Do you have the authority to speak for the ruler of your country?' He could hardly imagine their homeland, impossibly distant, filled with thousands of people who looked like Don Carlo, tall, pale skinned, beak nosed. Or did they look more like Renzo, powerfully built, the colour of polished cypress wood? 'What agreements have you made with the Nankoku lords, Lord Mizuta for example? I need complete honesty from you. If you fabricate information I will find out. I may appear to you to be young and alone, but I command resources that you know nothing about and I am here as the representative of the Empress. I expect from you not only cooperation but also truth and transparency.'

He tried to speak with conviction but he was all too aware of his inexperience in the face of these men, twice his age, who had sailed across oceans, had visited many countries and who more importantly enjoyed the favour and friendship of Terada Fumio.

The two men exchanged smiles as if they were thinking the same thing. Sunaomi burned.

Don Carlo said, 'You must meet my colleague, the companion of my travels, João da Alaça. I am thinking we should hold a feast to welcome you to Hofu. Lord Mizuta will join us.'

He spoke warmly but Sunaomi sensed the confidence behind his words, as if Hofu belonged to him by virtue of his friendship with Terada. The foreigner had more claim to the city than Sunaomi, despite his childhood connections and his family's residence.

'Let's make it in three days' time. Lord Terada graciously allows us to stay in his guest house. I know the residence is familiar to you but Renzo will come to escort you. I will write to Lady Kaede in the meantime, answering your questions and stating our case. I will give you the letter when I see you next.'

Sunaomi thanked him, assuring him he would look forward to that meeting. They conversed more generally for a while about the beauty of the garden and the identity of the various ships at anchor in the harbour. Then the two men left, expressing their gratitude and their pleasure.

Kaneda accompanied them to the gate but Sunaomi remained under the wisteria, idly stroking Chin's silky fur, gazing out over the sea and wondering how he was going to make any headway.

◆

That night Chin woke him while it was still dark. She sat upright, sniffing and quivering. He thought he could hear Kichizo and Kiyoko talking quietly outside, but he could not make out the words.

The next morning as he walked with Hiromasa to the library for his lesson with Shomei, his brother said suddenly, 'They were talking about you last night.'

'You heard them?'

Hiromasa smiled. 'Even they forget sometimes that I hear everything.'

'What were they saying?'

'Kichizo wanted to leave but Kiyoko said they must stay with you, since they had agreed to. Then he got angry and said she was being emotional.' He looked up at Sunaomi. 'I think she likes you.'

Sunaomi shook his head as though denying her feelings and asked, 'Anything else?'

'Kichizo found Masao.'

'What? He didn't tell me?'

'Kiyoko said he should but he didn't want to, not right away.'

Sunaomi wondered what Kichizo's secret reasons might be. He said, 'Tell Shomei I'll be with him shortly. I need to speak to our cousins.'

He found them in one of the small halls that, linked by cloisters, stood at the back of the temple. It was built of wood, weathered by wind, salt and rain, not painted red like the main buildings. They were practising as the Tribe did, every day, obsessively. Sunaomi sat on the verandah and watched through the open door as his two cousins fought, slipping in and out of invisibility, using all the subtle techniques of the Tribe that he himself had never mastered.

What had their teachers said? Falling out of practice was the worst thing that could happen to them, the difference between life and death.

The siblings took no notice of him, almost as if they did not know he was there, but of course they did. They would have heard his footsteps, smelled his scent. Their eyes seemed intent on each other but they did not miss even his slightest move.

Kichizo was stronger but Kiyoko was quicker. Her movements were instinctive and unexpected, as fast as a snake. Even though they were not fighting in earnest, Sunaomi sensed her rage and saw how she channelled it to increase her power. He saw how easy it would be for her to kill any man.

Eventually they came to a halt. They were covered in sweat but did not seem breathless. Kichizo made a gesture, acknowledging Kiyoko's mastery.

She laughed and said, 'I am still your older sister.'

She sat down next to Sunaomi. He could smell her sweat beneath the jasmine scent. Kichizo crouched down on the other side, as usual odourless.

Sunaomi said, 'So, you have found Masao? Why didn't you tell me?'

'Kichizo told me first,' Kiyoko said. 'I am the oldest and it's I who will decide what is to be done with Masao. Of course, I would have informed you as soon as I saw you, which is now. We agreed to work for you. You are our lord.'

Her eyes were bright with some deep excitement. Her desire hit him like a punch, taking his breath away.

'You really found him?' he said to Kichizo, trying to mask how Kiyoko was affecting him.

Kichizo did not raise his head but said, 'He wants to meet you but you must go alone, as he will. Just the two of you, like in the old days, the orphan warriors. Those were his words. I'll take you to the place later and wait outside.'

Sunaomi was suddenly transported back in time to Terayama when he and Masao found common ground: the forced suicide of their parents and all the loneliness and grief that followed. They had understood each other and formed bonds of friendship that had only strengthened over the years. Or so Sunaomi had thought.

'How did you find him?' he asked.

'Yasu and Yoshio get to hear of any new arrivals, so they knew he was in Hofu. In the end he approached me. You have been pursuing him and he had been watching you. He was thinking of boarding a ship for the Southern Isles, but maybe he is waiting for you, as ships leave every few days, but he is still in Hofu. He has taken a room near the harbour.'

'Does he meet with anyone? Has he started any more fights?' Sunaomi asked.

'I haven't heard of any fights, but Taro visited him yesterday,' Kichizo said.

'Taro?' Sunaomi felt a pang of betrayal. Taro had always admired Masao. He had known where Masao was and had not told Sunaomi. What purpose could he have had in meeting him?

'Could someone be plotting something?' Kiyoko said. Her

expression was like a cat choosing her victim among a flock of sparrows, while they squabbled over grains of rice in the dust.

CHAPTER SIXTEEN

The merchant came that morning with the new clothes, carefully folded in bamboo baskets, scented with camphor and rue. He also brought the bone white robes for Taro, asking where they should be delivered.

'Leave them here,' Sunaomi said. 'I will take them to him.' He had decided he must see for himself the Temple of the Poor.

The robes were as impressive as he had expected but he did not change into them immediately. He felt comfortable and anonymous in the monkish garment, and in the evening, since his own old clothes were dry, he put them on, wanting to walk through the town as inconspicuously as possible.

He had intended to leave Chin behind with Hiromasa but she fussed and yelped, so he let her come with him. As he and Kichizo walked towards the outer gates of the Daifukuji, they saw two strange men waiting just inside. They were armed with swords and their jackets bore the crest of the twin black sails of the Terada.

Sunaomi stopped and said to Kichizo, 'Is Terada Fumio here?'

At that moment deep laughter echoed from the Abbot's room and he recognised Terada's voice.

'Apparently they are old friends,' Kichizo said, giving his usual mocking half-smile.

'They are meeting without me?' Sunaomi felt disturbed and insulted. 'What are they talking about?'

'They drink together a couple of times a month,' Kichizo replied. 'Sometimes more. One of the monks told me. I don't think there's anything suspicious going on.'

Maybe not, but the idea that they were old friends made

Sunaomi uneasy. They were a different generation to him and would have long-standing ties of loyalty.

'I'll ask Kiyoko to listen to them, if you like,' Kichizo suggested.

He walked swiftly back to the guest room and spoke to his sister, who was sitting on the verandah with Hiromasa.

'Not a word will escape those two,' he said when he rejoined Sunaomi.

Terada's men stared at them without acknowledgement as they walked past, annoying Sunaomi even more. He felt stir within him his sense of rank and privilege, of what was owed to him by reason of his birth.

I will deal with Terada. I will not let him insult me.

Kichizo said, 'You know you reveal yourself too easily.'

'Really?' Sunaomi replied, in no mood for admonishment. 'So, what am I thinking now?'

'That Terada insults you and you are a son of the Arai.'

'Is it so obvious?'

'You make it so. You should mask your thoughts and emotions.'

Sunaomi knew Kichizo was right. He found himself wishing he was back in Miyako, riding Kiki through streets that were clean and safe, instead of walking through the narrow lanes and alleys which thronged with people, any one of whom might slide a knife between his ribs. He was afraid Chin, who wanted to stop and sniff at every unfamiliar smell, would get lost among the crowds, so he stooped to pick her up, thinking it would have been better to leave her behind, but it was too late to turn back now.

The quayside had many small drinking places, tucked between storehouses and shops, and street stalls offered all kinds of seafood, octopus, lobsters, crabs and shrimps, sizzling on hot grills. Iron pots held simmering soups and stews.

Kichizo stopped outside one place. 'This is where he said he would be.'

It looked narrow and dark inside. Sunaomi hesitated, fearful he was stepping into a trap.

'I'll wait here,' Kichizo said. 'Shout out if you need me.'

Sunaomi stepped inside, Chin still under his arm.

Oil lamps had been lit making the room smoky and uncomfortably warm. The floor was earthen, but there was a raised wooden area where customers sat. Around them servant girls hurried with trays, kneeling to refill bowls and remove empty flasks.

Chin wriggled against him, her ears pricked, her nose quivering. The noise was considerable so he could not hear her, but he felt the vibration of her growl.

Masao sat alone in one corner, a flask and two bowls in front of him. He did not look up as Sunaomi approached but filled both bowls and pushed one towards Sunaomi. His hair was greasy and dishevelled, his bare feet dirty. His robe was stained with dark encrusted patches and he smelled as if he had not bathed in weeks.

Sunaomi sat down. Chin was growling, showing her teeth, and then she started barking more angrily than he had ever heard. He had to hold her firmly.

Masao put out his hand. She laid her ears back and snapped.

'Your fluffy rat survived, then?' Masao said, pulling his hand away.

Sunaomi stared at him, unable to believe what the dog was telling him. 'Why would you do that?' he said. 'Were you trying to kill me?'

'I was angry when I saw you. Why did you follow me? Are you trying to make me kill you? You know if it comes to a fight I'll defeat you.' He gave a short laugh. 'The dog looked so stupid, flying through the air. I made a bet with myself that you would jump in after her.'

Chin snarled.

'And I won my bet,' Masao said. 'It would have been better if you had drowned then. I want you to leave me alone. Go back to Miyako and tell your aunt I have disappeared. I wanted to see you to say goodbye. I loved you once but that's over.' His speech came rapidly in short jerks. His mouth smiled but the smile did not reach his eyes, which glittered coldly.

'What happened to you?' Sunaomi could hardly recognise his old friend and nothing about him seemed familiar. 'Let me take you to Daifukuji. You can bathe and rest and then we will talk about your future.'

'Take me prisoner, you mean? I will kill you before I let that happen.' Masao shifted restlessly and drained the wine from his bowl. He was about to leave. 'Unless someone else gets to you first. Go back to Miyako now or you never will. That's my warning.'

The menace in his voice set Chin barking again. Sunaomi realised a stranger had approached them, a servant or a groom perhaps. As he looked up, the man fell to his knees and bowed, speaking in a language which Sunaomi thought was Sillan though he did not understand it.

Chin's attention was diverted from Masao. She whimpered and flattened her ears. He could feel her tail wagging. She was acting like a puppy. She knew this man from somewhere. She slipped from Sunaomi's grasp and the man picked her up.

He spoke again and this time Sunaomi could understand his words. 'What are you doing with the sacred dog? This one was sent to Lady Kaede, the noble ruler of the realm. I selected her myself, the prize of the litter. Did you steal her?' He stood up, holding Chin closely. She squealed and licked his face.

'No,' Sunaomi said, also getting to his feet. 'She was indeed sent by your countrymen to Lady Kaede but after travelling with me for weeks she became attached to me, and Lady Kaede, who is my aunt, my mother's older sister, entrusted her to me. I am the dog's guardian and I have papers proving it.'

'So, where are they?' the man said, looking at Sunaomi's old clothes.

'They are at Daifukuji, where I am staying. I am Arai Sunaomi.'

The man had been joined by three other Sillans who gathered behind him, silent and threatening.

'This is Saga Masao,' Sunaomi said desperately. 'He will tell you who I am.'

But when he turned towards the place where Masao had been sitting, his friend had gone.

'He was no more than a vagrant, like you,' the Sillan said. 'You stole the dog. Maybe he was your accomplice.'

Sunaomi felt a surge of rage, mixed with disappointment that Masao had left, irritation at being caught up in this trivial misunderstanding, fear of losing Chin. 'Kichizo!' he called and drew his sword.

The sword was more persuasive than his clothes or his words had been. The Sillans stepped back only to find Kichizo with drawn sword behind them.

The innkeeper came hastily between them, pleading with them to put their swords away.

'Lord Terada's men will come, arrest you all and close my place down.'

'We serve the honoured envoys from Silla,' the man said. 'This thief stole one of our sacred dogs. Let him be arrested.'

'I am also an envoy,' Sunaomi said. 'From the Empress and Lady Kaede.'

'Well, do what envoys are supposed to do: discuss, negotiate,' the innkeeper begged. 'Don't kill each other, especially not in my place.'

Kichizo made a gesture with his head towards the door and he and Sunaomi backed out, swords still drawn. The Sillans followed them.

'Now give me back my dog,' Sunaomi demanded.

'Certainly not! See how she knows me. I bred and raised her.'

Chin seemed quite content in the man's arms, causing Sunaomi a sharp pang of jealousy and annoyance. He was reluctant to get into a fight. He and Kichizo were outnumbered. A group of Terada's men were at the end of the street. He did not want to attract their attention. Yet it was unbearable to relinquish the dog.

He glanced at Kichizo. His cousin's attitude was tense and wary, his eyes watching the Sillans carefully. He sensed Kichizo did not want to get into a fight either, because it would be one they could not win.

'Come to Daifukuji,' he said, making one last appeal. 'I will prove I am speaking the truth and am not a thief. I can open discussions on the Red Seal ships, as Lady Kaede instructed me.'

The Sillan smiled contemptuously, not believing a word. 'Shall I call Terada's men and have you arrested?'

The idea was humiliating. Sunaomi stepped back with a gesture of surrender and sheathed his sword. The Sillans walked away but before they reached the end of the street he heard Chin begin to yelp in distress. Her cries tore at his heart. He did not think he would ever see her again.

'Wise decision,' Kichizo said as they reached the temple without further incident. 'Sillans use a form of bare-hand fighting which is lethal. I don't know enough about it to engage with it. We wouldn't have had much of a chance.'

'Even with swords?'

'One of them would have broken your arm with a kick, instantly. I'm going to consult Yasu about them.' As Kichizo walked away he added, 'It's a shame about the dog, though.'

'I should never have become so attached,' Sunaomi said, half to himself. 'It is just a dog, after all.'

Yet he felt as if he had lost one of his limbs.

Kaneda was outraged when he heard what had happened.

'I should have come with you. If they have taken the dog it's an insult not only to you but also to Lady Kaede. You must not go into the town without me again.'

'You could have done nothing either,' Sunaomi said.

'I'll go out tomorrow with the papers. Those men can't be hard to find.'

'You should not challenge them alone. They are more

dangerous than they appear, according to Kichizo. In the morning I intend to go to the Temple of the Poor for I must deliver Taro's new clothes.'

'That's ridiculous,' Kaneda said, showing his frustration. 'The Arai don't run errands like merchants!'

'I need to see the place for myself, and talk to Taro. You must come with me, naturally.'

Kaneda nodded, his lips pressed firmly together.

'Do we know where it is?' Sunaomi asked.

'Kiyoko has been there, I believe,' Kaneda replied.

'Then she can come with us.'

This seemed to mollify Kaneda. 'That will be fitting,' he said. 'She can carry the clothes.'

'I saw Masao,' Sunaomi said. His head was aching and he longed to be alone, but he needed to talk to someone and Kaneda was the only person he fully trusted. 'I can hardly believe it, but it was he who kicked Chin into the water.'

'Surely he was not trying to harm you?'

'I think it was more an impulsive act of cruelty or a sort of meanness, like boys torturing a stray cat for laughs.' Sunaomi paused and then said reluctantly, 'I did not know Masao had that in him.'

'It was characteristic of his grandfather,' Kaneda remarked.

'At the end of his life,' Sunaomi agreed. 'But I'd always thought it was the wound to his eye that made Lord Saga insane.'

'He was always cruel.'

'The terrible events of Masao's childhood must have had an effect on him,' Sunaomi said, wanting above all to understand his friend so he could help him.

'Yet your childhood has not made you cruel,' Kaneda said.

'I had many who stepped in and cared for me, you among them. But Masao had no one.'

'It's a two-way thing,' Kaneda said. 'You have to allow those who want to care for you to get close to you.'

'Masao has always turned against everyone,' Sunaomi said.

'And now that includes even me.'

I'll save him if it's humanly possible, he thought. But he had no idea how he was going to do it. The evening had been one of failure and loss. He felt deeply dispirited.

Kaneda said, 'Are you feeling all right?'

When Sunaomi did not answer, the warrior went on. 'I have been concerned about your health. Ever since the arrow wound you don't seem to be yourself. There are dangers here, it's true, but I am more worried that you are fading away. You are thinner than ever, and there is something insubstantial about you. Forgive me for speaking so frankly, but if you cannot appear bolder and more confident, then we are wasting our time here. We should return to Miyako.'

Sunaomi was briefly tempted by the idea, but it seemed weak to give in so quickly. Making an effort to reassure Kaneda and rally his own spirits, he said, 'Many people in Hofu want me out of the way, and now I am also the target of street-fighting Sillans who believe I stole their dog. But I cannot let any of them intimidate me.'

'At least you found Masao,' Kaneda said.

'Only to lose him again. But what can I do? If I cannot persuade him to come with me I cannot arrest him. I can do nothing without armed men. Terada's guards control the city.'

'You know that Terada came earlier to visit the Abbot?' Kaneda said. 'Kiyoko told me.'

'I realised they were together just as I was leaving. It worried me, to be honest. Did Kiyoko hear anything important?'

'Apparently they spoke only of trivialities. They did mention you but only as regards how long you were staying.'

'They probably communicate in code,' Sunaomi said. '*Have another drink* means I admit you control the city and *Try these nuts* means Let's kill Arai Sunaomi.'

'It's quite possible, though I am not able to be so lighthearted about it,' Kaneda said. 'Again, I urge you to leave.'

'I won't let Terada scare me away. I'll go to the Temple of the

Poor and meet once more with the foreigners as we arranged. At least then I'll have something to tell Lord Kahei. And I would like to make the effort to reach an understanding with Terada. We must have some common ground.'

He lay wide awake in the dark, thinking about what Kaneda had said. He had to admit there was some truth in it. Was it the loss of Utahime that had weakened his ties with the real world? His longing for her and his grief had lessened but in their place had come this lassitude and lack of substance. He felt Chin's absence keenly, almost ashamed to grieve so much for a dog and a ghost.

CHAPTER SEVENTEEN

In the morning Hiromasa was silent and miserable looking. He had prepared a bowl of meat for Chin the night before and it sat uneaten, beginning to smell.

'Take it to Shishi,' Sunaomi told him.

In a short time the boy came running back, calling out, 'Something happened to Shishi!'

Sunaomi hurried after him, Kiyoko following them. The Abbot's dog lay on its side, next to the empty bowl.

'He ate the meat, and I was patting him and suddenly his eyes clouded over and he fell asleep,' Hiromasa said, his voice breaking.

Could the meat have been poisoned? Sunaomi wondered, but Chin had eaten the same meat the previous day with no ill effects. The dog did not froth at the mouth or seem in any pain. He was just deeply asleep.

'Did you stare at him?' Kiyoko asked Hiromasa.

'Yes, but I wasn't trying to hurt him. I wanted to see what he was thinking, so I held his gaze.'

'It is the Kikuta sleep,' Kiyoko said quietly.

'What does that mean? Will he be all right? I haven't killed him?'

'He should be all right,' Kiyoko said. 'You are still young and this must be the first time; you are not yet fully powerful. But you must never look children or animals in the eye from now on. Can you remember that?'

He nodded, impressed by her serious tone.

'How marvellous,' Kiyoko said to Sunaomi. 'All the old Kikuta skills are returning in him.'

'Don't say anything about this.' Sunaomi did not think it

marvellous in any way, for the more skills Hiromasa demonstrated, the further away he would be taken from Sunaomi.

One of the monks must have alerted the Abbot, for he came from his room, not running but moving faster than Sunaomi had ever seen him.

'What's happened?' he exclaimed.

'I'm sorry,' Hiromasa said. 'I didn't mean to hurt him.' He began to cry in earnest, fighting back the sobs.

'He's been poisoned?' the Abbot demanded. 'Or is it that he was not accustomed to eating meat? You should never have brought animal flesh into the temple.'

'No,' Sunaomi replied. 'It's something else.'

'How can you be sure? We must try an antidote.'

Sunaomi felt he had to tell the truth. 'Hiromasa made him go to sleep, by mistake.'

The Abbot frowned, not understanding. 'When will he wake up?'

Sunaomi looked at Kiyoko. 'I'm not sure,' she said. 'By the end of the day, I suppose. You either wake up, unharmed, or ...'

'Or what?'

'Or you don't wake up ever.'

The Abbot stared at her, as if seeing her for the first time. 'It's something your people do?' he said.

She nodded. She looked unusually submissive and penitent. Sunaomi thought she looked like a maid being scolded by her employer and realised it was what she was making the Abbot believe.

'Carry him to my room.' The priest bent to touch the dog's silky fur, his eyes suddenly bright. Sunaomi felt his own eyes grow hot in sympathy.

Kiyoko lifted Shishi gently and began to walk away, followed by Hiromasa.

The Abbot said, 'Taku, their father, was a friend of mine and I sheltered your grandmother, Shizuka, for weeks. But I cannot allow the Tribe to practise their dark skills inside Daifukuji.'

'It won't happen again,' Sunaomi said. 'I am as distressed about it as you are.'

'Where's your dog?' the other asked abruptly.

'I ran into a Sillan last night who said he had bred her. He did not believe I was her official guardian and I did not have the papers with me. He took her, but I am sure I will have her back with me soon.'

'How long do you intend to remain here?' the Abbot said. 'My advice would be to return to Miyako.'

'Before I leave I have a few more questions to which I need answers,' Sunaomi replied.

'Then it might be better if you found somewhere else to live.'

'Is that something Terada Fumio asked of you?'

The Abbot spread his hands. 'I cannot risk upsetting him, for he protects and supports us in many ways.'

'I will stay until the end of the month,' Sunaomi declared, trying to control his anger and still sound forceful. 'For the service of the Empress should override Terada's wishes.'

'Of course I am not going to turn you out in the street,' the Abbot said, making an effort to return to his usual affable self. 'But you cannot stay here indefinitely, and that young woman and the boy must leave.'

Sunaomi returned to the guest room where the morning meal had been set out on trays. Kaneda was waiting for him. Kichizo had returned and was already tucking in heartily.

Under Kaneda's watchful eye Sunaomi forced himself to eat a little. They were joined by Kiyoko and Hiromasa.

Kiyoko said to her brother, 'Something very interesting just happened.'

He raised his eyebrows, his mouth full.

'Hiromasa has another skill we didn't know about,' she said.

'Is that so?' Kichizo continued eating in silence for a few moments. 'Why don't he and I spend the day together and we'll talk about it?'

Sunaomi wanted to keep his brother with him, but he also

did not want him to miss out on Shomei's lesson. 'All right,' he agreed. 'Just make sure he does not neglect his studies.'

'It will be a day of learning all round,' Kichizo promised.

Kiyoko led the way to the western edge of the city. She had tied the basket containing Taro's clothes behind Hitare's saddle. Sunaomi followed her, and then Kaneda came on the speckled roan, Baku. At first their progress was slow through the crowded streets that led to a section of the port where Sunaomi had not been before. On the edge of the water hundreds of men were working on building ships, shaping the wood, joining the planks. He did not comment to the others but took note of the extent of the work.

The road widened and there was room to ride three abreast. It was a hot day, the sky a deep summer blue, the trees lush and green, the water in the rice fields shining brilliantly. On their left a river ran full after the rain. Normally, riding Kiki and wearing new clothes would have raised Sunaomi's spirits, but he was anxious about leaving Hiromasa and about the Abbot's dog, and he missed Chin at every moment. They rode in silence until Kiyoko spoke.

'The river's shallower further up,' she said. 'We can cross there.'

'You've already been to this temple?' Sunaomi asked.

'Hitare needed to get out, so I've been riding around.' She smiled at him, no longer looking in the least like anyone's maid. 'I like to know my way round. I heard Taro talking about the Temple of the Poor and thought I would take a look for myself.'

'What was your first impression?' Sunaomi said.

'No one can change the world. I don't know why they try.'

'Maybe they seek a better life for everyone.'

'They strive and strive, but the years go round and still it's the strong who eat, the weak who are meat.' She laughed. 'Be one of

the strong and take pleasure where you find it. That's the sum
of my beliefs.'

Again Sunaomi felt the pull of her desire. He longed to lie
down with someone, be held and caressed, and maybe that was
what was needed to break the spell he was under, but he feared
entanglement with her and what it might lead to.

They rode between the rice fields towards the mountains.
The road was deep with mud, churned by the feet of oxen
and rutted by the logs that had been dragged along it to the
ship-building yards. More logs, attached by ropes, were being
hauled by men and oxen through the waters of the river.

On their left side the southwestern slopes were still thickly
forested with cedar on the lower part and oak and beech higher
up, but the northern hills had been cleared, the trees felled leaving ugly scars and landslips like waterfalls of mud and rocks.

'No one is abiding by the laws that control forestry,' Sunaomi
said to Kaneda.

'Or any other laws proclaimed from Miyako,' the warrior
replied.

'The land is being destroyed.' The sight filled Sunaomi with
despair and anger.

'It brings riches and power to the destroyers,' Kaneda said.

They came to the place where it was shallow enough for the
horses to splash across the river. Once a quiet ford for farmers, it
had become a busy crossroads where logs were piled up before
their turn came to be dragged downstream. Men worked with
lathes and adzes to remove the bark and stumps of branches.
Women had set up stalls serving tea and food, their little fires
making the air smoky.

One man was obviously the overseer, issuing orders and
solving problems.

'I should speak to him,' Sunaomi said, and Kaneda called
out, telling him to come over.

Looking surprised and a little irritated, the overseer walked
towards them, shading his eyes against the sun. Sunaomi tried

not to sound accusatory with his questions about the number of trees felled, the plans for replanting, the reason for such a large quantity of timber to be accumulated at one time but within moments the other had become defensive.

'Bring it up with Lord Terada. We answer only to him,' he said, turning away with a superficial apology. 'Sorry, I'm busy as you can see.'

'One more thing to discuss with Terada,' Sunaomi said, as they rode through the river and up the opposite bank.

'The most urgent matter is getting your house back,' Kaneda said.

'That's the lowest priority, in my opinion. There are many other more important things he needs to explain honestly.'

Kiyoko brought Hitare alongside, so close her knee brushed against Sunaomi's. 'The temple is just up ahead,' she said.

It was a series of wooden buildings, old and weathered, unpainted, concealed among trees that to Sunaomi's relief and gratitude stood unfelled, soaring tall and imposing towards Heaven, giving a deep and welcome shade.

As they approached, a woman came out to greet them. Sunaomi recognised her as Ame, who had led Taro away when they first arrived in Hofu. She called to a young boy to come and hold the horses.

As they dismounted Sunaomi heard a neighing from behind the temple. Kiki called back. Hitare and Baku had their ears turned forwards.

'It must be the nag that Sasaki lent us,' Kaneda said, giving his roan a pat. 'The one that Taro rode.'

'We don't get many horses here,' Ame said. Her face was calm, her gaze direct. In the dappled shade she had an unearthly beauty. 'We are the poor; we walk on our own feet. Nothing serves us but we serve the world. Here we welcome everything that is worn and broken, faded, fatigued. So, that horse fits in well. It was broken in body and spirit, until it met the one you call Taro, and was healed.' She smiled at Sunaomi. 'As you were.

We are all broken in some way. That's why we come here.'

'I'm not broken,' Kiyoko said. 'There's nothing wrong with me.'

'The Secret One sees your heart,' Ame replied gently. 'Nothing is hidden from its gaze.'

Kiyoko gave a mock shudder. 'I think I'd prefer to wait here.'

There was a low bench under the trees and she went to sit on it, pushing away two old cats with torn ears and stumpy tails who had approached her hoping to be stroked.

'I suppose you have come to see him?' Ame said to Sunaomi.

'I've brought clothes for him,' Sunaomi replied, untying the basket and giving it to the woman. 'They are a gift from the merchant, Hachizaemon.'

'They are white, I imagine,' Ame said. 'For that is what I was told: the Servant of the World will be clad in white clothes, will carry the book of teachings, will ride a borrowed horse. Come, I'll take you to him.'

They walked around the side of the main hall. It was so quiet Sunaomi had assumed it was empty but now he realised there were many people on their knees inside, praying silently. At the further end was a bare altar where a single lamp burned before a statue which he took to be the All Merciful goddess, with a child on her lap. On the wall above, sunlight through narrow windows formed the shape of a cross.

The buildings and garden had the kind of wild neglected beauty that had always appealed to him. Even the broom on the step with its sparse bristles and broken handle, the overturned bucket with a ragged cloth draped over it, the splintery wood of the posts and floorboards were pleasing to his eye.

Morning glories and hydrangea bushes grew unchecked in the garden, their blossoms vibrant hues of purple and blue. The place reminded him of the old house in Miyako, yet there the neglect had sprung from fear whereas here it was for some other reason; some deeply held belief underpinned it.

'We live in another realm,' Ame said, as if reading his

thoughts. 'This world means nothing. It will all pass away just as our bodies will age and die and decay. But the kingdom of heaven lasts forever. That is where our treasure and our hearts are.'

Ame led them along a mossy stone path, warning it might be slippery, and then told them to wait a moment while she went ahead with the clothes. Sunaomi could hear voices coming from the other side of a low roofed building to their left. He recognised Taro's and then realised the others with him were the foreigners, Renzo definitely, and Don Carlo, and a third he did not know. He could make out the particular rhythm of speech and translation, the soft sounds of the foreigners' language, their voices when they spoke his own halting and harsher.

'Why are they here?' Kaneda muttered. 'In what way are they broken? They are more likely to be the ones doing the breaking.'

Ame reappeared and beckoned to them, saying, 'He is changing into the new robes. Come and wait for him.'

The three foreigners were sitting on the verandah outside a small room. Ame went immediately into it, drawing the battered door closed behind her. It slid awkwardly in the groove and creaked. Renzo knelt, his feet tucked under him. Next to him a book lay open as if someone had just set it down. Sunaomi recognised it at once as the teachings of Yoshimori. The other two men let their legs hang over the side.

Renzo greeted them and said to the foreigner Sunaomi did not know, 'This is Arai Sunaomi.'

'We met him when he was a little boy,' Don Carlo said. 'Does Lord Sunaomi remember Don João?'

'As I said before, I remember meeting two foreigners, but I can't say I recognise either of you.' Sunaomi sat next to Renzo. The other two turned round, twisting their backs so they could see him.

Kaneda remained standing in the garden, keeping watch.

'You may be surprised to see us here,' Don Carlo said. 'We were informed of the arrival of a young preacher who bears ancient teachings. We were eager to meet him and hear about them. Renzo, explain further, if you please.'

Renzo picked up the book and leafed through it, saying, 'They find it extraordinary that what they call the Word has preceded them. They are enthralled by the teachings of the so-called Hidden, for their secret god and the foreigners' Deus may be one and the same. It seems like a miracle. But Don Carlo is worried that the beliefs of the Hidden might be heresy. He hopes these teachings, written down by the Emperor Yoshimori, will shed some light on this.'

Sunaomi thought, *It was I who taught Taro to read and he has learned much from Kaneda. But he has had no special education. What can he have to share with men like these?*

But then he remembered the feverish night, the journey on the horse, and Taro like an angel. Whatever Taro was he could not be judged by the standards of the world.

The door creaked and slid open, revealing Taro in the bone white robe. He stood for the slightest moment as if allowing them to see him, then dropped to his knees beside Sunaomi and embraced him as if they were brothers.

Kaneda made a startled sound but after the first shock at such familiarity Sunaomi recalled Taro's arms holding him, keeping him from falling, not allowing him to slip away into death. He returned the embrace warmly.

'Thank you for the clothes,' Taro said, drawing back and looking Sunaomi full in the face.

'They are a gift from Hachizaemon.'

'But you brought them yourself. That means a lot to me.' Giving Sunaomi a warm, open smile, Taro held out his hand and received the book from Renzo.

'Let us continue with our reading,' he said. 'Sunaomi will be able to help us.'

'*Lord* Sunaomi,' Kaneda corrected him from the garden.

Ame said quietly, 'Here in the Temple of the Poor we are all equal. We use neither titles nor honorifics.'

Taro smiled. 'As it is written by Yoshimori, "In the eyes of the

Secret One the lowest servant is as worthy as the greatest lord.'"

Don Carlo said something and Renzo translated, 'The last shall be first and the first last.' He added, 'It is in their Holy Book.'

Don Carlo spoke again and Renzo went on. 'He is amazed. He says it is proof of the universal and everlasting truth of their Deus.'

The reading and translation continued until the midday bell sounded from the temple, startling pigeons and doves who flew up with whirring wings. Briefly the drone of cicadas ceased and then resumed with greater intensity.

'It is time for communion,' Ame said, explaining to Sunaomi and Kaneda. 'It is our shared meal. As well as feeding the hungry we reaffirm our friendship with each other and our submission to the will of the Secret One. We receive, through food and drink, its essence for it exists in all things. You will join us?'

'Gladly,' Sunaomi replied and followed her, with Taro, to the front of the main hall where men, women and children sat in a large circle on the ground. He thought the foreigners would join them, but noticed they were hastening to leave. Renzo came and spoke to him.

'They wish to apologise to you for departing. They fear the meal is contrary to the teachings of Deus, so they will not take part. But we will see you in Hofu.'

'I look forward to it,' Sunaomi replied.

Taro tied back the sleeves of the new robe, saying in a clear voice so everyone could hear, 'These fine new clothes will become dirty but that is the way of the world. Nothing is pure, nothing lasts, everything decays as our own bodies will.'

There was a murmur of agreement as he and Ame served each person with a bowl of soup and a small rice cake, saying, 'May the Secret One nourish our bodies and feed our souls as we walk the luminous way.'

Sitting among these people, sharing the simple meal, Sunaomi found he was moved despite himself. Kiyoko came to sit next to him.

'So, you will listen to the teaching now?' he said quietly.

'I am hungry,' she retorted. 'I expect many people are. They are here only for the food.'

Sunaomi looked around. Most did look undernourished, thin and pale from poverty, and several were crippled: a woman with a twisted arm, an older one-legged man, perhaps a former warrior. Some could not walk or feed themselves and were supported and helped to eat by their relatives and friends. They received the food with bowed heads, murmuring their thanks, many reaching out to touch Taro's hands or robe as he paused in front of them.

After the meal first Ame, then Taro addressed the gathering, using simple words to deliver their message.

'Follow us on the luminous way. The giving and taking of life belongs to the Secret One alone. You should therefore let all things live.

'Split a piece of wood and I am there. Lift up the stone and you will find me there.'

Watching the faces of the people around him, Sunaomi felt Kiyoko was wrong. They genuinely believed the teachings and would follow them with all their heart.

He became aware of one man who kept glancing in his direction. He was tall with a frame that was all muscle and bone, his face as lean as a skull, his eyes deep set and intense. When the gathering was over and they were about to leave, this man approached Kiyoko and greeted her, whispering something Sunaomi could not quite hear.

Kiyoko turned towards him, saying, 'This is Maru Toma, the headman of the village where we bought the meat for your dog. He was asking after it. I told him it was stolen.'

Sunaomi tried to suppress the sudden wave of grief.

'Let's sit down for a while,' he said, indicating the bench Kiyoko had used earlier. 'I would like to talk to you.'

Toma hesitated and then sat next to Sunaomi. 'It's hard to remember, this "everyone is equal" thing. I know it in my head but my heart and body believe differently. Forgive me if I am presuming too much. In the normal world I would be prostrate at your feet.' He looked down, his face darkening from some emotion. 'I'm sorry about your dog.'

Sunaomi thanked him, his curiosity awakened by the headman's words which seemed so at odds with his appearance and his outcast status.

'The boy who came with the young woman described the dog to me,' Toma said. 'It sounded like a wonderful creature.' He paused and then went on awkwardly, 'I love all animals, especially birds. I know them all by song and can call to them in their own language.'

A trilling sound came from his throat and a surprised bush warbler responded from the forest.

'We deal in death,' Toma said. 'It is our trade. We slaughter horses and oxen, skin them and tan their hides. You can probably smell death on me, not like the lord's—I mean your—sweet fragrance. I treat them gently and accompany their spirits forward, praying for an auspicious rebirth, for as we heard, they all contain within them the essence of the Secret One.'

'You sound like a good man,' Sunaomi said.

'Thank you. I try to live well. It troubles me that I must take the life of other living beings yet this is what I have been born into and I must make what I can of it.'

He fell silent. Sunaomi said, 'Was there anything else that you wanted to speak to me about? You know I was sent by the Empress and Lady Kaede, so if you have any grievances or complaints you can tell me.'

Toma's face became expressionless. 'Lord Terada protects us. In return for our leather he makes sure the Jo-An laws are observed. We have no complaints.' As he stood to leave he added quietly, 'They should not cut down so many trees. The birds, the insects, the wild animals have nowhere to go. When they take so much the whole world goes out of balance.'

‘You should not have let the outcast sit so close to you,’ Kaneda said as they rode away. Behind them came the sounds of singing. Sunaomi had been aware of the warrior's disapproval and had noticed him recoil from Maru Toma. He himself was still under the spell of the teachings and the shared worship.

‘Nor should you have allowed Taro to embrace you. Either one of them might have stabbed you.’

‘Why would they do that? Apart from the fact that Taro and I have been friends since childhood, he expressly preaches against killing.’

‘Yet the foreigners do not shrink from it from all I've heard,’ Kaneda said. ‘I don't think Taro's teaching is going to disarm them. It is a strange mixture we saw today. Ame connects these people to Terada, the foreigners are linked to Lord Mizuta, and the headman from the outcast village ... there are many undercurrents of sedition. You should report all this to Lord Miyoshi.’

‘I saw only people seeking to be treated with respect and hoping for a better life for their children,’ Sunaomi said.

‘That's a delusion,’ Kiyoko said. ‘Neither food nor respect are given out freely. They are earned or they are seized.’

His companions' cynicism and suspicions brought Sunaomi back to earth. He rode on saying nothing. He had had a glimpse of another way of being, another kingdom, and he wanted with all his heart for it to be real. Was he deluded too?

The heat was intense. The horses' coats were dark with sweat. He longed for cool water and shade.

After a while he asked Kiyoko, ‘Do you know anything about Ame?’

‘Apparently she saved Terada Fumio's life. He was trying to evade Saga's warships and sailed his own vessel into a storm. The ship was lost with all its crew. Only Terada survived. He was washed up on the shore of Himejima. Have you ever heard of it? It's an island ruled by women where it rains for eleven months in the year.'

Kaneda said, 'It used to be claimed by the Arai but it never seemed worth fighting over. Is there anything of value on it apart from rock oysters?'

'The women dive for abalone and clams. They are skilled navigators and sailors. They take their small craft as far as Nankoku. Ame took Terada to Utsu where he became an ally of Lord Mizuta and met the foreigners again. With their help he rebuilt his fleet.'

'What are they to each other?' Kaneda asked. 'Are they lovers?'

'I don't know.' Kiyoko laughed. 'Naturally rumours abound that they are. He is a man in the prime of life who likes young women very much. But I think Terada values Ame for her purity and selflessness. Her nature is the complete opposite of his. If he slept with her he would destroy the very thing he loves.'

Sunaomi was surprised by Kiyoko's sensitive perception but then she said, 'Ame has a hold over him that she intends to keep. After all, when there are no men on your homeland why not latch onto the most powerful man in Hofu. She gives him something no one else can, a sense of forgiveness.'

'Surely Terada is not a follower of the Luminous Way?' Sunaomi said.

'He comes here often and joins in the worship. If anyone is in need of forgiveness it is him. But I have no idea what is truly in his heart. They say he kills with a smile on his face and has never known regret.'

'Are there truly no men on Himejima?' Sunaomi asked.

'Their men live and work in Nankoku and visit once a year, for the three weeks in autumn when it stops raining. They hold a huge festival and then the rain starts up again and the men depart, leaving the women with their babies and cats.'

'Cats?' Sunaomi repeated.

'There are a lot of cats on Himejima,' Kiyoko said gravely.

'Where did you learn all this?'

'You can learn anything if you know the right people,' she said. 'In other words, from your Muto family who you really should call on, you know. It's rude to be in Hofu so long without getting in touch.'

'I would strongly advise against that,' Kaneda exclaimed.

However, Sunaomi considered the suggestion seriously. Maybe the Tribe had never forgotten or forgiven his defiance, maybe Kichizo and Kiyoko were simply encircling him, like wolves around a deer, nudging him towards punishment. But no one else could give him the information they did and he had no other allies.

When they returned to Daifukuji the dog, Shishi, was awake. He sat on the steps next to Hiromasa, his eyes bright, his gaze alert. Hiromasa jumped up when he saw Sunaomi.

'Shishi woke up!' he cried.

'Thank heaven,' Sunaomi said quietly.

'But the Abbot still wants us to leave. Does that mean I don't have to study writing anymore?'

His education had hardly begun and now it would be cut short. 'I don't know,' Sunaomi said. 'Maybe we can still come every day to Master Shomei.'

'Where are we going to live next?' Hiromasa demanded as they dismounted and Kaneda and Kiyoko led the horses away.

'I'm not sure yet,' Sunaomi admitted.

'But we'll all be together, Kichizo and Kiyoko too?'

'I hope so.' They began to walk together towards the guest room. Sunaomi said, 'What did you and Kichizo do today?'

'He showed me some of the things he can do,' Hiromasa said. 'It was excellent.'

'Where is he now?'

'He went after the black-skinned man.'

'Renzo?'

'Is that his name? He came to remind you of the invitation tomorrow.'

'That's strange,' Sunaomi said. 'We were with him earlier.

Why should he come again? Perhaps he forgot he mentioned it.'

'Maybe because his real purpose was to speak to the Abbot,' Hiromasa said.

'Did you hear what they said?'

'I made sure I did! They talked about you. Renzo said you had been at the temple and were on your way home. The Abbot said he had asked us to leave and he'd tried to persuade you to return to Miyako. He said ...' Hiromasa's voice tailed away.

'What?' Sunaomi prompted.

'He did not want you dead. And Renzo said nobody wanted that but ...'

Sunaomi said, 'Well, that's good to know.'

'So, you are not going to leave Hofu?'

'Certainly not! I have not finished my investigations and I'm not going to let them scare me away. Besides, I won't leave without Chin.'

Hiromasa smiled. 'People think you are not brave, but I know you are.'

Sunaomi noted this backhand compliment and hoped he would not disappoint his brother.

'Where is this place you are going tomorrow?' Hiromasa asked as they came to the edge of the verandah.

'It is our old home, the former Arai mansion. I suppose you would not remember it.' He was dreading the visit, unsure of what memories would be stirred up and wondering if anything remained of his parents' spirits. He reminded himself that it was not in the Hofu mansion that they had killed themselves on Lord Saga's orders, but in the Arai castle town of Kumamoto. When the Arai domain had been restored to him after Lord Saga's death many ceremonies had been held to placate their spirits. He believed them now to be at peace. If they lived on it was in himself and his brothers.

He lay awake that night for a long time, thinking about the past, missing Chin, and trying to plan the future. When he finally fell asleep he dreamt vividly of Utahime. He went to meet her with a feeling of joy but when he took her in his arms he saw her face had changed into Kiyoko's. He awoke troubled and bereft.

CHAPTER EIGHTEEN

Since Kichizo had visited the mansion and checked it out, Sunaomi decided to take him and to leave Hiromasa in Kiyoko's care. Kichizo would stay with the horses and naturally Kaneda would accompany Sunaomi on the actual visit inside the house.

Only rarely had they been apart in years. Kaneda was as familiar as Sunaomi's own shadow. But at the back of his mind he knew that sooner or later he was going to have to send messages to Lord Kahei and he trusted no one but Kaneda to take them. Just the idea of being without the old warrior made his heart sink. The temptation to go with him was great. But as he had said to Hiromasa, he would not leave without Chin, and he still hoped to bring Masao with him.

He dressed in the second, more resplendent set of clothes: pale blue formal trousers under a wide shouldered robe with white arrows on a plum background, tied with a sash of deep purple. Kaneda looked as he always did and carried his old-fashioned long sword. Kichizo wore the leggings and jacket of a groom, beneath which, no doubt, were various concealed weapons.

The house had had a new gate built, grand and imposing, carved with exotic creatures, dragons, tigers and a kirin. Several guards standing there greeted Sunaomi more or less respectfully and ushered the three of them inside. Kichizo led the horses away along a stone path following one of the guards.

The garden was carefully tended, with many plants and flowers Sunaomi did not recognise. Presumably Terada brought them back from his voyages. Strange birds called from a large aviary beyond the trees and he caught the flash of their bright unexpected colours, brilliant reds and greens.

Nothing was as he remembered. Terada had remade it all

and stamped it with his own flamboyant personality. Sunaomi was both relieved and sad.

Terada himself stood on the verandah and welcomed them fulsomely. They removed their sandals and maids came with bowls of water to rinse the dust from their feet. Then Terada led them around the house, pointing out various aspects of the garden, to the reception room at the rear.

Sunaomi looked for signs that the Arai had once lived here, but he saw none. All had been erased. Only the way the summer light fell on the polished boards was familiar. For a moment he thought he heard his brothers' footsteps as they chased each other around the verandah. He could not help pausing and taking a breath. Then he saw Terada's shrewd eyes on him and became determined to mask his feelings.

He made a sign to Kaneda to remain outside and stepped into the room.

In there, already seated, were the two foreigners and Renzo, with a man Sunaomi had not seen before, rather short in stature but splendidly dressed, whom he assumed was Mizuta Yasunobu, and, to his surprise, his grandmother's husband, the doctor, Ishida.

Tiger skins lay on the floor, their heads showing the eternal snarl of their huge white teeth, and the room was cluttered with curios and antiques, giving it a foreign flavour, quite unlike the austere elegance that he remembered his parents had favoured. Among the carvings and statues the human faces seemed fragile, their eyes shifty, their expressions fickle.

As Sunaomi made a deep bow to them all, he remembered Ishida was an old friend of Terada Fumio's and had accompanied him on many of his voyages. Normally Sunaomi would have been delighted to see him but the doctor's presence now increased his sense of unease.

They all observed him with varying degrees of subtlety, apparently waiting for the person of highest rank, Lord Mizuta, to speak first. He finally spoke in a deep voice like that of a much larger man. 'Welcome to Hofu. I hope you will find time to venture further south and visit us in Utsu. You could return with me in a day or two, or I will send a ship at any time.'

Sunaomi thanked him and said he would consider the offer, wondering if he should take his investigations as far as Nankoku and what his chances were of returning alive from such a journey.

'Lady Kaede, my aunt, sends her greetings,' he said. 'She takes a keen interest in the provinces, even the most distant. If I do come to your domain it will be as her envoy.'

'Naturally, that is understood,' Mizuta replied. 'You will be treated with every honour.' The lord spoke with flattering courtesy, but Sunaomi suspected he aimed to trap with honey where Terada would use a dagger.

'It is not honours I look for, but the truth,' he said, hoping he did not sound too blunt. 'I have many questions.'

'Which we will of course do our best to answer,' Terada butted in. 'But our purpose today is pleasure, not business. We must get to know each other better. Ishida has already told me so much about you. I want to discover more for myself.'

His tone had changed from their previous meeting. He seemed to be making every effort to be polite.

'I did not know Dr Ishida was in Hofu,' Sunaomi said. 'Did you come from Kumamoto?'

'No, I have not been there for some months,' Ishida said, 'but I hope to return within the week. I thought you might come with me. Your grandmother longs to see you.'

'A perfect suggestion,' Terada said. 'We expect the wind change any day now, and after that will come the typhoons of late summer. You could go to Utsu with Lord Mizuta and the same ship will take you on to Kumamoto.'

Conveniently removing me from Hofu, Sunaomi thought. He addressed Lord Mizuta. 'I was told you are building a new castle. It must be magnificent.'

'So magnificent it is not at all practical in military terms,'

Mizuta replied, narrowing his eyes. 'It is more ornamental, a folly of mine.'

'And the numbers of ships you are building, are they follies too?'

'Ah, they are so beautiful,' Mizuta said with enthusiasm. 'We've learned so much from the foreigners. It would almost be a crime not to build them. They are all at the command of Lady Kaede and the Empress, of course.'

'For what purpose?' Sunaomi said mildly. 'I was not aware that we were at war with any other realm. The problem is that ships are not built from air. I've seen the trees that have been felled for timber. It looks as though too much has been cleared. Not only does it deplete the forests, it increases the risk of landslips and flooding.'

Mizuta looked affronted as if he did not care either for the lecture or the underlying reprimand.

Terada said, 'We will discuss this another time.'

Sunaomi persisted. 'Before then I hope you will prepare a report for me. I need to know exactly how many ships are in your combined fleets, both warships and merchant vessels, and their armaments, cannons and muskets.'

'Of course, of course.' Terada's expression stiffened for a moment and then he clapped his hands. A few moments later maids appeared with flasks of wine, bowls and dishes of an iced delicacy. It had become very hot in the room, the air heavy and motionless. Sunaomi could feel the sweat pooling in his armpits. The bear carving against his chest had become so hot he feared it would burn him. Did it move a fraction or was it just sweat trickling behind it?

The welcome taste of ice transported him back into childhood. The syrup was sweet and fragrant with a flavour of citrus.

'We have an ice pit,' Terada said. 'You would know that.'

It was the first flick of humiliation but Sunaomi ignored it. He was remembering when the ice pit had been dug out following his mother's wishes. Blocks of ice were cut from frozen lakes in winter and transported, wrapped in straw mats. It always amazed him and Chikara that the ice did not melt, even in the hottest days of summer. Heavy boards covered the mouth of the pit and the boys were forbidden to play near it but they loved to watch the ice being cut and shaved for the cool treats that helped alleviate the summer heat.

The wine loosened tongues and made the foreigners less stiff and awkward. The conversation turned to various journeys they had made and to their native land, its different customs and foods.

All the men wore strings of beads and Sunaomi noticed how their fingers touched them constantly. He wondered if it was a sort of secret communication between them, allowing them to say one thing with their mouths, another with their hands. He felt he could almost read their thoughts. He saw clearly they were co-conspirators. This meeting had been designed to demonstrate their solidarity and Terada's power. He touched his own string of pearls, saw that the others noticed, and resolved not to wear them again.

From time to time the foreigners spoke in their own tongue, understood by everyone except Sunaomi. Once they all looked at him simultaneously and Terada laughed loudly while the others tried to hide smiles. Ishida's expression was one of pity.

The afternoon wore on, the wine bowls were filled and drained and filled again. Sunaomi tried to drink sparingly and Ishida, he noticed, drank only tea. Terada teased the doctor and pressed him to taste the wine but he steadily refused, turning the conversation towards his discoveries among the plants of the Southern Isles, their medicinal qualities and the gardens he had established here and in Kumamoto.

'I will show Sunaomi,' he declared, getting to his feet and beckoning to Sunaomi.

Sunaomi followed him swiftly and for a few moments they were alone and beyond earshot in the lush garden.

Ishida said quietly, 'You must leave immediately. You are not safe here.'

'What are they going to do? There is some plot, isn't there? You must tell me their plans.'

'I can't divulge their secrets. My loyalty and life are all Terada's. But I know how much you mean to your grandmother. It would break her heart to lose you. For her sake I'm warning you. You are becoming a nuisance with your questions and your prying. They will swat you out of the way like an insect. Worse, there's a serious risk that Terada will seize you to use as a hostage against Kaede and Kahei. Leave tonight, tomorrow at the latest. After that no one will be allowed to enter or depart. Don't make the trip to Utsu or you will be putting yourself in Mizuta's hands.'

'Why are you going to Kumamoto at this time?' Sunaomi asked.

'I am returning to my wife.' It was a plausible answer, yet Sunaomi felt Ishida was hiding something from him. As he had said, he was Terada's man. Was it possible he was going to the Arai domain to persuade Chikara and Shizuka to join him?

The doctor looked uncomfortable. With a visible effort he changed his voice to a lighter note and began to discuss the plants, lilies, orchids, various forms of ginger and other herbs, plucking and crushing leaves to release their fragrance.

'Terada will drink till dawn,' he said. 'I never drink alcohol now. Once I betrayed someone when I was drunk. I've never forgiven myself.'

Sunaomi wanted to question him further, but Ame appeared silently beside them. Ishida held out a leaf to her, saying, 'Smell this, it is refreshing.'

She bit and chewed it. 'It is like perilla but sharper.'

The scent hung in the air as if it could mask all trace of Ishida's warning.

'Let's take the horses for a gallop,' Sunaomi said when they left the Arai mansion. He told Kichizo to make inquiries about a new lodging place and he and Kaneda rode on side by side.

They followed the road to the east, letting the horses canter once they were clear of the town. It was late afternoon, still very hot. The horses were glad to stretch their legs after standing all day. They turned off on a track that led towards the sea and came to a deserted stretch of marsh and wetland with spongy sedge-like grass and flocks of water birds. The horses slowed to a walk at the muddy shore.

'What did you make of that?' Sunaomi asked.

'There is some conspiracy going on,' Kaneda replied briefly. 'What did the doctor say to you?'

'That I should leave at once, that I am not safe. He would not tell me anything more. Only that from tomorrow the town will be closed off.'

The wind blew from the west, the tide was ebbing away from the shore. The birds swooped around them, their cries harsh and urgent. Sunaomi looked out across the Encircled Sea and, to his right, back to Hofu.

Ships were departing from the port, their sails golden in the setting sun. Sunaomi watched them, hardly understanding what he saw.

'The fleet is sailing east,' Kaneda said.

'Towards Akashi and Miyako, before the wind changes. They will be ready and waiting for the land army. This is a real insurrection, far greater than I thought. You must go at once and inform Lord Miyoshi.'

'I cannot leave you here alone,' Kaneda protested.

'There's no time to waste. I'm not going to appear to be running away, and I can't go without Hiromasa. But you have a chance to escape now. Give me the writing tools. I'll write quickly and you must take my letter to the lord.'

They both dismounted and Kaneda produced the writing case.

'What else are you carrying?' Sunaomi asked.

'A few coins, our letters of passage.'

'Give me the one about the dog but keep the others, you may need them.'

'What about you?' Kaneda asked.

'I think they have become worthless in Hofu,' Sunaomi replied.

He wetted the stone with water from the pools on the shore and quickly wrote all he had seen in Hofu, the conspirators, the ships and weapons, the link with the Hidden which he did not fully understand, Taro, Masao. When he had finished he shook the paper to dry it and rolled it carefully. Kaneda took it, tried to speak but could not.

'I'll be all right,' Sunaomi said with assumed confidence. 'As long as you reach Lord Miyoshi.'

'I promise I will.' Kaneda leaped on to Baku's back and cantered away.

Kiki neighed and cavorted, wanting to follow. Sunaomi spoke to him to calm him, wishing he too were riding away from Hofu. He watched until horse and rider were no more than a speck in the distance.

CHAPTER NINETEEN

By the time Sunaomi came to Daifukuji it was twilight, the lingering dusk of midsummer, the moon pale above the water. The town gates had been closed behind him, and he suspected they would not open again for some time.

Kichizo met him outside the temple, raising his eyebrows when he saw Sunaomi was alone. Sunaomi shook his head slightly, indicating he did not want to speak where they might be overheard.

'No one wants to offer you lodging,' Kichizo said quietly as they walked through the cloisters to the guest room. 'They all fear offending Terada.'

'They probably don't want the trouble of dealing with a corpse or the expense of a funeral,' Sunaomi replied.

Kichizo laughed. 'I've arranged for us to go to the Muto house.'

'I suppose they are accustomed to disposing of the dead.'

'You will be safe there,' Kichizo assured him.

And then what? He was only just beginning to grasp the enormity of Terada's ambitions. If he succeeded, if Nankoku and the Three Countries became a separate realm, Sunaomi would have failed completely. He would never return to Miyako. If he were not murdered in Hofu he would have to take his own life.

Is it possible to persuade Terada to abandon this madness? he thought and the idea came to him that he should return one more time and speak with him alone. By now he had nothing to lose.

Kiyoko and Hiromasa were already eating. Kiyoko pushed a bowl towards Sunaomi, saying, 'Now you are out of favour with everyone the quality of the food has deteriorated.'

'Human nature is fickle,' he said, shaking his head. 'Even in a temple. Thankfully I am not hungry.' Anxiety and the wine he had drunk earlier had left him with a dry mouth and a headache.

'I'm so glad you are back,' Hiromasa said. 'You were away so long, I was worried.'

Sunaomi looked at his brother. His thoughts had become very dark. He imagined having to cut Hiromasa's throat before opening his own belly. The full force of his father's suicide hit him, driving the breath from his body and nauseating him. There was no future for Hiromasa as his brother. He had to return to the Tribe and remain hidden there. But the Abbot and Shomei knew who he was. Was there any chance they would keep that from Terada?

'Kichizo, take Hiromasa now to your family's house. You can slip away without being noticed. Take Hitare, I'll bring Kiku tomorrow.'

'But Chin won't know where we are if we leave here,' Hiromasa said.

'She is not coming back,' Sunaomi replied. 'You must resign yourself to never seeing her again.'

'You can't give up hope. Today Kiyoko and I searched the streets. Tomorrow we'll do the same.'

Sunaomi looked at Kiyoko questioningly.

'No one seems to know where the Sillans have gone,' she said. 'Maybe they have already set sail. Am I to go to the Muto house too?'

Sunaomi felt a rush of longing. They would be alone together. He would be held by her. Even the Abbot had assumed they were already lovers …

'Yes,' he said. 'I will spend one more night here and leave openly tomorrow. Meet me at the gate in the morning.'

'If that's really what you want,' she murmured, with a slight smile.

After they left, Sunaomi took off the formal clothes, folded them neatly and prepared his belongings for his departure. He placed Utahime's flute and the bear next to the head rest and dressed in his old travelling clothes. But when he lay down he was too hot, so he pulled the clothes off and lay naked. There was not a breath of wind. He thought of Terada's ships and hoped they were becalmed somewhere on the Encircled Sea.

Slowly the air cooled. A breeze sprang up, pleasant on his bare skin. He thought the wind had changed direction and prayed for the easterly. Finally he fell asleep.

He woke suddenly. He had been dreaming but the dream fled immediately, leaving him only with the feeling that someone else was in the room. It was still lit by moonlight, but the moon had crossed the sky and was sinking towards the west. From the temple hall came low chanting, broken by the note of a bronze bowl being struck. It was past midnight but not yet dawn.

The room smelled of jasmine. Slowly a shape began to form out of invisibility. Although he had seen it many times, the impossibility and the reality always shocked and thrilled him. Present and not present at the same time, the invisible body was a link with *that other world*.

'Don't say anything,' Kiyoko whispered. 'I want to be with you tonight.'

Her hands when she caressed him still seemed half-formed. Her touch fluttered on his skin. But when he surrendered and drew her closer her body was firm and determined. He felt a wave of regret and grief for Utahime, but Kiyoko was alive and in his arms. And she was warm, so different from the icy touch of the ghost girl.

Afterwards she said, 'I wanted that for a long time. I think you did too.'

'Maybe I did, but it didn't seem like a good idea since I am betrothed to someone else.'

'You can marry that someone else, I don't care. It would be nice if we were allowed to be married, but it's already been decided who my husband will be. That doesn't have to stop us being lovers.' She traced his face with her fingers. 'You are beautiful, Sunaomi, you must be aware of that. Right now your beauty is at its peak. I wanted to possess that.'

Her praise made him uncomfortable. 'Who is he, your future husband?'

'It is Jun.'

'Jun? You can't be serious!'

'I don't mind. I like him, he's brave and skilful.'

'But he's so old!' Sunaomi exclaimed. An alternative future had been playing out in his head, that he and Kiyoko would marry, that he would disappear into the Tribe with Hiromasa. He felt disappointed and unreasonably jealous. He thought of the empty marriage that he had agreed to with Kinu. At this moment Kiyoko's physical affection, her animal desire were far more appealing. He pulled her closer again. She responded with joyful eagerness.

She said later, 'He's not that old. He seemed so much older because we were children.'

'He was my uncle's bodyguard for years,' Sunaomi said. 'He must be thirty-five at least. Twice your age.'

'Not too old to make children.'

'Is that what you want?'

'The Tribe always want more children. That's why they took you all those years ago.'

The monks' chants became louder. The dawn bell rang out.

'I must go,' Kiyoko said, reaching out for her sash, discarded on the floor. Her fingers encountered the flute. 'What's this?' she said.

'A flute,' he replied briefly.

'I can see that. Whose is it? Do you play?'

'A little. I studied it for a time.'

She put it to her lips even as he said, 'Don't!'

She blew into it, her eyes not leaving his, but no sound came out.

'It's harder than it looks,' Sunaomi said, taking the flute from her.

'Show me,' Kiyoko demanded.

He started uncertainly for he had not dared try it since Utahime left him but as soon as he breathed into it the notes emerged true and clear almost as if it played itself.

'Beautiful,' Kiyoko said, her expression wistful. 'And what's this?' She held up the bear. 'I remember this. You used it to threaten my mother and me. Where did it come from?'

'Hisao carved it,' Sunaomi said. 'Kaneda mended it.'

Again she held his eyes as though she sought truth there. 'Is this the bear that killed the innkeeper?'

He nodded. It seemed like months ago yet it was still the same summer.

'So, you can still breathe life into objects? That isn't over?'

Before he could take it from her Kiyoko held the bear up to her own face and breathed on it.

'It's warm,' she said, 'as if it is alive. I can't waken it, though.'

'Maybe it's only the Arai who can, because the bear is the symbol of our clan.'

'What happened to the ghost girl's doll?' Kiyoko said, putting the bear down.

'It burned,' Sunaomi said after a moment's pause.

'You lost her, your ghost lover? Was the flute hers?'

Sunaomi nodded.

'So, it is enchanted,' Kiyoko said. 'Everything about you is wonderful! Am I your first human lover? I hope so.'

'I suppose you are,' he replied. He was already half in love with her.

'I imagine there would have been boys. Was Masao one?'

Her question brought up memories that were too painful: the comradeship he and Masao had shared, their mutual trust and understanding, their orphan status.

'He was, wasn't he?' Kiyoko persisted. Something in her voice alarmed him.

'It's all over. Masao has changed beyond recognition. He has come to hate me.'

'And you hate him? Then you will not mind if I kill him?'

'What?' he stared at her, barely understanding her words. Her playfulness had vanished, revealing her real character, implacable and unforgiving.

'He and his friends tried to rape me. Have you forgotten that? He is going to pay.'

'The whole purpose of my journey is to find him and give him another chance,' Sunaomi said. 'You must swear to me that you will not kill him.'

'I've already sworn to myself that I will. It is the whole purpose of *my* journey, the reason I came with you.' A flash of regret shone in her eyes. 'I suppose I will lose you now. But at least you will know that I have not lied to you. I kept that promise.'

He saw her wild eyes, her vital energy, all completely beyond his control. For a little while he had been caught up in her passion and her desire but he knew it was far from love. She would never change her mind to please him, never give up that vow to kill his friend.

◆

The following morning Sunaomi went to say goodbye to the Abbot and thank him. The priest seemed unusually uncomfortable and disturbed.

'I'm afraid you've left it too late to leave,' he said. 'I've been told the gates are closed and no one can enter or depart.'

'I have found other lodging in the city,' Sunaomi replied.

'Where?'

'It may be better that you don't know,' Sunaomi said.

'Yes, you are right. I wish I could protect you more but it's not possible. Disappear as best you can.' The priest gave him a shrewd look. 'Your man did not return last night?'

'Again, for your sake and my own, I prefer not to share anything with you.' Sunaomi patted the dog which sat beside the Abbot. 'Has Shishi recovered completely?'

'Physically, I would say so, but something has changed in his nature. He is calmer, almost meditative. I feel he understands every word spoken.'

'Not everything the Tribe does has evil effects,' Sunaomi said. 'I have one request of you, that you do not mention to anyone the young boy who was here with me, whom Shomei was kind enough to teach.'

'I will say nothing, but, you know, the two of you are so alike that others may have already drawn their own conclusions.'

Sunaomi did not reply, simply bowed deeply and gave Shishi one last pat.

Kiyoko was waiting at the temple gate. It was as if the previous night had been a dream. She gave him a half-smile but did not speak, bowed with assumed deference and took his bundle of clothes from him.

'I must get Kiku,' he said.

'Didn't Kichizo take him last night? I went to get him but he wasn't there.'

'I said I would bring him.' Sunaomi felt anxious, fearing to lose the horse.

'I'm sure he'll be hidden somewhere safe. Don't worry.'

She walked a little way ahead of him. The wind had dropped again, the sea was as flat as a silken cloth. No ships came or left. Even the seagulls were silent and still. Kiyoko led Sunaomi by a roundabout route, ducking through alleys, and even other houses, to a shop house near the port. It was pervaded by the smell of fermenting soy beans. In the front part a woman and two men were adjusting the stones on huge vats of beans. The house seemed narrow but it extended a long way back, and Sunaomi guessed it would contain concealed rooms and hidden ways in and out, in the Tribe tradition.

The woman stopped work to stare at Sunaomi. She had a terrible scar down one side of her face across an empty eye socket.

'That's Nori,' Kiyoko said. 'She looks after the shop and prepares the food.'

'How many people live here?' he asked, already made uncomfortable by the smell and the cramped feeling.

'It varies. People come and go. Muto Yoshio stays here most of the time. Kuroda Yasu is a frequent visitor. At the moment someone else is here who is eager to see you.'

'Mai, I suppose.'

'You spoiled my surprise,' Kiyoko said, with a return of her playful manner.

At the end of the house was a kitchen and a small garden in which a few herbs and vegetables grew in pots around a citrus tree, heavy with greenish yellow fruit. On one side stood a building with a dirt floor and no door. Sunaomi could see a fire smouldering in a hearth. He felt its heat on his skin.

Inside, Hiromasa was kneeling next to an older man. He was heating a piece of iron in the fire, holding it with long tongs, turning it this way and that.

'Bring it out now,' the man said. Sunaomi recognised his voice. It was Muto Yoshio, whom he had met in the Tribe village he had been taken to when he was a child.

Hiromasa laid it on the stone and Yoshio brought the hammer down on it several times, making sparks fly upwards.

Sunaomi watched them for a few moments, trying to identify the smell that hung around the back of the house, different from the soy beans. He thought it might be nitrate, or some other substance used to make gunpowder.

His brother was rapt in the work and looked completely at home. When Sunaomi turned he saw a woman bending over the plants. She straightened up. It was Mai.

'Little cousin,' she said, delighted. 'Not so little anymore!' She gave him an appraising look and then glanced at Kiyoko and shook her head, with a rueful smile.

Sunaomi could not help being pleased to see her but she also made him uneasy. He remembered how relentlessly she had pursued Hisao and in the end had poisoned him. Now Kiyoko would do the same to Masao, unless Sunaomi could prevent it.

Mai said, 'I've had news of you from time to time, mostly from your grandmother. I am on my way to Kumamoto, as soon as the wind permits.'

'Dr Ishida is also waiting for the wind,' Sunaomi said.

'Yes, we will be travelling together.'

Was she going with the same purpose, to bring the Arai into this alliance of the southwest clans? Were the Tribe already aligned with Terada? Had Sunaomi been led, eyes wide open, into a trap?

He did not say anything but gazed into the forge, watching Hiromasa. His brother had looked up at the sound of his voice and smiled at him. Now he had returned to his work. He seemed less distracted and more diligent than he ever had with Shomei.

Mai sat down on a small bench and gestured to him to sit beside her.

'I'll get us some tea,' Kiyoko said. She touched Sunaomi's arm lightly. 'Are you hungry?'

He shook his head. He felt empty but also nauseated.

'I think you must be after last night!' she said. Soon after she left the smell of grilling fish wafted through the house, making his mouth water.

'That was really not a good idea,' Mai remarked.

'What?'

'You and Kiyoko.'

Sunaomi made a movement with his head towards Hiromasa. 'Speak quietly. He will hear everything you say.'

The hammer blows masked her whisper. 'You know she is to be married to Jun?'

'Kiyoko does what she wants,' Sunaomi replied. 'He must know that already.'

'Jun is pragmatic by nature. It is not him you have to worry about. It is Kichizo. He is jealous and possessive of his sister, and has always idolised Jun. You don't want to antagonise him. Stay away from Kiyoko while you are in this house.'

'Tell her that,' Sunaomi whispered as Kiyoko came through

the garden.

'Food is prepared,' she said. 'Come inside.'

Sunaomi and Mai followed her to a room in the middle of the house. It looked like the typical living space of a merchant family, with a stack of account books in one corner and a few pieces of furniture, a low desk, a mirror of foreign design, and some head rests in another. Doors on both sides were open onto narrow alleys with stands of bamboo and water-filled channels. The trickle of water and the slight rustle of the leaves, as well as being away from the forge, made the room seem a little cooler but after a few moments Sunaomi became aware of the stifling heat. The old house had retained years of the smell of fermentation and cooking, seeping into the wooden walls and the straw matting. His head was aching.

Nori came in carrying trays of food which she placed on the floor with a few murmured words, inviting them to eat. Kiyoko brought the rest of the trays and sat down with them.

'She is always so sad,' she complained, taking a large piece of fish and eating it in one bite. 'What happened to her?'

'Nori?' Mai whispered. 'She fancied she loved Hisao, and she let someone escape. She was punished cruelly by Akio.' She turned to Sunaomi. 'It was Maya, your cousin—they are all dead now, so it does no harm to tell you.'

'Maya was imprisoned here?' he said, astonished. Sudden memories came back to him; she had teased him unkindly, she had resented him and he had never understood why. And a memory returned to him in a flash, something he had not thought about for years, of the night he had gone to a deserted house by the shore in Hagi, and had seen the ghost of Akane. They had told him he had mistaken a statue, but he had been convinced he had actually seen her spirit, and now he had spent so much time in *that other world* he realised he probably had.

'Maya was captured when the Tribe—Akio and Hisao— killed Taku and Sada. Kiyoko's father, and my sister,' Mai said.

'Why were they together?' Kiyoko said, her eyes wide. 'Oh, of course! They must have been lovers. I never knew that. No wonder my mother was so angry and wounded. That explains a lot.' She stared at Sunaomi. 'I thought it was just that she hated you.'

'It was as if she wanted to punish everyone who had any connection with her pain,' Sunaomi said.

'Taku loved Sada in a way he had never loved her,' Mai added.

'How do you know so much about it all?' asked Kiyoko.

'I wanted to find out as much as I could before I carried out my revenge.'

Kiyoko was looking at her with admiration. 'How did you do it?'

Mai tapped her bowl of tea with her eating sticks. 'Poison.'

'Hmm.' Kiyoko frowned. 'I don't like poison. I'd rather use a knife.'

'It depends who you want to kill.' Mai glanced at Sunaomi. 'He has gone pale. He does not like to remember it.'

'Sunaomi was there?'

'I was a child,' he said shortly. *There was nothing I could do.* Yet he would always feel guilty, would always grieve for Hisao.

He heard the splash of water outside. Hiromasa and Yoshio were washing and a moment later they came in. Yoshio was middle aged with a domed, balding head and an unremarkable face. Sunaomi wondered if he would have known him if he had seen him anywhere else.

As they both sat down Hiromasa said, 'I'm glad you're here.'

Yoshio gave Sunaomi a nod. 'It's good to have two of Zenko's sons back in the Tribe.'

'I'm grateful to you for having us here,' Sunaomi said. 'But it doesn't mean we are back in the Tribe.'

'You don't have anywhere else to go, though, do you?' Yoshio gave a short laugh and devoted his attention to his food.

When he had finished he said, 'I'll talk with Arai Sunaomi. Mai can stay. Hiromasa, clean up in the forge. Kiyoko, help Nori.'

Even Kiyoko obeyed without question. Mai filled the tea bowls and Yoshio said to Sunaomi, 'I don't know that you would be much use to us within the Tribe. You had few skills as far as I remember.' He spoke in a matter of fact way, like a merchant assessing the quality of the soy bean harvest. 'Your brother is different. We'd certainly like to keep him.'

'Sunaomi may be more skilled than you think,' Mai said. 'Like Hisao he has a talent for carving; he brings dolls and toys to life. And, like Hisao, he can summon and control ghosts.'

'Not anymore,' Sunaomi said. 'That part of my life is over.'

Mai reached forward, touched the cord around his neck. 'Yet you still carry the bear.'

Yoshio held out his hand. 'Show me.'

Sunaomi lifted the cord over his head and drew the bear from inside his robe. He was aware of its warmth as he placed it in Yoshio's palm and the other man exclaimed as he felt it too.

'Is it alive?'

'It sleeps as if in hibernation.'

'And you bring it to life when you need it?'

Sunaomi nodded. 'Twice it has come alive. But every time it is more destructive and harder to control.'

Yoshio said, 'I remember you had another carving, a black fox. I thought it had some power but we never looked at it further. What happened to it?'

'I burned it.' Sunaomi did not want to think about the terror of the black fox. It was one thing he should never have breathed life into.

'I remember Tomiko coming back with Jun saying we could not touch you, but she did not explain why.' Yoshio looked questioningly at Sunaomi.

'I threatened her with the bear,' he said, and because it seemed important to be truthful, 'I would not have known how to do that without the time I spent in the Tribe.'

'She said you needed more hardness and then you used it against her.' Yoshio laughed again, seemingly without resentment. 'So often the way, isn't it? How old are you now? Sixteen or seventeen, if I remember?'

'I am seventeen,' Sunaomi replied, not trusting the other man's affability.

'But you have not yet made your coming-of-age?'

'I am to do it when I return to Miyako if Lord Miyoshi is there.' *And Kinu and I will be married.* He did not really believe either event would ever happen.

Yoshio sat in silence, deep in thought. Finally he said as if thinking out loud, 'We have never had anyone so close to the government and the court as you would be. Even your father's influence did not stretch that far.'

'In what sense would you have me?' Sunaomi asked cautiously.

'Nothing anyone else would need know about. You would give us information and in return we would protect you from your enemies.'

Mai said, 'I don't mean to offend you but because of the way you look and act no one will ever suspect you are anything more than a frivolous young nobleman who enjoys the favour of his aunt.'

'Hiromasa we will have in another sense,' Yoshio said, with a bland smile. 'His skills are too great to forgo.'

He will be a hostage for my compliance, Sunaomi thought.

'It's best if we get you out of Hofu and back to Miyako,' Yoshio said. 'Kichizo will go with you and be your bodyguard.'

'You are fortunate,' Mai said, with a smile.

Sunaomi was not so sure. Kichizo was skilful and fearless but their childhood mutual dislike still lingered. And now Kiyoko had come between them.

'Remember what I said to you earlier.' Mai gave him a warning look.

'Don't I have any choice in the matter? I still have things to accomplish here,' Sunaomi said. 'I must speak with Saga Masao once more, and I would like to find my dog.'

They both smiled as if his foolishness amused them.

'We'll take care of Masao, and find the dog if it's possible,'

Yoshio said. 'But you must leave.'

'I also wanted to visit Terada, and plead with him to see reason.'

'You may have to see him to be allowed to depart,' Yoshio said. 'And to get from him papers of passage. It's most important that you achieve that. Don't expect him to change his plans or ambitions because of anything you say.'

Sunaomi remained silent, trying to come to a decision. Someone called out from the front of the shop.

'I must go,' Mai said. 'My ship is ready to leave with the easterly and the ebbing tide.'

'I wish I had time to write to my grandmother,' Sunaomi said.

'I will tell her everything she needs to know,' Mai replied and left swiftly without saying anything more.

'My first loyalty must always be to the Empress and Lady Kaede,' Sunaomi said to Yoshio. 'I hope you understand that.'

'It's been an aberration,' the other man replied. 'Women are not designed to rule over men. When Otori Takeo made Shizuka head of the Tribe we were torn apart. We are only now recovering.'

'Yet the country is at peace, people are content. They are not starving, terrified, persecuted.'

Yoshio laughed. 'You can see for yourself how that lack of fear, that contentment, makes people eager for something else. They are bored. They want drama and spectacle, things that thrill them and make them feel alive. Of course, from our point of view unrest and sedition are good for trade. In a time of peace no one needs an assassin or a spy. But Terada Fumio starts an insurrection and suddenly many new opportunities arise.'

'I am one, I can see that. But you have to agree you will not support anyone else.'

'We work for whoever pays us the most,' Yoshio replied, no longer laughing.

'I suppose my aunt will pay highly for my safe return,' Sunaomi said.

'Kichizo will collect the money in Miyako.'

'You are vouching for this agreement, but who is the real ruler of the Tribe?'

Yoshio said nothing, just bowed his head.

'It is you?' Sunaomi found it hard to believe that this unassuming, ordinary-looking man should have so much power.

'Kichizo may take over when he is older, but for the time being, yes, it is I.'

'Must I seek permission from you for everything I do?' Sunaomi asked, half-sarcastically.

Yoshio shrugged. 'It would probably be a good idea. Once you are on the road Kichizo will prevent you doing anything misguided.'

Sunaomi felt he had come to a dead end. He could see no way out other than accepting Yoshio's offer, leaving Hiromasa in the safety of the Tribe, and returning with Kichizo to Miyako. Chin ... well, she was being well looked after. She would forget him in time. And Masao? That was his greatest failure. For he was abandoning Masao to Kiyoko's justice which he had no power to impede, just as he had not been able to prevent Mai's execution of Hisao.

'I will prepare to leave,' he told Yoshio. 'I will call on Terada on the way. Will Kichizo come with me?'

'Of course,' Yoshio said.

CHAPTER TWENTY

Sunaomi went into the adjoining room where Kiyoko had left his bundle of clothes. He unwrapped the formal garments, smoothing out the wrinkles with his hands. Maybe Masao had left Hofu already, had set sail for the Southern Isles where he would start a new life. He did not think he would ever see him again or know what had happened to him.

He took the flute from his sash and placed it on the floor, along with his sword, then unlooped the cord from his neck and put the bear next to them.

Hiromasa came quietly into the room.

'I am leaving to return to the capital,' Sunaomi said. 'I would like to take you with me, but you will be safer here.'

'I'll miss you,' Hiromasa said. 'But I like being here. I'd rather learn how to make weapons than study letters.'

'Maybe you can do both,' Sunaomi said, forcing a smile.

'I'm glad we are brothers but we did not grow up together and I'm not used to it. Here I can be myself. Do you understand that?'

Sunaomi nodded, his heart too full to speak.

'Can I have this?' Hiromasa held up the bear. 'I like it, it feels so warm.'

'Yes, take it. It will remind you that you were born Arai. It will protect you. But don't awaken it, it is very powerful.'

'How do I do that?'

'When we next meet I'll tell you.' He embraced his brother wondering how long that would be.

He put the flute and his sword in his sash. As he passed the kitchen Kiyoko, who had been washing dishes with Nori, called out to him.

'Where are you going?'

'First to Terada, then on to Miyako.'

'You won't be back tonight?' she questioned, coming close to him.

'No, I am leaving Hofu.'

She reached up and touched the side of his face. 'I wanted us to be together again.'

He moved away from her, aware of Nori stolidly staring into space, and of Kichizo, standing at the entrance.

Hitare waited patiently in the street but there was no sign of Kiki.

'Didn't you take Kiki last night?' Sunaomi asked Kichizo.

'No, you said you would bring him.'

'So, where is he?' Sunaomi said. The horse's absence made him very uneasy. 'I cannot ride to Miyako without him.'

'It's all right,' Kichizo said. 'You can ride Hitare, and I'll run.'

'Did someone steal him?'

'Possibly. He's a valuable horse,' Kichizo sounded dismissive, adding, 'We can't delay now.'

As Sunaomi prepared to mount Hitare, Kichizo said, 'I can smell her on you. You should not have done that.'

'Your sister makes her own choices,' Sunaomi replied.

'It will never happen again,' Kichizo said quietly.

'That sounds like a threat. Your orders were to protect me,' Sunaomi returned.

'Maybe I also make my own choices.'

Taking Hitare's bridle, Kichizo began to lead him through the streets. They made the rest of the short journey without speaking.

The wind blew briskly from the east. The port was full of ships jostling each other to catch the tide. The streets were crowded. Sunaomi's mind felt similarly jumbled and teeming. How would he be received by Terada and what was he going to say to him? He disliked the feeling that he was going to beg a favour but Terada had wanted him to leave. Sunaomi did not expect him to stand in his way now. He wondered where

Kaneda was, if he had got away unhindered, how far Terada's power and influence stretched.

At the gate one of the guards took Hitare's reins and another told Sunaomi to wait while he informed Lord Terada of his presence. As the man walked away, Hitare gave a loud neigh, which was echoed by another horse from inside the walls.

'That is Kiki!' Sunaomi exclaimed.

'Maybe,' Kichizo said with his habitual lack of expression.

'Why is my horse here? Did Terada have him stolen?'

'You'll be able to ask him yourself,' Kichizo replied.

The guard returned saying, 'Arai Sunaomi is to enter alone.'

'I'll be around,' Kichizo said.

Sunaomi gave him a brief look, hoping for some indication of his intentions. If Kichizo wanted he could follow him in, using invisibility or the second self. Sunaomi had seen him do this often enough when they were children. But Kichizo was unreadable.

Sunaomi walked into the garden of his family's former residence as if walking into the cave of a tiger.

Terada Fumio sat in the main room, two of his men on either side. Though Sunaomi did not at first see her in the dim light, Ame knelt to one side, her head lowered.

He knelt and bowed, careful not to appear too submissive, aware that he, the eldest son of the Arai, far outranked the former fisherman turned pirate, and spoke at once. 'I intend to return to Miyako today. I would be grateful if you will issue permission to leave Hofu, and I will take my horse, which for some reason is in your stables. Before I go, however, I want to make one last appeal to you.'

Before he could continue Terada interrupted, saying in a furious voice, 'You are very bold to make such demands in your position. The time for negotiating is long past and so is the time for departure. You should have left when you were first warned. It is too late now.'

'I must urge you to confirm your loyalty to the Empress,'

Sunaomi persisted. 'Only you can put an end to a pointless rebellion in which hundreds will lose their lives. Let me take a message of reconciliation back to Miyako. If you have genuine grievances they will be addressed.'

Terada did not respond to this but studied Sunaomi's face. 'You are all Shirakawa,' he said finally. 'Devious and cowardly like the Shirakawa women. I would not trust you for a moment.'

Sunaomi thought, *I have walked in worlds this man cannot imagine. I have listened to the dead.* He touched the flute in his sash and felt the departed all around him.

Terada mistook the gesture. 'Are you reaching for your sword?' He addressed the guards, 'Take it off him.'

Sunaomi drew the sword out himself and laid it on the floor. 'I intend you no harm,' he said calmly. 'I have merely come to plead with you. We can work together. Treaties can be made with the foreigners and the Sillans. We will recommence the Red Seal ships. The foreigners and the Nankoku lords will be invited to Miyako.'

Terada replied, 'You know I have firearms from the foreigners which will destroy Kahei's army. My ships are already nearing Akashi. You would do better to join me. Dr Ishida is already on his way to Kumamoto to persuade your brother and grandmother to become my allies.'

'I hope you are not trying to insult me,' Sunaomi said. 'I believe I have made it clear where my loyalties lie.'

Terada again fell into silence, biting his lip.

'If you will provide me with letters of passage and my horse, I will take my leave,' Sunaomi said.

Ame spoke quietly to Terada and the former pirate nodded, making Sunaomi think he was about to acquiesce but at that moment a man came running in, dropped to his knees and said, 'May I approach you, lord?'

Terada made a beckoning motion with his fingers and listened with growing anger to the man's hurried whisper.

Pushing him aside he stood and came close to Sunaomi. He

bent down and stared him directly in the face.

'Your man rode away last night?'

Kaneda is captured. Sunaomi felt despair descend around him but Terada went on.

'He will not get far. My men are pursuing him. What did you think, that you would bring Miyoshi Kahei down on me?'

He began to pace up and down the room. 'But now I have to keep you here. Your aunt is devoted to you, I am told. You are like a son to her. And Kahei hopes to marry you to his daughter—I've heard the rumours of a betrothal. You will be my hostage to their surrender. But don't expect to live in luxury. Zenko's son in his former home is too much of a provocation. You have seriously offended me now.' He turned to the guards. 'Put him in the ice pit.'

Ame made a slight movement. Sunaomi caught a glimpse of her expression and thought he saw pity in it. She seemed about to speak but then the guards' hands were on him. Their grasp outraged him but there was no point in struggling. They were much taller and stronger, and he was unarmed. He wondered if he should call out to Kichizo. Surely his cousin had heard everything. But there was no sign of him.

They walked him through the garden, past the aviaries and the fish ponds, through a small grove of fruit trees where he and Chikara used to play. The peaches and loquats were over but the summer oranges were ripening among the dark glossy leaves.

He could smell horses and again heard Kiki's neigh. He was so close to him yet might as well have been a hundred miles away. Now he was being guided to the back of the garden, where there were sheds for gardening tools. One of these was an open structure erected above the ice pit. Axes, hooks and knives to handle and cut the ice were arranged neatly on benches around three sides. The pit itself was covered by wooden planks, weighed down by heavy stones. Two of the guards held Sunaomi by the wrists while the other two removed the stones and the boards. A rough ladder leant against the inside wall. One guard pulled it up while the others pushed Sunaomi to the edge and lowered him down by the arms.

When they let go he dropped onto the straw mats that wrapped the ice. He heard the thud as the boards were replaced and the guards' footsteps as they walked away.

At first he thought the darkness was complete but chinks between the boards let in a little light. After weeks of heat the coolness was almost a relief at first but it was not long before he was shivering. He felt his way around the walls; the earth was crumbling and he feared if he tried to climb out they would collapse on him. The ground was muddy. Everything dripped moisture and was cold. The blocks of ice were kept frozen by their size and the depth of the pit.

'Kichizo!' he called without much hope. 'Kichizo!'

What would his cousin do? Would he return to the Muto house and report what had happened or would he disappear, pretending he was riding towards the capital with Sunaomi?

No one will ever know where I am.

There was a movement above and his heart leapt but the voice that spoke was a woman's.

'I've brought you some food,' Ame said.

She shifted one of the boards and let down a bucket on a rope.

He untied the knot and found inside a small flask of luke-warm tea and some rice cakes wrapped in leaves.

'Use the bucket if you need to relieve yourself,' she called down. 'I'll come back to empty it before dark. But I am not allowed to bring more food, so make it last till tomorrow.'

Sunaomi lost count of the days. Ame's visits merged into each other. Sometimes he heard her praying above him before she removed the plank and recognised words from The Hidden Wisdom of Yoshimori, Taro's book. How strange and distant was that day when Taro had requested the book and Sunaomi had given it to him, and with it the scribe's house. As his flesh dissolved and his body wasted away he mourned the person he had been then, in possession of so much, able to be so generous.

Every time Ame lifted the plank he felt the wave of hot air from outside. Once men came to lift out one of the blocks. They did not speak to him but one held him out of the way while the other fastened cords around the ice to lift it. He heard their conversation as they walked away and knew they despised him. The man's hands had felt as hot as coals.

He dreamed of the heat of the bear, and of Utahime and Kiyoko. Their faces blurred into one. He dreamed he heard music and woke holding Utahime's flute in his hand but he did not have the strength to play it.

In his delirium he imagined he was in hell, condemned to this punishment for falling in love with a ghost. Creeping things infested his limbs and his bones were gnawed by worms. He stood before the lord of Hell, and was shown his father's sins in a misty mirror. Tears flowed for his parents and himself, caught in the web of earthly passions.

The heat must have been increasing, for the ice was melting, making the ground muddier. He was never dry. There came a day when Ame called out and he could not stand nor tie on the bucket. A draught of hot air swirled in like the wind that preceded typhoons. Ame called again but he did not answer.

He heard the ladder drop. She must have climbed down, for a few moments later she was shaking him.

'Wake up. Wake up,' she murmured. 'You must eat and drink.' She held the flask to his lips and he drank without thought. He could not stop shivering. His throat and chest burned.

'I am dying,' he said. 'Is that what he wants? What use is my corpse to him?'

'He does not want you dead,' she replied. 'Only to remain hidden. I will bring you something to keep you warm.'

He had a short vivid dream that Chin was licking his hands and then Ame was back with a fur in her arms. His fingers sank into it as she wrapped it around him and he knew it was a bearskin.

She gave him some rice cakes and he ate them, tasting the morsels of fish inside them. Slowly his body regained a little warmth.

'How long have I been here?' he asked. 'What is happening outside?'

Ame did not answer directly but said, 'Through your suffering will come great good. Join us, become one of us. We will spread the knowledge of the Luminous Way throughout the realm and bring Heaven's kingdom into being.'

'How will you do that without fighting?' Sunaomi asked.

'For hundreds of years we have followed the teaching that we should not kill. Now we believe that era is over. A new age is beginning. The foreigners brought other teachings, apt for this new sacred time. We are not to bring peace, but the sword. There is a time for peace and a time for war. Even Maru Toma is taking up arms alongside us. He and his people are tired of being passive and despised. It is warfare that brings respect and honour in this land of ours.'

'And Taro will fight?'

'He will lead us, riding your former horse.'

'Did you steal Kiki for that purpose?'

'I was led to by the spirit,' she replied. 'The same that spoke to me about Taro coming.'

Sunaomi was silent.

'Taro does not need to be armed,' Ame went on. 'For the power of Deus protects him against bullets or arrows. And Saga Masao will be at his side. The north-eastern domains will join us when they learn Lord Saga's grandson is with us.'

'Masao?' Sunaomi said, confused.

'He has been many times to see Taro. They pray together. Masao is healed from his madness, just as you were healed. Think about what the purpose of that healing was. Surely your fate is tied closely to Taro and to Masao. You should be with them.'

Her words had the deranged logic of a dream. To be again with his friends from childhood, to put an end to his suffering: he only had to submit to the divine will. He also wanted to see the kingdom of heaven on earth. She was right; he was being called to this.

Above their heads the shed shook in the wind. Something blew loose and fell down on the ice blocks. The sound brought him back to reality. It was not Deus or the Secret One who had him thrown into the ice pit. It was Terada Fumio, and Sunaomi would never bring himself to submit to him.

'A typhoon is coming,' Ame said. 'I must go. The Sillan envoys have returned and are visiting. Fumio needs me to confirm what they say among themselves. And now they may have to stay the night. I must make arrangements. Pray about what I said.'

'Surely they are not going to join you as well?' Sunaomi said.

'If it is the will of Deus.'

She tied the bucket to the cord and began to climb the ladder. He thought, *I could overpower her, climb out ...* he remembered the iron hooks and knives in the shed above. But he knew he was deluding himself; he did not even have the strength to stand. As Ame pulled up the ladder and replaced the plank, he wrapped the bearskin more closely round him.

It became suddenly as dark as night. The wind rose to a howl and drumming, driving rain began to fall. Sunaomi drifted into sleep, waking to the unearthly lightning and the crash of thunder. When a little light returned, the rain still fell in torrents. Water was rising from the floor of the pit. First there was an inch of water lapping around him, then two, then six. He climbed on top of the ice blocks, clinging to the straw with frozen fingers. He felt the blocks shift and sway as they began to float.

Something drifted against him and he grabbed at it. It was a broom that must have been blown down before. The bearskin had become waterlogged and fatally heavy. He pulled it off with the other hand. It floated in the water like a dead animal.

The ice block tipped and he half-slipped half-fell into the water. It was waist deep and rising. The bearskin swirled around his legs, entangling him. He saw he was going to drown. No one was coming to rescue him. The pit would fill, the sides would crumble and collapse, the heavy planks and stones would crash down and trap him under water.

He thought stupidly, *I don't want to die scrabbling for my life in mud and dirt.*

The broom floated upwards taking him with it. He could no longer stand but the planks above were still beyond his reach. As his fingers grazed them he called out, desperately, not expecting anyone to hear him.

He heard a dog yelp, a bark he would have recognised anywhere. Chin.

I am dead and she is waiting for me on the banks of the three-strand river.

'Chin,' he said. 'I am here. Let's cross together.'

The yelping became louder and more excited. The rising water pushed him up against the planks. He felt one of them give way and his head was out in the open air. He looked into the astonished eyes of the Sillan groom.

'Is that you, Arai Sunaomi, the dog's master?' the man said.

'Yes, get me out of here!'

Gusts of wind blew the rain sideways. The planks and the

edge of the pit had become as slippery as ice. The Sillan took one of the hooks from the bench and caught Sunaomi by the back of his robe, raising him like a fish. For a moment he lay gasping for breath on the planks, then the man pulled him away from the pit into the garden. A torrent of water came rushing down the hillside. The side of the pit gave way and the remaining planks and stones crashed in.

Chin jumped around him, crying out like a human baby, dancing on her back legs, her ears flat against her head, her tail wagging, her whole body wriggling in joy.

He sat up and let her jump on him and lick his face.

'She's very thin,' he said accusingly, and then, 'I'm sorry, I should thank you.'

'She hasn't been eating,' the man said. 'She pined for you. This morning she was whining and restless. I brought her out, despite the rain. She came straight here.' He was shaking his head in admiration at the dog's intelligence and loyalty.

'Just in time,' Sunaomi said. The rain poured over him but he felt nothing, just the shock of relief.

'You are rather thin yourself,' the Sillan said. 'You look like a living corpse. How long were you in there?'

'I don't know. What day is it?'

'It is the beginning of the seventh month.'

Nearly three weeks had passed. 'You are not going to hand me over to Terada?'

'I don't think so. That would make the dog sad again.' The man was silent for a moment, then said, 'I will take you to the ambassador. She will help you, I think.'

'How will you get me there?'

'Terada has gone to the port to inspect the damage to the ships. There are many people entering and leaving. The house is also badly damaged. No one will notice you.' He gestured to a pile of mats in the corner of the shed. 'I will wrap you up in those and carry you like a package.'

He spread out one mat and Sunaomi crawled onto it. The

Sillan placed another on top of him and tied them with cords.

'If anyone asks, I will say you are a corpse,' he said. 'You don't mind?'

'It's not the first time,' Sunaomi said, but his voice was muffled by the straw and the Sillan could not hear him. The man picked up the bundle as if it were no more than mats and slung it over his shoulder.

Chin whined anxiously as she followed them through the garden. The gates were open. Sunaomi caught glimpses of servants carrying large red umbrellas and two palanquins. His rescuer greeted someone in Sillan but did not pause. Instead he quickened his pace and they were outside in the street.

Sunaomi heard a shout. 'You, stop! What have you got there?'

He could not see enough to know what happened next. He felt the flow of energy race through the Sillan's muscles and a jolt like a lightning strike as the man kicked out. He heard the crack of bone on bone, a cry of pain and shock. Then he was spun round like a top as the Sillan turned a delivered another blow. There came a gasp, a shriek of agony.

Still holding Sunaomi firmly over his left shoulder the Sillan walked swiftly again, Chin barking excitedly, the rain splashing around them.

◆

Afterwards he remembered only a few vivid details: the rain pouring from the eaves; a woman in a curious long-skirted dress; the warmth of water as he was bathed and made clean; his own tears; a hot drink which made him nauseous; dreams of drowning. Then, not that night but sometime later, hours of dreamless sleep.

When he woke, it was day. The rain had stopped, birds were singing, sunlight fell on the wooden boards of the floor. The air was fresh and clear.

Chin lay deeply asleep against his side, her small body rising and falling with her steady breathing.

He heard footsteps and a woman came to his side and knelt beside him, placing a tray with two bowls on the floor. Her cheeks were red, her hair in braids.

Sunaomi sat up. He was clad in a loose white garment, woven from hemp or possibly cotton, tied with a sash dyed red as if with safflower.

'Eat this,' she said. 'The dog and you can eat the same thing. You've both been starving.'

It was a broth of some kind with egg stirred through it. The smell made him immediately hungry.

'Not too fast,' she said. Her manner was stern but beneath it lay laughter, as if everything amused her.

Chin opened her eyes and stretched. Her tail moved and she licked her lips. The woman set the second bowl on the floor by the door and clicked her tongue to call the dog over.

Chin would not move from Sunaomi's side. The woman laughed. 'All right. I will bring it to you.'

They both drank together.

'Now,' the woman said. 'Can you walk?'

She helped him up and walked with him round the narrow verandah and through the garden to the privy.

Chin ran after them. When the dog squatted to urinate on the gravel path the woman brought a bowl of water to rinse it away. She returned with another one for Sunaomi to wash his hands and face.

His hair was loose around his shoulders and still damp. His face and brow felt stubbly. He had not shaved or plucked his beard for ... he had no idea how long. Everything seemed to be moving slowly as if in a fog. His mind shied away from remembering what had happened.

From inside the house he heard voices. He wondered why he could not understand them, then realised that they were speaking in Sillan. The man who had rescued him appeared on the verandah. Chin ran to him but when he bent to pet her she dashed back to Sunaomi.

The Sillan shook his head ruefully. 'She is happy now. That's all that matters.' He looked at Sunaomi carefully. 'You are recovered?'

'I think so,' he replied.

'You know, we were preparing to set sail, but the threat of the typhoon kept us in Hofu. Then we were summoned by Terada Fumio. But I wished I had not taken the dog, for she would not eat, and cried for you. I wanted you to know that.'

'She found me in the end. You and she saved my life. I'm very grateful.'

'I was just doing my job,' the man replied, 'looking after the noble dog and following her instincts. But you must tell the ambassadors how grateful you are and what your aunt will do in return. They want to see you now.'

'I should get dressed,' Sunaomi said, wondering what had happened to the beautiful robes and feeling a moment of regret for them.

The woman said, 'We washed your clothes but they are not dry yet.'

There had been something else, something important. What was it? It came back to him. 'Did you find a flute?' he asked her.

'It's in the room,' she said. 'It has also been washed. It was clogged with mud.'

Sunaomi stepped into the room and saw it lying on a low table. He picked it up thinking what a miracle it was that it had not been lost. It looked and felt different. Its colour was lighter as if the wood had been bleached. He put it to his lips and played a few notes. Its tone was purer than ever. Under his fingers he could feel tiny swellings like buds that had not been there before.

'Is it enchanted?' the woman said behind him, as if it were natural that it should be. 'I've heard of flutes like that. They burst into leaf or play themselves.'

Sunaomi tucked it into his sash without replying, for he did not think he had the words to explain the enchantment of both the flute and himself.

'I will tie back your hair,' she said, again with barely suppressed laughter. She ran her fingers over his face and chin. 'What a boy you still are. You have barely any beard yet.'

Sunaomi felt embarrassed at appearing before the Sillan envoys in what seemed to be a nightrobe, but when he entered the main room he saw the others gathered there, two men and a woman, were also dressed informally, in loose garments of coloured gauze, pale reds and blues.

He knelt and bowed to them, then sat up with Chin at his side.

The woman welcomed him, saying, 'We are happy to see our dog thief recovered. Forgive us for taking her back. Of course we had no idea who you were.'

'I must thank you for saving my life and sheltering me,' Sunaomi said.

'How fortunate that we were able to be of service to you,' she said. 'We hope it will be a mutual benefit.'

He sensed she was both shrewd and well informed. She was middle aged but her face was unlined and her hair deep black.

'I speak for my colleagues and will translate for them. You may call me Lady Nin.'

'I am Arai Sunaomi. I am sorry for the confusion over the dog. Lady Kaede deeply appreciated your gift. The dog became attached to me so I was entrusted with her.'

She shook her head, smiling a little. 'Once these dogs have given their heart and their loyalty it is for life.' She was gazing into his face. 'I am going to ask you to make a decision. I hope you are well enough.'

He was not sure he was, but he bowed to her again and waited to hear her offer.

'We are returning to Silla today,' she said, 'while the east wind holds. War is about to break out in your country and we do not want to be caught up in it. Terada has made approaches to us to join him, with the lure of future trade treaties, but before he became a great admiral his acts of piracy along our coast caused immeasurable suffering and loss. We cannot forgive him for that and will never become his allies.'

'So, he has not yet set out from Hofu?' Sunaomi asked.

'He has been waiting for Lord Mizuta's forces to arrive from Nankoku. The winds delayed him, and then the typhoon. His own fleet had to put in for shelter on the way to Akashi. But he will take advantage of the fine weather now. We hope Lady Kaede, your aunt, and the Empress will prevail and we are prepared to help you escape. Terada was going to use you as a hostage to buy time for himself but because he prefers confrontation to negotiation he did not care if he killed you. We can take you to Maruyama, if you decide to come with us. But we must leave immediately.'

Sunaomi did not reply for a moment. His attention had all been on the east, on Miyoshi Kahei and his aunt's government in Miyako. He had hardly thought of Maruyama, of Hiroshi and Shigeko. He did not want to go so far away. It would take him weeks to get back and meet up with Kahei, which he felt, with a strong urgency, he had to do before Terada launched his attack.

One of the men spoke quickly.

Lady Nin said, 'We must leave. Please make up your mind. I don't see that you have any choice. You are not strong enough to survive in the city alone. Wherever you seek to hide, you will be discovered and handed over to Terada.'

She's right. I have no choice, Sunaomi thought. *The Tribe betrayed me before. I can trust no one here.*

'Thank you,' he said. 'I will come with you.'

Even as he spoke a sense of shame and failure shot through him.

'I will give you some of my clothes,' she said. 'You must dress as a woman and travel as one of my companions. We have no time to talk now but once on board and safely underway we will discuss what arrangements can be made with your aunt and her government.'

Sunaomi was taken by the servant to the room where he had slept and hastily dressed in a long-skirted dress like the one she wore. She braided his hair like a girl's and swiftly shaved his chin. He walked alongside her to the gate, matching his step to hers. Here two palanquins waited. Lady Nin rode in one, Sunaomi and Chin in the other. The other Sillans, the groom among them, walked in front and behind.

Throughout the city were signs of the damage done by the typhoon, and the streets swarmed with people hurrying to repair houses and shops. The air was fresh and clear, the sun sparkled on the water and the wind blew steadily from the east. The tide was full, just about to turn.

They climbed into small skiffs and were sculled out to the ship. It was built in the Sillan style, part trader, part warship. Its red and white flags fluttered in the wind, as it swayed and rocked like a living beast eager to depart.

Ropes were lowered. Sunaomi did not think he had the strength to climb, but the groom appeared at his side, took Chin from him, and half-lifted half-pushed him up. He felt the sailors stare at him in his women's clothes.

Once on deck he looked back at the hills behind the city. Where the forests had been cleared were ugly gashes left by the flooding rains and the landslips that had followed.

'Keep your head covered,' Lady Nin said, 'and sit with me out of sight.'

'Will we be pursued?'

'Don't worry. Terada has many other concerns today, and, though he thinks he's the only man who's ever handled a ship, our sailors are no less skilful. And our ships are faster.'

The water was muddy and full of debris: planks of wood, logs and branches, old straw mats, drowned animals, but after the anchors were raised and the sails hoisted, the ship began to move into clearer waters and then the open sea.

Sunaomi thought how the sea took everything, all the trash

of human life, and absorbed it into its trackless, uncharted depths. He could drop into it and disappear beneath the waves. They would wash away the shame that ate away at him, as corrosive as rust. Out on the ocean under the blue dome of heaven and, later at night, the vast stretch of stars, human activity, its struggles and passions, seemed meaningless. He longed to retreat from it. He did not think he could take any more wounds.

He changed into his own clothes which had been spread on the deck to dry. They smelled of salt and aloes. They had shared his ordeal but they had been washed clean of all trace. He did not think he ever would be.

Lady Nin made no reference to his state other than to say, 'You will recover. You are young and resilient.' Instead she spoke of her country, its history and its customs, telling him how for centuries they had paid tribute to the great empire of Shin and in return received protection from the north.

'Before his death,' she said, 'we feared Saga Hideki was planning to invade. He had delusions of conquering Shin, and our country lay in his path. But he died before he could begin his attack. Our king and queen were relieved and grateful. That is why we hope to sign agreements and let the Red Seal ships trade again.'

He forced himself to answer that Lady Kaede had spoken of that very thing but he was only half-engaged. He did not think he would ever recover. He had known fear, hunger and pain as a child, as well as terrible grief, and he had recovered, but this wound, among all the others, went too deep.

♦

The ship rounded the coast and headed northeast. Behind them the mountains of Nankoku faded into the haze.

'There is Himejima,' Lady Nin said, pointing out a distant rounded shape that seemed to float over the water.

Ame's island of women and cats but no men.

'And over there, in the east, is Kumamoto,' she said.

He recognised the familiar shapes of the mountains of his home town. Dr Ishida and Mai must have arrived there weeks before. Were the Arai, his brother and grandmother, even now preparing to join Terada's rebellion? Was his domain also lost to him? He was indifferent, just glad that the ship passed by without stopping.

During the night the wind dropped and the sailors put out the oars, keeping a steady rhythm until dawn. Then a southerly breeze sprang up and the sail was raised. The wind held and two days later they were in Maruyama.

CHAPTER TWENTY-TWO

The Sillans were well known in Maruyama. It was four months since the noble dog had been given to Lady Shigeko and entrusted by her to Sunaomi to take to Miyako. They had both travelled a long way to return here.

Around midday the ship sailed slowly up the deep river on the rising tide. Town and port were bathed in sunshine. Beyond lay the deep green of forest and mountain, unscarred by clearings.

'Now we come with another gift,' Lady Nin said as they disembarked into a flat-bottomed boat. 'I think your cousin will be glad to see you alive.'

But Sunaomi dreaded telling Shigeko of his failures, especially that he had lost Kiki, the horse she had given him, for her horses were as dear to her as children.

He had lived in Maruyama on and off over the years. His cousin and her husband, Sugita Hiroshi, had been like foster parents to him. It should have felt like a homecoming, but all he felt was his failure and shame.

Terada should have killed me. It would have been better. Now maybe I should take my own life. Death beckoned to him, offering an escape from pain.

The Sillans kept a residence near the harbour. Lady Nin and the envoys planned to rest here while the ship reloaded and the groom was sent with a message to the castle. He returned soon afterwards with one of the retainers, a man Sunaomi remembered, Naida Sadaaki.

'You are to come back with me at once,' he said, after greeting Sunaomi. 'Lord Hiroshi cannot wait to see you.' Then he addressed the envoys, saying with deep respect, 'You are invited to the castle tonight.'

'Thank you,' Lady Nin replied, 'but we will catch the afternoon tide and the south wind to return to Silla. We will await your messengers and pray peace will prevail.'

Sunaomi thanked her and the envoys, bowing to each one in turn, and then spoke to the groom.

'You saved my life. I am forever in your debt.'

'The noble dog saved you. She showed me where you were. Now you are reunited, there is no debt between us.' The man bent down and rubbed Chin behind the ears, speaking to her in Sillan. She wagged her tail.

'What did you say?' Sunaomi asked.

'I told her to look after you. You are a good master to her. You must never abandon her.' He spoke with deep seriousness as though he had seen Sunaomi's thoughts of suicide.

'I hope I will never have to,' Sunaomi said.

Yet when he walked with Naida through the familiar streets to the castle and people greeted him, recognising the boy who had grown up among them, he wanted to lower his head and hide his face. He wondered if his bond with Chin was strong enough to tether him to this world.

The white-walled castle rose above the town. Its lower floors were built of pale stone, its upper ones of wood. Above the keep the banners of Maruyama and the Otori heron were stretched out by the south wind.

Hiroshi was in the ground floor armoury where documents were kept and weapons stored, since the stone walls and slate ceiling would protect both in the case of fire. It had a distinctive smell of oil, whetstone, old paper and gunpowder that made Sunaomi recall the hours he had spent there, and then he remembered another house, in Miyako, where Hiroshi had taught him to read and write, and Sunaomi had shown him the spirits of the dead. Hiroshi had been hostile to him then. Later he had forgiven him and had treated him like a son.

Now he received Sunaomi with affection, though he could

not hide his surprise.

'I've sent for my wife. She will be overjoyed to see you. Then you can tell us why you are here.'

Naida went to help him to his feet, handing him a dark, silver-topped cane. Hiroshi still limped and often had an expression of pain, from wounds suffered at the battle of Takahara, ten years earlier.

It was always cold inside the lower floors of the castle, even on the hottest days. Sunaomi was trembling, and tried to control it. He heard Shigeko's footsteps hastening down the corridor that linked the castle and the residence. She still walked with a quick light tread like a young girl, though she was now the mother of two daughters.

'Sunaomi!' she exclaimed. 'What's happened? Have you been ill? You are so thin and pale!'

'Apparently he came by ship with the Sillan envoys,' Hiroshi said.

'From Hofu?'

Sunaomi nodded.

'Was the town hit by the typhoon? We had heavy rain but escaped the worst of it. It is the season, what can we do? We are powerless against the weather.'

He felt she was talking to fill in his silence, to give him time to collect himself. Her gaze was perceptive and concerned.

'But we should not stay here,' she said. 'You look cold.'

'Who could be cold on a day like today?' Hiroshi said, trying to joke, after a quick glance at his wife.

'Let's go back to the residence,' Shigeko said.

The little girls were playing in the garden with one of the maids. They ran up excitedly when they saw who had arrived and petted Chin in delight, squealing when she licked their bare legs and faces.

'She remembers us, I think,' Shigeko said.

'She never forgets anyone she meets,' Sunaomi replied.

'Let the children play with the dog outside for a while,'

Shigeko told the maid. 'We will talk to my cousin.'

They went inside and sat down. Shigeko asked, 'Are you hungry or thirsty?'

Sunaomi shook his head. For a few moments he gazed out at the garden without speaking. Then he said abruptly, 'I had to leave Kiki, the horse you gave me. In fact, he was stolen from me. I'm sorry, I don't know what will happen to him.'

'That's a shame,' Hiroshi said. 'He's a fine horse. But we have others, you must choose one of them.'

'If he is still in Hofu he can be recovered,' Shigeko said. 'We'll send one of the grooms.'

Sunaomi realised they had heard nothing of events in Hofu. They lived in their own realm, content and secure, blinded by their own happiness. They had no idea war was about to break out.

'You've had no word from Lord Kahei, or from Miyako?'

'Should we have?' A look of concern crossed Shigeko's face. 'Is my mother all right?'

'When I left in the fourth month, she was.'

'We have heard nothing,' Hiroshi said. 'Why were you in Hofu? Were you alone? Where is that faithful warrior of yours, Kaneda?'

'I sent him to Lord Kahei, I'm not sure how long ago, maybe three weeks, but I don't know if he ever reached him. Immediately after, I was held captive by Terada Fumio.' He stopped, the memories surging up, threatening to overwhelm him. 'I don't want to talk about that. What I must tell you is that Terada is planning a rebellion with the support of the Nankoku lords, the foreigners, and several other groups, sects he has favoured, possibly even the Tribe. We must muster whatever forces you have and arms, and ride to save first Hofu and then Miyako.'

Even to his own ears his voice sounded deranged.

'You must be mistaken,' Shigeko said. 'Fumio is an old ally of the Otori. He helped my father take the city of Hagi. His daughter has been my friend since we were children.'

'We can negotiate with him,' Hiroshi suggested. 'You are in no condition to go anywhere. You must rest and recover, and I will dispatch messengers to him. We'll find out what his grievances are and reach a solution together. Riding out with an army against him will only antagonise him further.'

'He is past any negotiation. The only way you will get him to talk to you will be if you defeat him in battle. His fleet is already halfway to Akashi, waiting to back up his land forces. I will rest for as long as it takes you to prepare your men. Then we must leave. The typhoon will have delayed them; there is still time, if we can move swiftly.' He stopped and took a deep breath. 'You don't know how deeply he hates your mother,' he said to Shigeko, 'and how much he longs to punish her.'

His impatience and frustration made him agitated. He could not sit still. Pretending he was checking on Chin, he stood and began pacing up and down the verandah.

Behind him he heard Shigeko whisper something to her husband. Hiroshi came out to join him.

'I'll get some men together and ride out tomorrow. But you are in no fit state to make the journey back so soon. You must stay here and regain your strength.'

It was so tempting. Sunaomi wanted nothing more than to sink into the cocoon of beauty, comfort and safety that Maruyama offered. He dreaded returning to Hofu. But Terada possessed his house, his sword and his horse. He had insulted and humiliated him. He would know no peace until he faced him.

'I will come with you,' he said.

'Well, we'll decide later. Either way you must choose a new horse.' Hiroshi moved to embrace him like a father but Sunaomi pulled away. He did not want to be made to feel like a child.

However, everything seemed designed to weaken his resolve. Shigeko led him into an adjoining room where bedding had already been spread out. The outer shutters were closed, the light dim, the air cool. A maid came with warm water. It was Haruka, whom he had known since he was a child.

'Welcome back,' she said, with delight. 'The children are very happy to see you here again. I'll bring you something to eat. I am sure I can find one of your favourite dishes.'

Sunaomi shook his head but she patted his arm saying, 'When you smell the food your appetite will return, I promise.'

Shigeko said, 'After you've eaten you must sleep.'

'I don't want to sleep,' he replied. 'There is no time, and I have nightmares.'

'Sunaomi, something terrible has happened to you. I see it in your eyes, in your body. Talk to me about it.'

Her gentle voice, her beautiful face so filled with concern and tenderness towards him made his eyes grow hot but he refused to weep.

'I can't,' he replied. 'It was nothing.' Then, under her steady gaze he said, 'Terada held me captive for a while.'

Shigeko said, 'I was like a captive in my marriage to Lord Saga. I gave myself willingly to him. My father desired it and the marriage was to bring peace to the Three Countries and the whole of the Eight Islands. But to my husband I was a prisoner of war, to be humiliated and made to suffer. Every night was like a battle. He knew nothing of love or tenderness. He could only be a conqueror, an occupying force. I was the daughter of his enemy. He never stopped being jealous of my father, even after Lord Otori was dead. I bore it all for the sake of peace, and I felt I deserved punishment for it was my arrow that pierced his eye bringing on his madness. And to some extent I was able to calm him. I took the brunt of his rage to spare others.'

'You could not spare Masao's family, though.' Sunaomi thought of his beloved ghost girl, Masao's sister, who had been murdered by her parents on Saga's orders.

'That was when I saw the extent of his insanity. But Fumio is not mad in that way, surely?'

Sunaomi shook his head. Were not all men insane when they were carried away by their rage? He knew Shigeko's words were meant to comfort him and he was grateful to her for speaking so frankly, but the knowledge of her humiliation did nothing to alleviate his.

He said, 'You know Masao, Lord Saga's grandson and heir, will be at Terada's side in the coming war?'

'Masao? I did not even know he was in Hofu.' For the first time Shigeko's calm seemed shaken.

'It was one of the reasons I went there. There is so much I have not told you. In short, I wanted to save him, but it is too late now.'

Haruka came back with a tray of food, a broth of small clams, grilled sweetfish and the braised eggplant that had indeed been one of his favourites.

Shigeko said, 'I'll talk further with my husband while you eat. Maybe things are more serious than we thought.'

'They are and probably far worse by now.'

Sunaomi did not want to eat but Haruka persuaded him to try the food, and to please her he took a few mouthfuls. Then his body told him clearly it needed this sustenance and he ate swiftly and silently like a starving animal.

'That's good,' Haruka said. She took the tray and stood, still as lithe as a girl. 'Now sleep.'

He stared at her, grateful and angry at the same time.

'You think you are not tired? Like you thought you were not hungry?' Her teasing calmed him a little. 'I'll wake you, I promise, as soon as Lord Hiroshi is ready.'

'You swear it?'

'I do,' she replied solemnly.

He lay down. Chin crept close to his side. For a few moments he dreamed, then fell abruptly into the deep well of sleep.

•

He woke feeling Chin growling quietly at his side. It was still light but he could tell from the rays of the sun shining through the chinks in the shutters, and the birdsong, that it was evening, just before sunset.

The door slid open and his cousin, Miki, Shigeko's younger sister, came in. She knelt beside him, studied his face with her steady penetrating gaze, and felt his forehead.

'No fever,' she observed.

'No, I am fine, perfectly healthy.'

'I am not convinced of that,' she said. 'You have been through some terrible experience. It has left you in deep shock.'

When he did not reply she went on, 'You don't want to tell me about it?'

'There is nothing to tell. I am over it, or I will be when I return to Hofu.'

'I told my sister and brother-in-law that the danger is real,' Miki said. 'Hiroshi is taking you seriously now.'

'Thank you.' Sunaomi remembered her powers of clear sight and her deep, uncanny knowledge.

'I am glad you are here, though,' Miki went on. 'I have something to tell you. I wanted to write to you but it felt better to tell you in person. I will say it now for we may not be alone together again for some time.'

She spoke quickly and quietly. 'You know my father often suggested you and I should marry.'

Sunaomi opened his mouth but she said, 'Let me finish. I am not looking for any professions of sentiment from you. I have made up my mind. Once, I was drawn to the idea. As you grew up I liked you more and more, and I was attracted to you as anyone would be. But I am called to another path. I am going to Terayama where I will become a nun. Many young girls seek refuge there now or are sent by their parents for their education. A new wing will be built to house them and I will be their teacher and eventually their Abbess.'

'So, you will never marry?' he said.

'No, that is not to be my path. I'll tell you what I have never told anyone else. I loved my sister, my twin, Maya, more than any other human being, and when she died a part of me was extinguished. No man will ever fill that emptiness but I believe it will make me a vessel for the divine.'

'Lord Miyoshi wants me to marry Kinu, his youngest daughter,' Sunaomi said. 'He suggested a betrothal, but I was unable to decide. Among other things I did not know if your father's wish constituted a promise between us. I'm glad you have told me of your intentions. There is no barrier to the betrothal now, as long as your mother gives her approval.'

The other barrier had been Utahime. She no longer possessed him. However, memories of Kiyoko's body and passion troubled him. Was he to forgo all that in a marriage which offered friendship but not love?

'It is a good choice for you,' Miki said. 'You are not strangers to each other, you are close in age, and you share many interests: music, learning, a love of horses.' Her gaze fell on the flute which lay on the floor between them. She picked it up and ran her fingers over it. 'This is beautiful. I never learned to play. I wish I had.'

'You will have the opportunity to study with a master at Terayama,' Sunaomi replied.

'That's true.' Her face stilled as if she were listening to some inner voice. Then she smiled. 'You are to give this to Kinu. It will be a betrothal gift for her.'

The night was hot and still. After the long daytime sleep Sunaomi was wakeful and restless. Around midnight he rose and went to the cistern in the garden to splash water on his face. Its trickling sound made him feel a little cooler. The half-moon was bright in the sky, dimming the stars, casting shadows.

From the verandah he heard the murmur of voices. Shigeko and Hiroshi were talking together. He could not make out the words but the quiet intimacy, the ripple of their conversation, touched him. Perhaps they were saying farewell, knowing that they might not see each other again.

He went quietly back and lay down, wishing that he were not the cause of their separation.

In the morning Hiroshi selected a new sword for him and then they went to look at the horses in the water meadows. Tenba and Ashige, older and staider now, grazed with the herd. Sunaomi could not help recalling the day he had chosen Kiki and he deliberately picked a horse that looked nothing like him, a smallish bay with a clever look.

'He's always reminded me of Shun, Lord Takeo's horse,' Hiroshi said with a smile. 'It's a good choice; he's intelligent and reliable. Of course we hope you will be able to get Kiki back, but whatever happens this one is yours.'

'Does he have a name?'

'Just the bay, so far. You can call him what you like.' *Maybe I won't give him a name. The bay will do fine.* He led the horse back to the castle while Hiroshi rode his calm, wide-backed grey, one of Ashige's sons. There he found a suitable saddle and bridle, and a woven saddle bag in which he could put Chin. About thirty men had gathered and were preparing their horses.

'They are so few,' he said.

'It's close to harvest,' Hiroshi replied. 'Many have returned to their land. I've sent out messengers, and more will follow us as they can. But we don't keep a large army here in Maruyama; there has never been any need for one.'

Shigeko, Miki and the children, with Haruka, waved goodbye, and many townspeople shouted words of good luck and safe return. Once beyond the town they rode down a steep track into a ravine where a ford crossed the Asagawa, the horses carefully picking their way between the boulders.

'There was a fierce battle here when Lord Takeo took the town,' Hiroshi said. 'I was only a child and did not witness it myself but it was I who told Takeo about this route and suggested he should trap the enemy here. They were all slaughtered.

Some were men I had known all my life.'

It was dark and cool in the shade and in the babble of the river easy to imagine the voices of the dead.

'I never forgot it,' Hiroshi said. 'I had not understood that madness that drives men to kill each other. I was raised to be a warrior. I loved the art of sword and bow, the development of character, courage, loyalty, endurance. All this is beautiful and admirable, even noble, but I did not want to use that beauty to end the life of a stranger. The Battle of Takahara was for me a defeat, even though we were the victors.'

'I have never been in a real battle,' Sunaomi said. 'There was the fight on the execution ground when I was a child, and recently I defended myself in an ambush, and I suppose I killed then, maybe two men. But that was the first time.'

'Despite the tragedies of your childhood you grew up in a realm at peace. For almost ten years we have had no threats either from within or without. A strong, just government makes it possible for all to live in tranquillity. But maybe this very tranquillity makes us overlook the men who arise to challenge, who seek power and domination of their own, who imagine grievances that must be redressed. We should have been ready and dealt with them swiftly, but it is endless work. I see I have grown complacent and a little weary. I wish time might stand still and I could stay forever with my wife and daughters, but here I am, riding away from them, planning for a war I don't want, against an old ally.'

Hiroshi rode in silence for a while and they emerged from the shade of the ravine onto the road that led towards the east. Then he said abruptly, 'I wish evil would lie down for once and accept defeat but it never does. It always springs back up when we least expect it.'

CHAPTER TWENTY-THREE

The moon swelled to full as they rode across the high plain, where Sunaomi's grandfather had liked to go hawking when he was a young man. To the south lay Sunaomi's own domain. Was it also in rebellion or did it remain loyal to the Empress? There was no way of knowing. None of the remote villages along the way had any news, and the land that lay baking under the summer heat gave no hint of any uprisings.

Sunaomi burned with impatience. The days seemed endless, always the same landscape of dry grass, heat haze and dust. He resented having to pause at night, and hardly slept. Sometimes on horseback he fell into feverish dreams and woke with a start to find they were still riding across the plain.

As Hiroshi had said, the bay horse took good care of him.

The track steepened. The slopes of the plain gradually became hills and then mountains. The grass gave way to forests. Finally they came through the pass to the small town of Kibi where they were able to bathe and eat without stint. From here it was only a day's ride to Terayama or Yamagata, the Miyoshi castle town.

'We'll go straight to Yamagata,' Hiroshi said. 'Much as I would like to consult with Makoto and Gemba, I cannot take so many men to the temple, and it might just be wasting our time.'

'Lord Kahei uses messenger doves to keep in touch with his sons,' Sunaomi said. 'So, possibly we will have some news in Yamagata.' He was thinking about Kaneda, wondering if the warrior had reached Lord Kahei, or if he had been captured by Terada's men before getting far from Hofu.

'Let's hope so.'

Yamagata had been the heartland of the Middle Country,

the Otori domain, second in importance only to Hagi, but for years it had been Miyoshi Kahei's. Kahei had three sons but of the direct Otori line no one remained alive. Miki would have no children, and Shigeko's daughters would carry the name of Maruyama. Sunaomi thought about this with sorrow. An era was ending, ending in war.

They came to the city at night. The full moon was rising behind the walls. The gates were closed and guarded. Willows along the river had been cut down. The town was prepared for attack and siege.

Sunaomi rode forward with Hiroshi, identifying himself. Behind him the tired horses stamped and jostled, impatient to be unsaddled and fed. One of them neighed and loud replies came from horses within the walls, like an alarm waking up the town.

The guards were suspicious and reluctant. They would not open the gates but spoke through the bars.

'You are not expected. There are many rumours of insurrection. Maybe you are part of that.'

'Is Katsunori here? Or Kintomo?' Sunaomi thought the brothers might remember him.

'I cannot give you that information,' the captain said woodenly.

'Please tell Lady Miyoshi that Arai Sunaomi is here, with Sugita Hiroshi. We are friends, allies. We've ridden for eight days to come to Lord Kahei's aid.'

'Wait a little,' the captain said and spoke to one of his men.

After a while he heard Kinu's voice. 'Sunaomi? Is that you?'

'It is.'

A guard held a burning torch behind her. A mixture of relief and tenderness rose in him at the sight of her pale delicate face. Her eyes lit up.

'Open the gate and let them in,' she ordered without hesitation. 'Take the horses to the stables and feed them. The men can go to the barracks. Wake the cooks and tell them to prepare food. Lord Arai and Lord Sugita will come with me.'

'Thank you,' Hiroshi said, 'but I prefer to stay with my men. Please convey my respects and gratitude to your mother. I will thank her myself in the morning.'

They dismounted and Hiroshi led the horses away. Holding Chin under one arm, Sunaomi climbed the steps to the castle at Kinu's side.

'I did not expect to see you here,' he said. 'I thought you would be with your father in Miyako.'

'I will explain everything to you.'

'I'm sorry to wake everyone so late at night,' he said.

'I was awake. I don't sleep much, as you might know.'

When they came to the long verandah that wrapped around the living quarters, maids were waiting with bowls of water. Kinu took Chin from Sunaomi. The dog allowed herself to be held by the young girl, even nestled into her arms.

'I've been so worried about both of you,' Kinu said. 'We've had no news for so long.'

'If only Chin could talk,' Sunaomi said. 'But you probably would not believe the adventures she has had.'

One of the maids went ahead of them with a lamp. Once inside, Kinu looked carefully at Sunaomi. 'And you, you look as if you have had some adventures. You have become so thin and changed. What happened?'

'I was very close to death,' he said. 'And now, I don't know if I am alive or dead.'

'You are here, talking to me. You are alive.' She touched his arm briefly. 'Do you want to bathe? Or eat?'

'I'm not hungry,' he said. 'But I would like to bathe if it's not too much trouble.'

'I'll ask the maids to prepare a bath and bring you a night robe. They can sponge and air your clothes. I imagine you will leave tomorrow.'

'I wish I could stay longer but I must reach your father as soon as possible.'

Kinu went to the verandah and spoke quietly to the maids.

When she returned, she said, 'I will not be here myself much longer. I am to leave for Terayama in a day or two.'

He stared at her, not understanding.

'I am so glad you are here, so I could tell you myself. My father has finally given me permission to become a nun. In a way it is thanks to you, for I found myself telling him about our agreement. It distressed him very much but he could not make me change my mind. In the end he admitted it would be better for me not to marry.' She gazed on him, her eyes luminous. 'I hope you will not be too disappointed. I'll never forget that you agreed to do that for me. But now there is no need. We are both free.'

A wave of emotion swept over him. He had not realised how dear she was to him. He thought, *I could have made her happy.* His eyes grew hot. He turned away so she would not see.

'Now I have angered you,' she said.

'No, not at all. It is for the best. I am happy that your father has acquiesced to your desires, and I don't believe I have much of a future.'

The maid came with the nightrobe and he began to undress. As he unfastened his sash his fingers touched the flute. He remembered Miki's instruction.

'This is for you,' he said, holding it out.

'Thank you! It's beautiful. Where did it come from?'

'I'll tell you one day,' he said, not believing he ever would.

'Is it maple? I can almost feel the buds in the branch. I'll play for you while you bathe.'

He walked back down the steps, through the garden to the hot spring. The moon threw deep shadows. Insects were chirping loudly. It was still warm but something in the air spoke of autumn. He sluiced the dirt from him and slipped naked into the hot water.

He hardly heard the first notes but slowly became aware that Kinu was playing. She must have been sitting on the verandah above for the music fell over him. At first it sounded like Utahime and his heart quivered in sorrow. But Kinu's style was different, peerless. The music entwined around him. It was the steam, the water, the insects, the moon and stars, as old as memory, as new as this moment. His heart cracked and tears flowed down his cheeks. His shame was washed away, his mistakes forgiven.

Barely discernible beneath each note lay its echo, as though two flutes played in a duet. He could almost believe the two girls played together, but when he returned to the verandah, Kinu was alone. Chin slept beside her.

The girl finished the melody while he watched without speaking or moving. His heart was filled with regret for what might have been.

She lowered the flute and gazed on him, her eyes wide, her face flushed.

'Sunaomi,' she murmured.

A bewitchment took hold of them. He stepped towards her, trembling with emotion. The flute slipped from her fingers and she came into his arms as if she flew to him.

They clung to each other, fiercely and tenderly, their bodies curving together, demanding, fulfilling.

'What is this?' Kinu whispered. 'Is this love?'

'Yes,' Sunaomi said, his heart overflowing with gratitude for Utahime's last gift to him.

'This longing to be held by you, to take you into me, is this desire? Do you feel it too?'

'I do. Kinu, let us be married. Don't shut yourself away from the world and from me.'

'All those things I said before, what a fool I was. I was going to deny us this just because of my fears. Of course we will be married. As soon as possible. I cannot wait!'

'War may force us to delay,' he said.

'No, you might die in the war. I cannot bear to let you go.' Her caution and fear had all melted away in the fire of her passion.

Footsteps echoed beyond the corner of the verandah.

'My mother is coming,' Kinu said. 'Usually she sleeps like the dead. Why does she have to be so vigilant on this night of all nights?'

Lady Miyoshi appeared. They had stepped away from each other but they might as well have still been embracing. The air itself was infused with their mutual desire.

'Well!' she said in surprise. 'I am happy to see you again, Sunaomi. My husband wrote with the news that you were to become our son-in-law, and then my daughter returned home telling me she was going to become a nun and there would be no marriage. Can it be that you have changed her mind?'

'I hope so with all my heart,' Sunaomi replied.

'And, Kinu, you have reconciled yourself to marriage after all?'

'If it is to Sunaomi,' Kinu replied, flushing even more.

'I see,' Lady Miyoshi replied, trying to hide her amusement. 'I suppose we should arrange the wedding as soon as possible.'

'I cannot bear to wait even one more day,' the girl cried.

'You will have to be patient. Your father must be present, but we do not know when that will be.' She addressed Sunaomi, 'I imagine my daughter has not yet told you, but our sons left a few days ago with half our men. As you saw when you arrived, those who were left have fortified the town.'

'Did Lord Miyoshi send for his sons?' Sunaomi asked. 'What news have you had?'

'One of the messenger doves came. My husband uses a code in case the bird is intercepted. It was brief and enigmatic, but Katsunori took it to mean that his father needed him and was to meet him outside Hofu.'

Did that mean Kaneda had succeeded in reaching Lord Miyoshi? For the first time Sunaomi felt a twinge of hope.

'Hiroshi and I will follow them at daybreak,' he said.

'Kinu, you must leave Sunaomi to sleep now,' her mother said. 'I will wait here.'

As they stepped into the room Sunaomi bent to pick up the

flute. He cried out in surprise.

'What is it?' Kinu asked.

He held the flute out to her. It had sprouted leaves, fresh and green, like a living branch.

'I will be back before they turn red,' he promised.

'What if they wither and fall? Will it mean you are dead?' Her voice was desolate. 'I have a terrible premonition I will never see you again. It will be my punishment for being so blind.'

'You must look after Chin for me,' he said. 'She has accepted you as part of me. She will be your companion until I return.'

They rode fast, resting only briefly at night, taking advantage of the light of the waning moon. Every evening clouds like priests' heads gathered over the mountains. Thunder echoed but the storms did not break. The air was sultry. Biting insects troubled the horses, and columns of gnats often enveloped them. At night the men hardly slept for the whining of mosquitoes.

On the fifth day, as they neared Hofu, the road became busier, clogged with people fleeing the city, speaking of the outbreak of war and an army led by angels whom neither arrows nor bullets could wound. For weeks, one man said, the gates had been closed and no one allowed in or out, but they had just been reopened.

At the marsh where Sunaomi had said farewell to Kaneda, Hiroshi signalled a halt. Sunaomi looked across to the harbour, which seemed more filled with ships than ever. They were too distant for him to make out their banners but several were the distinctive shape of carracks.

A little way ahead the road was guarded by a band of men. Among the horses Sunaomi recognised Kaneda's roan, Baku. His heart leaped and then dropped like a stone, for Baku was riderless and he could not see Kaneda among the group.

The men's crests showed they were Otori and Miyoshi. Hiroshi said, 'It's Katsunori.'

'What have they done with Kaneda?' Sunaomi asked. 'That's his horse, Baku.'

'Are you sure?'

'I'd know him anywhere.'

The horse lifted its head and whinnied at the sound of Sunaomi's voice.

Lord Miyoshi's eldest son, Katsunori, came forward, his youngest brother, Kintomo, at his side.

Hiroshi told him their names and Katsunori gave a brief nod. 'Have you come to our aid, or were you hoping to take us by surprise from behind?'

'We are all on the same side, I believe,' Hiroshi said.

'You can never tell with the Arai,' Katsunori said with a glance at Sunaomi. The insult did not touch him. *I am to marry your sister. Wait till you learn that!*

Sunaomi said, 'We have just come from Yamagata where we saw your mother and Lady Kinu,' and realised it was a joy just to speak her name. He wanted to ask immediately about Kaneda, but waited for Hiroshi to speak first.

'What's the situation here?' Hiroshi asked. 'How far away is your father?'

'We stopped a man who came up riding fast, demanding to be allowed into the town. He said he was a messenger from our father but we didn't believe him.'

'He was lying and hoping to give us false confidence,' Kintomo added.

'What did you do to him?' Sunaomi demanded, fearing the worst.

'We're holding him prisoner until we find out if he's telling the truth,' Katsunori said.

'It is my man, Kaneda Sunamori,' Sunaomi said. 'I know his horse. Bring him here at once. I myself sent him to your father. He has never told a lie in his life, other than to protect me.'

He leaped off the bay's back as two of Katsunori's men brought the old warrior forward. His sword had been taken from him and his hands tied in front of him.

'Lord Sunaomi,' he said, a smile breaking out on his face. 'You come at just the right time!'

'Untie him,' Sunaomi ordered. 'I am sorry they have treated you like this. It's a poor reward for your courage and endurance.'

'You are alive, that's all that matters. Once again you've saved my life. It's like being released from the fox death.' He shivered, rubbing his wrists, and looked at the bay. 'Where is Kiki?'

'He was stolen from me in Hofu. But I recovered Chin and she is in Yamagata with Lady Kinu.'

I had to say her name again! I am about to ride into battle and may never see her again.

Kaneda raised his eyebrows, his smile becoming a grin. All he said though was, 'Where's my sword?'

When it was handed back to him, he said, 'I also had a spyglass, a loan from Lord Miyoshi.'

Kintomo produced a long polished tube and gave it to him, looking a little embarrassed. 'I should have recognised it,' he said.

Katsunori added, 'We're sorry.'

'It's always wise to be cautious,' Kaneda replied. 'I'm sure your father has written a precept about that. Now that the misunderstanding is behind us may I convey his messages to you?'

Telling his brother to keep watch, Katsunori withdrew to the side of the road with Hiroshi and Sunaomi to hear Kaneda's words.

'Terada's fleet has not reached Akashi,' the old warrior began. 'They had to put into port to shelter from the typhoon and many ships were damaged. They are still heading for Miyako, but they will meet half of Lord Miyoshi's army now. They have lost the advantage of surprise. In the meantime the east wind has protected us and given us time to ride back. Your father and his men are a short way behind me. His orders are to refrain from attacking the city until he arrives. He hopes the combined size of our forces will intimidate Terada and his allies into surrendering. Their land army is small, compared to the fleet.'

'But Mizuta has been transporting men and horses from Nankoku for weeks,' Sunaomi said. 'And then there are the foreigners, and all the others who support Terada.'

Kintomo called out to them, 'An army is riding out from the city!'

Katsunori stood, saying, 'That is not small by any measure.'

Sunaomi saw clouds of dust, golden in the afternoon sunshine, stirred up by the feet of hundreds of men and horses. Banners flew above their heads, red crosses on a white background.

Kaneda had the spyglass to his eye. 'Isn't that Kiki in front?' he said. He handed the spyglass to Sunaomi, his face grim. 'Guess who's riding him.'

Sunaomi squinted through the eye piece and saw his ivory-coloured horse, Kiki, with his black mane and tail, and on his back, in his bone white robes, Taro.

'He is not armed,' he said and scanned the throng. 'None of them are.'

Katsunori took the eyeglass from him, surveying the army from east to west. 'Is it some kind of sorcery?' he exclaimed. 'Or is it divine protection they are under?'

'We cannot fight against unarmed men,' Kintomo added. 'Where's the honour in that?'

'Are they outcasts, or the Hidden, or others who vow not to kill?' Katsunori sounded bewildered. He passed the spyglass back to Sunaomi. 'Do you recognise any of them?'

Sunaomi looked through it again. 'Next to Taro is a man called Maru Toma. He is an outcast.'

'And Taro is who?' Katsunori asked.

'My former servant. He has become a spiritual leader to these people. He is no danger to us. He will do us no harm.'

Sunaomi scanned the throng again. His gaze was arrested by a figure he had not spotted before, walking at Kiki's side. It was Masao.

He also seemed unarmed. It was too far away for Sunaomi to see the expression on his face but his stride was forceful and fearless. Taro rode while Masao walked. Truly the world was turned upside down. Could Masao really have given up the way of the sword? Masao who had loved to kill?

'Can you see Terada or Mizuta?' Katsunori said.

'No sign of either.'

'They are hiding behind these farmers and outcasts,' Kintomo said in disgust.

'Or using them as some kind of decoy,' his brother said. 'Lord Sugita, you are older and more experienced than us. What should we do?'

An ethereal sound drifted towards them. The men were singing as they approached, the same sacred hymns Sunaomi had heard at the Temple of the Poor. The back of his neck tingled.

'That's eerie,' Kintomo muttered.

The horses laid back their ears and stamped restlessly.

Hiroshi said, 'I'll ride out to meet them, unarmed, as they are.'

'No,' Katsunori said. 'That would be madness!'

'It will be a demonstration of the Way of the Houou,' Hiroshi replied. 'We have always taught that our aims can be pursued without violence. Now I will put that to the test.'

'The houou are long gone,' Katsunori said. 'Those days are over forever. These people cannot be allowed to advance, for their dreams and delusions will incite the whole countryside. We have firearms, we can wipe them out and take the city.'

'And destroy all those ships as well?' said the more cautious Kaneda. 'The foreigners have muskets and cannons. Better to retreat and wait for your father.'

'I am determined to go,' Hiroshi said. 'We will show our peaceful intentions and pay heed to their grievances.'

'I must go with you,' Sunaomi said. 'Taro will listen to me.'

'Then I'm coming too,' said Kaneda.

'Wait here,' Hiroshi said to Katsunori. 'Don't advance and above all don't fire.'

The three of them removed their swords and entrusted them to Kintomo, then mounted the horses and rode forward. The bay walked calmly, ears pricked forwards, Baku close behind.

'I can't believe we've been through so much together only to die on this marsh,' Kaneda said.

I don't want to die today, Sunaomi thought, though it was as fine a day as any to die. Lord Miyoshi Kahei had written something along those lines but he could not remember it.

The beautiful sound of men's voices singing washed over him, growing louder all the time. He could make out some of the words.

Split the wood and I am there
Lift the stone and I am there

In the distance thunder rumbled. The horses' manes stood upright in the charged air, and the hair of the approaching men looked like halos in the intensity of the light before the storm. He felt the ardour of their hope, the courage their beliefs gave them. Truly it seemed that the Kingdom that Taro had promised was about to be revealed.

'Taro,' he shouted. 'Stop! We can talk!'

Kiki flung up his head and gave a loud neigh. Masao seized the reins. The singing died away.

Taro looked in the direction of Sunaomi's voice and smiled. 'My friend,' he said, 'I am no longer yours to command. I obey the Secret One now and I am bringing the kingdom into existence.'

'We are unarmed but Lord Miyoshi's sons will not let you pass,' Hiroshi called. 'Disperse now before you are all slaughtered. Go back to your homes quietly and you will not be punished.'

'Who are you to speak of punishment?' Taro replied. 'Only the Secret One can judge us. Bullets and arrows cannot touch us.'

A cheer rose from the surrounding men and they began to sing again.

'Terada Fumio is using you for his own ambition,' Sunaomi said. 'He does not believe what you teach.'

'He is an instrument of Heaven, sent to further our cause,' Taro replied.

Kiki was trying to get closer to Sunaomi and the bay. Masao was still holding the reins, steadying him. Sunaomi glanced at his face and saw in it the old eagerness and passion for life, but somehow refined and made new.

He has changed. He can be saved.

Lightning flashed around them and thunder cracked almost directly overhead. A curtain of rain was approaching from the west beneath clouds the colour of indigo. A rainbow appeared over the marsh and the swirling birds seemed an even brighter white.

'We are not enemies,' Hiroshi called. 'We are your kinsmen, men of the Three Countries. Like you, we have no weapons.'

Sunaomi's vision was dazzled. For a moment the world held its breath. Then he heard another crack, saw Hiroshi's horse rear, realised it was not thunder but gunfire. The bay leaped sideways, almost unseating him. The grey staggered and fell, shot in the chest.

'Hiroshi!' he screamed.

Gunfire sounded behind him. He saw the jolt of Taro's body, a look of surprise on his face, blood on the bone white robe.

Kiki rearing, Taro falling, falling into Masao's arms.

Sunaomi threw himself down from the bay and knelt beside them.

Taro's eyes were wide open, the pupils dilated in shock.

'I thought,' he said, and then, 'I saw ... I see ...' Blood gushed from his mouth and he died.

The singing faltered as the unarmed farmers and outcasts began to flee. Behind them there appeared a line of soldiers, wearing steel foreign made armour and carrying firearms. On a command they knelt and fired through the fleeing farmers towards Katsunori's forces.

So, they were a decoy, Sunaomi thought, half in shock, *and no one cares if they are hit as they run away.*

The quick-thinking Kaneda dismounted beside Sunaomi and pushed him behind the fallen horse. The warrior was still holding Baku's reins and with the other hand he caught the bay.

Hiroshi knelt beside his horse. He seemed unhurt, but the horse was mortally wounded. Eyes rolling, legs twitching, nostrils red and inflating, it tried to whinny to its master.

'Hush, hush,' he said, 'Good man, brave fellow. Be still now.' He stroked the soft coat under the black mane as its spirit fled.

Masao crouched down beside them, his eyes bright.

'Kintomo was right,' Hiroshi said. 'It was an ambush all along.'

'Taro did not know that,' Masao said. 'He would never have deliberately deceived anyone, least of all Sunaomi.'

Lightning and thunder cracked almost simultaneously. The horses jostled and bucked in fear. Another round of gunfire echoed above their heads and then the rain was upon them, falling like a river, so dense and heavy they could hardly breathe.

The marshy ground began to flood immediately.

'Let's make a run for it while we can,' Kaneda said. 'The horses will shield us and the rain will prevent the enemy from reloading their guns.'

Sunaomi gripped Masao's arm.

'Leave me here,' Masao said. 'I don't mind dying here.'

Sunaomi did not answer. He pulled Masao to his feet and took Kiki's reins with his other hand.

He heard a different thunder, of horses' hoofs, and through the rain he saw Katsunori's men galloping, swords drawn, halberds at the ready. For a moment he thought they were going to be cut down by their own side but he heard Kintomo shout, 'It's Sugita and Arai. Let them pass.'

The wave of horses flowed around them. Baku and Kiki reared and tried to follow, but the bay walked steadily between Sunaomi and Kaneda.

When they came to the rear where they had left their swords, Masao said, 'What are you going to do with me?'

'Take you back to Miyako,' Sunaomi said. 'You can tell us honestly what happened in the street brawl where the Kono youth was killed. My aunt will decide then what is to happen to you.'

'I did not kill him,' Masao said quietly. 'The girl did.'

'The girl you and your companions were about to rape.'

'That is her side of the story,' Masao said. 'She was just a woman of the streets.'

Sunaomi said, 'I want to save your life, you know. That's what I've always wanted.'

'And I don't care if I live or die, so you are wasting your time.'

'There's every chance we're both going to die before the day ends, so let's not have this discussion now!'

Sunaomi called to one of the grooms, who were waiting anxiously, half-prepared to run for their lives, and told him to bind Masao's hands and guard him. He turned to Kaneda, who was checking the horses for injuries. Baku had a long shallow graze on his rump but Kiki and the bay were unharmed.

Hiroshi already had his sword at his waist and his bow in his hand.

'Give me the bay,' he said. 'I'll follow Katsunori. Kaneda must stay with you and take you to Kahei.'

'I agree,' Kaneda said.

The rain sluiced over them, plastering their hair to their skulls. Their feet were deep in mud.

Sunaomi did not want to fight but nor did he want to run away. He took up the spyglass which Katsunori had left with their weapons but he could see little through it. He wiped the moisture from the lens with his sleeve and looked in the other direction, behind him.

There was something approaching through the rain, a churning rhythmic movement of galloping horses.

'Lord Miyoshi is here,' he cried.

CHAPTER TWENTY-FIVE

Kahei was leading a troop of men who looked as though they had come a long way at great speed. The horses were breathing hard and their legs were caked in mud. At Kahei's side the banners of the Miyoshi and the Otori hung sodden.

He halted at the sight of Sunaomi and Kaneda, acknowledging their bows with a brief nod and taking the scene in at a glance.

'You are alive,' he said to Sunaomi. 'You have Masao with you and you may have prevented a rebellion spreading further. You have done well.' A look of distress crossed his face. 'We will talk later. I have some news for you which may be a disappointment. It is a great one for me.'

Sunaomi wondered what he could be talking about and then remembered that Lord Kahei believed Kinu, his daughter, was even now beginning her new life as a nun. But there was no time for explanations.

'Will you ride with me to finish the work?' his future father-in-law asked. 'You are not dressed for war, though. You have no armour?'

'I was not really expecting to fight,' Sunaomi said. He did not know what he had been expecting, still in shock from Taro's death.

'Dress for peace and you will encounter war,' Kahei said sternly. 'Dress for war and you will encounter peace.'

He ordered one of his men to give his armour to Sunaomi and to remain to guard Masao. While Sunaomi was lacing up the chest plate, Kahei questioned him.

'Katsunori already engaged this army? They have been forced to retreat? Some will be in flight, the rest will make a stand in Hofu, before escaping by boat. We can't stop them, we have no ships, but I'd like to get my hands on Terada. Where will he be?'

'In his residence'—*my residence*—'or possibly at Daifukuji, if he's not already aboard one of his ships.'

'When we reach the town I'll go to Daifukuji, you go to the residence. Meet me at the temple; if I'm not there, at the harbour. My men will sweep through the town, and deal with deserters and stragglers.' Kahei glanced up at the sky. The storm had come from the southwest. 'This wind will keep them pinned to the shore.'

Half the men dismounted and left their horses with grooms. Those who carried provisions ate and drank quickly before preparing their halberds. Those who had firearms were positioned on the flank. Among the horsemen were many archers.

'Give me the spyglass,' Kahei said. Looking through it, he said, 'The town gates are open. My sons must be already inside. Let's ride.'

Giving the spyglass to the groom who held his horse, he urged the animal forward. A cheer rose from the men as they followed.

Sunaomi took Kiki's reins and sprang up onto his back. He put him into a canter.

Bodies lay in the mud; riderless horses wandered around, some neighing at Kahei's men and trotting after them. Sunaomi caught sight of a splash of white next to the dead grey horse. *It is Taro. I must retrieve him later and bury him.*

A few stragglers from the enemy forces were cut down but there was no real opposition until they were in the town. Here pockets of soldiers had been stationed to defend the retreating men and give them time to get away. As they were overcome and fell back they set fire to the surrounding houses.

Sunaomi found his own house ablaze. He watched for a few moments, heard the cries of the caged birds and wished he could free them, imagined all Terada's treasures being reduced to ash, along with his childhood memories and his adult ordeal.

'He is not here,' Kaneda said at his side.

'No, let's join Lord Miyoshi at the temple.' Sunaomi was con-cerned about Hiromasa but pushed his fears to the back of his mind. His duty now was to assist in the capture of Terada. He had to trust the Tribe to look after his brother.

Trust the Tribe! Hadn't they already betrayed him and sold him to Terada?

At the gates of the temple he found Kahei with his younger son, Kintomo.

'Any sign of Terada?' Kahei asked.

Sunaomi shook his head. 'The house is burning. No one remained.'

The temple gates were closed, barred from the inside.

'They have cannon,' Kahei said. 'They are using them to protect the ships until they can get away. One is here inside the temple, the other on board a ship on the opposite side of the port.'

'We'll wait for the next volley and then rush them,' Kintomo suggested. 'Katsunori and Sugita are almost at the quayside. They will draw their fire.'

Kahei agreed with a grim face. Sunaomi wondered how he could bear to risk his sons' lives, but recognised the calm ruth-lessness that made Lord Miyoshi a great warrior.

There was a loud boom as the cannon fired, echoed from across the water. Kintomo made a sign to his men and two of them threw grapples up onto the top of the wall and swiftly scaled it. Cries came from within, shouts of fury and pain. The gates opened and the soldiers rushed in.

The small cannon was positioned on the seawall, ugly and incongruous in that place of peace. The gunners drew swords and knives, two fumbled with muskets, but they were quickly overcome and their bodies thrown into the sea.

Kahei had dismounted. He strode to the wall and gazed over the harbour. 'I can't see Terada on the wharf.' He turned back to

Sunaomi. 'Check inside the temple.'

Leaving the horses outside, Sunaomi and Kaneda, swords in hand, went to the main hall. Lamps had been lit inside and the monks were kneeling in prayer. One or two looked up; the rest did not move. Sunaomi walked swiftly along the ranks, in case Terada was hidden among them. None of them appeared to be armed.

Hearing sounds from Shomei's study, he looked in. The monk was packing up manuscripts and texts into boxes.

'You're back,' he said when he saw Sunaomi. 'Maybe you can help me. There's a smell of smoke and I must move these to the storehouse.'

His movements were erratic and confused.

'Is Terada here?' Sunaomi asked.

'I don't think so,' the old monk said, his voice vague.

'Where is the Abbot?'

'He is not to be disturbed,' Shomei said, with a shifty look which alarmed Sunaomi.

'What has he done?' he cried.

'It is atonement,' Shomei looked Sunaomi in the face. 'He should have given you protection from Terada, but he did not. Even after everyone thought Terada had killed you he still supported the pirate. And you wrote so beautifully. He allowed our temple to be used in warfare. Now it will be purified by fire. But first I must save my texts.' He stopped abruptly and then resumed. 'But perhaps it is better if they burn. I am too attached to them. What are they? Nothing but paper and words. They are not the truth.'

He formed a piece of paper into a spill and held it to the lamp. Tenderly he touched the flame to the manuscript on his desk.

'Look, Lord Arai. See how your work and mine are so swiftly consumed as though they never existed. That is human life.'

'Try to put it out,' Sunaomi told Kaneda. 'I must find the Abbot.'

The smell of smoke grew more intense. As he ran down

the cloisters he heard Shishi barking wildly. The door to the Abbot's room was closed. He slid it open and saw the Abbot slumped on the ground. His eyes were rolled back in his head. Beside him lay an empty glass; a flask stood on a tray.

The dog ran to Sunaomi and ran back again to the dead priest, pawing at him and whining.

Sunaomi knelt, his heart full of sorrow. What had happened? Had the Abbot taken his own life or had Shomei poisoned him?

Fire was crackling, closer now. He heard Kaneda call his name.

What was he to do with Shishi? The dog would probably pine to death without his master, yet he could not leave him here to burn alive. He would kill him quickly now.

An image came into his mind of Chin with her puppies. He reached out to pick Shishi up. The dog growled at him, showing his teeth, and pressed more deeply into the Abbot's robes.

'Come,' Sunaomi said. 'I will be your master.' Shishi's red–brown eyes held his gaze. What had the Abbot said, after Shishi recovered from the Kikuta sleep? *I feel he understands every word spoken.*

'You are mine now,' Sunaomi said firmly. The dog's tail moved slightly. When Sunaomi reached out again Shishi allowed himself to be picked up.

Kaneda shouted, 'Get out quickly. The fire is spreading.'

Someone was striking the great bell. Its booms echoed through the temple as Sunaomi ran outside, clasping the dog. Monks came pouring from the hall, gathered buckets and began to form a human chain to fetch water from the ponds.

'What have you got there?' Kaneda demanded.

'The Abbot is dead. I must look after his dog now.'

Kaneda clicked his tongue and shook his head, but said only, 'Lord Miyoshi's gone to the quayside.'

'We'll follow him,' Sunaomi said.

Kiki and Baku waited by the gate. Mounting the horses, they rode through the narrow street, the fire behind them. Crowds were running, jostling, weighed down by their possessions, as they tried to escape the spreading flames.

The wind had persisted from the southwest but as they drew closer to the quayside, Sunaomi realised it had dropped and a calm had descended over the waves.

The second cannon was on board one of the carracks. Sunaomi could see the foreigners in their distinctive black clothing beneath their steel armour and helmets. He saw Renzo beside them. A shot was fired from the cannon, and bowmen released a hail of arrows, but both fell short.

'The tide is swinging the ship out of range,' Kaneda said.

Katsunori's men were lined up on the quay, their muskets at their shoulders. Kahei and Hiroshi were both there.

The water below was churning with men in small boats, trying to escape, and others swimming for their lives. One by one they were struck and sank beneath the surface.

Kahei spotted Sunaomi and beckoned to him. 'Can you see Terada?'

Sunaomi scanned the boats, saw a bulky figure in the prow of a skiff, face wrapped in black, beneath a black helmet. A young woman sat close beside him as if seeking or offering shelter. Her face was lifted to the heavens, her hands folded in prayer.

Sunaomi pointed. 'That's him, I'm sure of it.'

He is running away, he thought. *Whether he lives or dies I will never forget his cowardice.*

'Katsunori,' Lord Miyoshi said. 'Can one of your men shoot Terada?'

The oarsman was sculling with all his force. The skiff was sweeping away on the ebbing tide. On Katsunori's order two men stepped forward, one armed with a musket, the other with a bow. They fired at the same moment, the oarsman fell, but Terada was unhurt. Another sailor stepped up to take the oar.

'They are beyond our range,' Katsunori cried.

'Hiroshi, you try,' Kahei said.

'I will try not to kill him,' Hiroshi said quietly.

'Kill him! That's an order!' Kahei returned.

The bay stood as still as a rock while Hiroshi pulled back the arrow and let it fly.

Sunaomi saw it hit Terada in the shoulder, saw the jolt the man's body gave, heard a shout of anger and shock from the sailors. Then the skiff disappeared behind Terada's ship. Within minutes the anchor was raised. The ship turned obedient to the flow of the tide and began to move steadily away. Terada's flag was hoisted in defiance. The foreigners' carracks followed, and in their wake a vessel carrying Mizuta's banner.

'We cannot pursue them without ships,' Kahei said in disgust. 'But it offends me that they will all escape without punishment.' He gazed after the ships for some moments before turning away and saying, 'Kintomo, gather your men and put out the fires.'

'We should let them burn,' his youngest son said. 'Teach them a lesson.'

'Let the lesson be that we are magnanimous in victory,' Kahei replied. 'Katsunori, finish off ...'

He was interrupted by a series of loud explosions that shook the ground, making the horses startle and neigh shrilly.

'Sunaomi, take Kaneda and check that out,' Kahei said. 'But be careful.'

Alarmed by the smell of smoke, Kiki did not want to go back into the burning town. Sunaomi held Shishi firmly and urged the horse on. People were running from the quarter where the noise had come from. When he shouted at them they pointed behind them.

He recognised the street. Kiyoko had led him through it to the Tribe house. His heart was pounding, his throat dry, his hands trembled.

Flames were licking at the houses on either side but where the Muto house had stood there was a gap. Twisted beams and paper screens were scattered and smashed. The walls had collapsed, exposing secret rooms and cellars, the remnants of a hidden staircase, a trapdoor.

Two bodies had been flung into the street. He dismounted, thrust Shishi at Kaneda and ran to them. One he recognised from the scar on her face: Nori, the serving girl, already dead. The other was Muto Yoshio.

Sunaomi knelt beside him. The man's eyelids flickered. He was still breathing.

'Where is Hiromasa?' Sunaomi said. 'Where is my brother?'

Yoshio said in a faint, pain-filled voice, 'He was never your brother. Just some brat from the Tribe. Kiyoko said it would be amusing, and it was.'

He whispered something else and Sunaomi bent over him to catch his final words.

'I curse you, Arai Sunaomi!'

'Burn in Hell!' Sunaomi cried savagely.

Kiyoko had promised not to lie to him but it had meant nothing. He had been a mere amusement to her, a toy, a doll. He had trusted Yoshio and Kichizo and they had handed him over to Terada. His chest burned with rage.

Were his cousins and Hiromasa buried beneath the rubble or had they escaped before the explosion?

A movement behind him made him spin around, his hand on his sword, but it was only Kaneda, Shishi tucked under his arm, the reins of the horses in his other hand.

'What happened here?'

'I suppose they were storing weapons, gunpowder. It was a Tribe house.'

'Were there any survivors?'

Sunaomi shook his head. 'It doesn't look like it.' He would talk to Kaneda about what Yoshio had said later.

'We'll go back to Lord Miyoshi then,' Kaneda said.

The clouds were clearing and the sun was setting, throwing an unearthly light over the sea and the burning town. Smoke drifted upwards, black against the orange glow.

Some of the Miyoshi men were searching the buildings for

stragglers, and then for food; others were helping the towns-people control the blaze.

'We must find somewhere to spend the night,' Kahei said. 'My men are exhausted after the long journey made at such speed, followed by this battle for the town. Can you suggest anywhere?'

'What about that place we went to?' Kaneda suggested. 'Where the sects had gathered.'

'The Temple of the Poor?' Sunaomi had no desire to go there, yet it made sense. It would have escaped the fire, there was space for many people and the surrounding farms would provide food.

'My sons and Hiroshi can keep watch in the town,' Kahei said, and Sunaomi heard his relief and pride when he spoke the words *my sons*. 'You can show me the way.'

'Give me Shishi,' Sunaomi said to Kaneda. 'Go and find Masao and bring him to the Temple.'

Kaneda bowed his head and handed the dog over.

'Did you ride into battle with a dog?' Kahei said, a smile lightening his usually stern face. 'There is no one like you, Sunaomi.' He peered at Shishi more closely. 'I did not see it clearly before but I thought it was a different colour.'

'This is another one,' Sunaomi explained.

'What? Are they multiplying? How many will you end up with?'

Sunaomi smiled too, thinking of the puppies he hoped the dogs would have, and then berated himself for dwelling on such a frivolity. Yet it was a comfort in this time of destruction and grief. The smallest things, the morning glory flowers, the evening star in the twilight, seemed unbearably beautiful.

Perhaps at the rumour of their arrival the remaining members of the sect had fled or perhaps they had made their way to the marsh to retrieve their dead. For whatever reason when Kahei and Sunaomi arrived the Temple was deserted. Only Maru Toma, the outcast leader, was in the open space in front of the main hall, kneeling beside the body in the bloodstained bone white robes that Sunaomi had last seen on the marsh.

Toma opened his eyes at the sound of the horses and immediately prostrated himself before them.

Sunaomi remembered how they had sat as equals and saw in Toma's actions all the tragedy and pathos of the uprising. The world had been turned upside down but now, for good or bad, the old order had been restored. Promising himself he would devote his life to bringing justice, he dismounted and spoke gently. 'Sit up. Lord Miyoshi needs shelter for his men. Can you provide it?'

'You are not going to execute me?' Toma said. 'I halfhope you will. Send me after him into glory.' Tears streamed down his face. 'I brought him here. I did not know where else to take him.'

'We will bury him tomorrow,' Sunaomi said. He gazed on Taro's face, his own eyes hot. What fate had decreed the boy's strange journey, ever since his path had crossed with Sunaomi's all those years ago? 'Do as I request and when everyone is fed and sheltered I will keep vigil with you.'

Kahei had also dismounted and stood beside Sunaomi, staring at the dead boy. 'So young,' he murmured. 'It is a fine face. You must tell me how it all came about. But first let's wash and see to my men.'

Sunaomi put Shishi down and led the lord to the cistern where they washed their hands and faces and drank deeply. Apart from the noise of the men as they filed into the Temple and were directed by Toma to various rooms, the only sound was the soughing of the wind in the cedars and around the eaves. The dog lapped water from Sunaomi's cupped hands and followed him as closely as Chin as he took Kahei to the room where Taro had discussed the writings of Yoshimori with the foreigners.

When they had taken off their armour, Kahei said, 'While we are alone there is something we must discuss. I have this great disappointment to reveal to you. It distresses and embarrasses me, especially after seeing how bravely and diligently you have fulfilled everything I asked of you, even finding Saga Masao.'

'What will happen to Masao?' Sunaomi asked.

'We must take him back to Miyako and let Lady Kaede decide.'

'He was not the murderer of the Kono youth,' Sunaomi said.

'Whether he killed him or not, he was involved and he ran away. He must be punished. But that is not what I wanted to talk to you about.' He took a deep breath but seemed to find it hard to continue. His gaze fell on Shishi, who sat close to Sunaomi. 'Where did you leave the other dog?'

'In Yamagata in the care of your daughter, Lady Kinu.'

'You saw my daughter? I thought she would be in Terayama by now. So, you probably already know what I have to say. I am profoundly sorry to break the betrothal but I could not allow the marriage under the conditions that she told me you had agreed to. She has won my permission to become a nun though it has broken my heart. I can only ask for your forgiveness.'

'Lord Miyoshi,' Sunaomi said, 'there is nothing to forgive. I talked with your daughter at length and she was persuaded to change her mind.'

'What?' Kahei was speechless for a few moments. Then he said, 'She is not going to be a nun?'

'Not at the moment. Maybe I will be an unsatisfactory husband and she will run away to a convent but ...'

'She wants to get married?'

'We both desire it with all our hearts,' Sunaomi said. 'Of course it may be only because she fell in love with my dog, Chin, but she has put aside her wish to go to Terayama. She is waiting in Yamagata for our return. She has told her mother, who is pleased, I believe.'

'Pleased? I can guarantee she is delighted! I have never heard better news. I would embrace you like a son but for all this battle filth that still clings to me.' Kahei turned away for a moment.

Sunaomi thought the old warrior had tears in his eyes but he could not be sure.

♦

Lamps were lit and fires prepared. Soon the smell of cooking wafted through the temple. Kahei went to eat with his men, but Sunaomi had no appetite and decided to fast during his vigil to honour the dead.

He knelt beside the body. After a while Maru Toma returned with oil lamps which he set at Taro's head and feet, together with an iron bowl of smouldering incense. He went away and came back, bent double under a large wooden slab. With Sunaomi's help he lifted the body onto the slab, saying, 'If you will remove the stained robe, lord, I will bring the other one to dress him in, after we have washed him.'

Sunaomi tenderly removed the garment, easing it away from the wound that had taken Taro's life and took one of the cloths that Toma brought, along with bowls of water.

'I don't suppose you have done this before,' Toma said as they began to wash the body.

'I have,' Sunaomi replied, remembering the dead boy who had been his substitute, buried under his name, and then he began to weep in earnest, his tears falling, mingling with the water.

When the body was washed and clad in the fresh robes, Toma began to pray, the prayers said by the Hidden in the moments before death. Sunaomi had heard them years ago, before he had even met Taro, and had never forgotten them. He had not dreamed he would hear them spoken for his friend, who had been his servant, and had become the servant of the world.

How will I break the news to his mother? The thought of Saya's grief shattered his heart anew.

He felt a hand on his shoulder. Kaneda said quietly, 'Saga Masao is here.'

Masao did not speak but fell to his knees at Sunaomi's side, folding his bound hands in prayer. Kaneda also knelt, head bowed.

Sunaomi heard the noise of the men settling down to sleep, and then the sounds of the night took over, the autumn insects, the trees rustling, leaves gently falling, the hooting of owls.

There was so much he still did not understand, so many questions to put to Masao, but they could all wait. Now was the time to sit in silence with his oldest friend, his companion, Kaneda, the outcast and the dog, Shishi, keeping vigil until dawn.

CHAPTER TWENTY-SIX

It was not until a few days later that he and Masao were alone. They were within a day's ride of Yamagata, staying at one of the inns along the highway. Kahei's plan was to rest in his castle town before returning to the capital with Sunaomi and his daughter, to celebrate their marriage and Sunaomi's coming-of-age. His sons remained in Hofu to complete the pacification of the town and repair the damage caused by the fighting and the flooding. Hiroshi had already ridden on to return to Maruyama.

The inn had a small detached guest room and Lord Miyoshi suggested Sunaomi spend the night there with Masao and Kaneda.

'Once we reach Yamagata, Masao will be a prisoner, under armed guard for the journey to Miyako. These will be your last hours together.'

Sunaomi was grateful for this thoughtfulness and deeply saddened by what the future held. Masao would not attend either his marriage or his coming-of-age; he would be under sentence of death or exile. How could he deliver his old friend to this fate? He imagined letting him go, giving him his own sword and Kiki to ride away on, but that would be a betrayal to both his aunt and Lord Miyoshi.

Maybe Masao was aware of his conflict for he said, after they had finished eating and Kaneda had gone outside to keep watch, 'Don't blame yourself for anything. What I did was my choice alone. The punishment will be mine alone. You don't have to share it.'

'I hope my aunt will be merciful,' Sunaomi said.

'For a long time it hasn't mattered to me if I live or die. The only thing that has changed is that I used to feel that out of despair and now I feel it out of hope.'

'Were you really expecting the Kingdom of Heaven to be revealed?' Sunaomi asked.

'It seemed a possibility,' Masao said, his face serious. 'For a moment, out there on the marsh, I believed it had come true. I thought I saw something.'

'I saw it too,' Sunaomi said.

'And then Taro died in that moment? Did the Secret One call him home? Did it use bullets to achieve its ends?'

Sunaomi had no answers to these questions. Who had fired first in that moment? Or had both sides fired simultaneously? Hiroshi's horse had been hit first, and then Taro ... he would never know.

'The last thing he gave me was his book. I have it here.' Masao took out the copy of the hidden writings of Yoshimori and passed it to Sunaomi, who held it with a heart full of memories: Taro asking permission to take the book, reading it so earnestly all the way from Miyako, Taro welcomed as a prophet, dressed in white, an angel, a sacrificial victim.

'He changed me,' Masao said. "He healed me of all my old pain. If I live I intend to follow his example and continue his teaching.'

Sunaomi was silent. He could only pray Kaede would show mercy.

It was nearly the end of summer, still very hot, the days long, the evenings light. All the doors of the inn were open. Shishi lay in the doorway where the air was cooler.

Sunaomi called to Kaneda to come in, meaning to show him the book, but there was no reply. The dog stirred and growled.

'Strange,' Sunaomi said, getting to his feet. As he walked to the door he felt something pass by him. The air moved as though a wind had sprung up though outside not a leaf stirred. A scent of jasmine lingered, and the smell of a young boy's sweat.

Kaneda was slumped against the wall, deeply asleep.

Shishi started barking. Sunaomi caught and held him,

feeling the mane ripple beneath his grasp. The dog was almost hysterical as the invisible ones slowly appeared.

Masao sat without moving, gazing at Kiyoko and Hiromasa.

'It is you,' he whispered. 'The woman of the streets who murdered Kono. I never expected to see you again. But I see you are not what I thought you were. Now I understand how you were able to kill and disappear so swiftly.'

Kiyoko's lips curved in a slight smile. 'And now I've come for you.' She glanced at Sunaomi. 'Don't call for help.'

Sunaomi said, 'I'll do anything if you spare him. What do you want?'

'Sunaomi, would you come back to the Tribe and marry me?'

He saw all he would sacrifice, the pain he would cause Kinu, the dark world of lies and deception he thought he had escaped. 'I will,' he said.

'Let her do what she pleases,' Masao said. 'It is my fate. I did not kill Kono but I took the lives of many and I deserve punishment. I ask forgiveness of you and all the others I have harmed.' His gaze turned to Hiromasa. 'You too,' he said softly.

Hiromasa stared back, without speaking.

'I can't have both, can I?' Kiyoko said almost wistfully. 'Once I have my revenge I will lose you forever. It makes me sad. I enjoyed our night together. But it's nothing compared to what I feel now, with the man who humiliated me at my mercy.'

Sunaomi thought he might overcome her with the bare-hand techniques they had both learned as a child. He pushed Shishi aside and threw himself at her, his arm rigid to knock the knife from her grip, and felt someone's fingers at his throat, the one with no smell, the invisible assassin, Kichizo.

Sunaomi struggled, bit, kicked, tried to call to Hiromasa to help him. He heard the sounds he dreaded, Masao's one cry of pain and the gush of blood. He felt a wetness on his face and sobs rose in his throat, choked by Kichizo's iron grip.

We vowed always to help each other but I could not save you.

Night was falling rapidly or was it his vision darkening

forever? He saw the faces of those he had loved, his parents, his brother, Utahime, and Kinu. Shishi was snarling. He thought of Chin.

Under the slippery blood Kichizo's grip weakened and Sunaomi was able to call out. 'Hiromasa!'

Hiromasa shouted in a shrill voice. 'Stop, stop, you didn't say you were going to kill him too. Just Masao, and he deserved it.'

'Be quiet,' Kiyoko said. 'We work in silence. That's a lesson for you. And another: there is no sentiment or brotherly love in the Tribe.'

'I will never stay with you if you kill him!'

'You will never escape,' Kichizo said. 'Just as he did not.'

Kiyoko said in an urgent whisper, 'Kichizo, he has the bear! Hand it over, Hiromasa.'

'I won't,' Hiromasa replied, defiantly as Kichizo's hold tightened.

Sunaomi could not see or move. He could fight no more. He felt his body signal surrender and his will follow. He heard, faintly, Hiromasa shouting, calling for help, and then a strange growling, deeper than the dog, followed by a cry of amazement from Hiromasa.

Suddenly he could breathe again. Kichizo had released him. He struggled to sit up, gasping for air, groaning with the pain of living.

Kichizo and Kiyoko were backing out of the door as the bear rose on its hind legs, swiping at them with its huge paws, its claws like knives.

They were both bleeding from mauling to face and hands. Even as they took on invisibility the blood dripped to the ground.

Then the sibling assassins were gone, leaving the bear snarling in frustration, while Shishi danced around it, yapping.

Sunaomi caught the dog and tried to quieten him. 'Hiromasa,' he said in a rasping whisper. 'You have to call it back. You released it. Now you must control it.'

'How do I do that?'

'Go to it and grasp it. Thank it and make it smaller with your will.'

'It will bite me,' Hiromasa said. 'Can't it just stay?'

'No, it can't. And it will bite you but that's the price you have to pay.'

The bear dropped onto all four feet and swung its head from side to side. Hiromasa looked tiny beside it. He grabbed at its fur but it ignored him. Sunaomi could see that it was about to run.

'Quickly!' he said in his strange hoarse voice. 'You are Arai. It has to obey you.'

The bear evaded Hiromasa and moved with surprising speed but at the door it halted. Kaneda stood there, bleary eyed, swaying.

'Look out!' Sunaomi reached for his sword. He would kill the bear himself rather than see it hurt Kaneda—but could it be killed?

Kaneda knelt in front of the bear and touched the silver fur round its neck. 'I know you. I mended you with silver. Am I dreaming?'

Sunaomi saw he was still in the trance of the Kikuta sleep.

The bear lowered its head submissively.

'Do it now,' Sunaomi said to his brother.

The boy stepped cautiously towards the bear and knelt beside it. 'Thank you for coming to my aid, for saving my brother's life,' he whispered. He thrust both hands into the thick fur and started kneading it.

The bear gave a deep, almost human sigh. Slowly its bulk diminished. Its eyes became glass-like, its tongue and teeth wooden. It did not resist or try to bite.

Hiromasa is its master, Sunaomi realised. *He is my brother, one of the Arai. The bear was his all the time.*

His brother hung the carving on its cord round his neck without speaking.

Sunaomi knelt beside Masao's body, tears beginning to flow, his heart aching as painfully as his throat.

'Farewell,' he whispered. 'You are with your parents and sister now, no longer an orphan.'

Shishi licked his hand as if to comfort him. The night sounds deepened around him. In the cries of insects, the squeaking of bats, the calls of owls he heard echoes of music, of the enchanted flute, his ghost lover saying goodbye forever, Kinu calling him back, to where she waited with Chin.